HE
+SHE

A spontaneous, offbeat **romance**

MICHELLE WARREN

HE + SHE

Editing and Formatting by:
Pam Berehulke
www.BulletproofEditing.com

Cover and Book Design by:
Michelle Preast
www.facebook.com/indiebookcovers

JENN STERLING
USA TODAY BEST SELLING AUTHOR

"With twists and turns I never saw coming, He + She is a beautiful story about finding love, redemption and yourself. Everyone needs to read this story!"

MELISSA BROWN
AUTHOR OF PICTURING PERFECT

"Quirky, fun, heartfelt and sexy—this book knocked my socks off. This is Warren's first New Adult Contemporary Romance…and I sincerely hope it won't be her last! One of my favorites of 2014!"

CONTENTS

WHEN LOVE IS NOT MADNESS, IT IS NOT LOVE

Pedro Calderón de la Barca

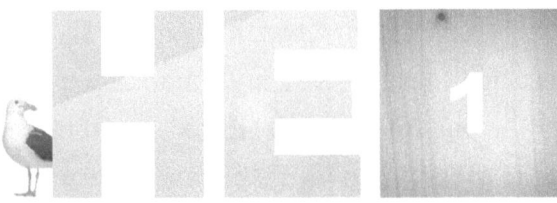

1

tep Nine: Make direct amends with the people I've hurt.

That's part of AA's recovery plan, but it's easier said than done. At least, it is if the prick staring at me from the front door of his farmhouse has anything to do with it. I grip the handle and pull, releasing the Jeep's door. It creaks open as I step out into the night with determination. Before I'm five paces into the yard, the dickhead meets me chest to chest with the usual look on his face— like he wants to kill me. And the truth is, he has every right to feel that way.

"I told you she doesn't want see you," he spits out.

"I know you did." I meet his gaze, puffing up my chest like some rooster in a cockfight. I set my jaw. "But I need her to know I'm sorr—"

He presses his large hands into my shoulders and shoves me away. I fall backward and slam into my car, making a futile grab at the side mirror before I hit the ground. Sollie Winters is standing over me so fast, all I have time to do is brace myself for the impact of his steely fist before it makes contact with my nose.

I don't fight back, since I'm desperately trying not to be a fighting person. Instead, I don't defend myself, I just lie still, allowing him to purge his anger. He owes me every strike to the jaw, every punch to the gut, every spurt of blood, and so much more. Though I didn't come here for a confrontation, I expected the less-than-warm-and-fuzzy welcome. It mirrors the two previous times I've tried to apologize to her since I learned she came home. But I needed to finish this, to finally say I'm sorry so I can get the hell out of town and move on with my life. There's nothing for me here after what I've done. I've ruined everything.

These are the words that run through my head as he pummels me one last time. He twists his fingers into my shirt, lifting my wobbling body to my feet, and shoves me back through my open car door.

"If you're not gone in five fucking seconds, I'm calling the police!" Sollie's slight Southern twang is more pronounced when he's pissed. He kicks the door shut and I sprawl across the front seat, a bruised and bloody mess. In the yellow haze of the front porch light, I see his wife run to his side, and though a frail thing, she forcefully ushers him back into the house, where their dogs are barking wildly. She looks over at me, giving me the same apologetic look she's given me before as they disappear into the house. That's when I notice a silhouette standing inside the lit window of an upstairs room.

Ignoring his warning, I sit up in the driver's seat, grip the steering wheel, and lean forward, looking closer. She could be at that window. Right there, watching me get my head split open, painting the front yard red. If she's looking out, it might make her happy to see me this way. If I were her, I wouldn't be happy until I was dead.

When the silhouette moves across the room and disappears, I contemplate one more go of it, despite the fact that my face resembles a rotting pumpkin smashed in the road. I take a second to consider and think of my counselor, who urged me not to return for a third time for a third beating. "You've done all you can," Mrs. Mankin drilled into me at our last session. It's true, I have, everything just short of stalking the girl, but I won't allow myself to do *that*. I don't need more problems than I already have.

I slam my palm to the dashboard, fumble for my keys, shove one in the ignition and turn on my car, revving the engine. Slamming the stick shift into reverse, I peel out of the dusty driveway, swerving as I back out, barely missing the rusted mailbox before I speed away. If I don't get out of here soon, I know that dickhead will have the cops all over my ass.

oday was supposed to be one of the best days of my life; a day I would never forget.

Come to think of it, that last part's true. I'll never forget it for all the reasons that make you ache inside, the reasons that make you want to give up completely, the reasons that make you want to fold in on yourself like origami paper, folding in and over, making the shape smaller and smaller until you disappear into an infinitesimal dot. And because of this there's only one thing I'm completely sure of in my soul—I must leave. Right now.

The glass doors glide open and I stomp through, legs weak and stomach hollow from crying my eyes out in the back of a taxicab. I make my way to the end of a winding line of people. Cheery faces turn when they see my big white dress and absurdly long lace train out of the corner of their eyes, but just as fast as their gaze settles in my direction, ready to greet me with well wishes, it slides away with an obvious pinch of uncomfortable guilt. And honestly, I can't blame them.

"You can go ahead of me." An older man's voice wavers

as he gestures nervously. With his shifting posture, I can tell he's trying not to look too closely, but with black mascara dripping down my cheeks, mixing with my face powder, red lipstick, and peach blush, it's clear that I'm a hot mess.

I make my way to the counter as each person in line shoos me forward in quick succession.

"May I help you?" The airline agent greets me with an unsure smile.

"I really hope so." I place my handbag on the counter, unzip it, and riffle through the contents as I continue to talk. "I need a ticket for the first plane out of here."

From the edge of my vision, I see that there's a moment of pause on her end, no typing, and no rushing to help, so I look up. The woman purses her lips as if she doesn't believe me.

"Seriously, not kidding." My raccoon eyes widen with an attitude.

The agent nods with a heavy sigh, and after a moment of assessing me, her long fluorescent nails tap the keyboard. "Looks like the first flight that you can make if you hurry is San Francisco."

"Sounds great," I say but frown. The irony of this location being the first option is a slap in the face. I try not to think about the pain and present my credit card and ID.

"It's $627 with taxes and fees," she adds, as though this will make a difference. A few years ago, it probably would have, but not on this god-awful day.

I shove the card closer. She reluctantly takes it, looking at me from over the rim of her glasses, the way she probably does when her kids give her lip.

"Any baggage?" Her gaze scans the floor behind me.

At this question, I laugh loudly and too obnoxiously, because I'm practically manic and sleep-deprived. I have so much baggage, and all I want to do is desperately leave it behind.

"I'll take that as a no." She raises a graying eyebrow and continues typing.

I think I'm almost done, free of Maryland, until she pops up on her tiptoes and peers over the wide counter that separates us. "But with the size of that dress, dear, you'll need two seats."

"Come on!" I slam the counter with my palm in a moment of frustration because I can see she's serious, but for the love of God, I hope she's not.

"Sorry, you'll never fit into one seat in that thing." She waves her arm through the air. "Unless you have something else to change into?"

"No," I say grimly. "I don't." I look down at my beautiful wedding dress. It doesn't mean what it should; it hasn't since the moment I shimmied into the lace and silk earlier today. Instead, the stupid white cupcake represents everything I'll never have; at least, not with the person it was meant to be with.

I glower at the thought of what I must do and take a pen

from my bag. Using it as a makeshift knife, I punch the ballpoint through the outer layer of the fancy fabric, creating a hole large enough to stick my finger through. When I find the perfect grip, I rip off the length of the dress, shredding the hell out of it with all the resentment and sadness that's boiling over inside. I grit my teeth, holding back more tears. If I break down now, again, they may not let me board the plane.

Around me, people gasp and chatter in reaction. "What's she doing? That dress must have cost a fortune," they say. In the commotion, a security guard saunters over. He stands nearby, but as far as I know, it's not illegal for a crazy girl to trash her own wedding dress in an airport.

By the time I'm done, the skirt looks more like a long, uneven tutu than anything appropriate enough to wear while walking down the aisle. Vera Wang would be horrified. I step out of the extra fabric and kick it aside with my boots. I'm happy that I had the good sense to wear them instead of those stupid heels that Bren's mom picked out for me.

"Bren." I say his name under my breath and bite my lip. The vision of his beautiful Crest smile dances behind my eyes. I used to live for that smile.

Somehow, in the wake of my obnoxious behavior, the agent stops giving me crap about the second seat and finishes printing my ticket. She hands it to me along with my ID and credit card. "Your gate's B62. You better make a run for it."

She walks into the cramped plane cabin with a huge release of breath and face red from running. I mean, I can only guess she's been running. And by the look of the mascara tracks that have dried over her rosy cheeks and her mangled wedding dress, she's running away from an important day. She doesn't look at my face when she squeezes by my seat and down the aisle, she only zones out, stepping slowly in pace with the person in front of her like a zombie.

"Poor thing," The older woman next to me leans over. She places a hand on my arm, as if she's getting ready to share gossip in a hushed tone. "She made quite a scene at the security line when they pulled her aside, but I can see how her appearance could cause concern. Looks like someone really pissed her off."

I laugh at the word *pissed* coming from this little old lady.

She gives my bruised face a once-over. "By the sight of you, you could have been the groom!" She pats me on the arm, as if she just solved the puzzle.

"No, I'm afraid not." I rub my jaw, still raw from Sollie Winters's beating last week. "If I was lucky enough to have a girl like that," I nod in the bride's direction, "I wouldn't let her run away from our wedding day."

Underneath the ruined makeup, it's easy to see that the girl is beautiful. Thick hair, pouty peach lips, and the gentle curve of her body, a fullness that suggests she's still young, probably early twenties. Unable to look away, I watch as she makes her way to the last row. She ends up sitting in the center seat between two hefty men. With her petite frame, she's lost in a cavern between them, but as she sits she does something unexpected. Despite her obviously shittastic day, she looks to each neighbor with a genuine smile.

I'm immediately in awe of this. I wish I were that optimistic on my bad days. There have been so many of them. And just because the moment is so pure, I wish I had my Canon to take a photograph of the authentic smile from the train-wreck bride. I'm half-tempted to jump up and retrieve it from the overhead bin, but when I look back to her, the simple moment is lost. She's resting her head back with her eyes shut.

I turn forward, trying to return my thoughts to what they should focus on: my upcoming interview. A new job in San Francisco could be my new beginning. And if I'm not nervous enough, in my head I continually reel through answers to possible questions that they may ask. I can't help myself; I've never wanted a job so badly in my life. Never wanted to escape so much. Maybe the bride and I have that in common.

When the plane takes off, the lady next to me settles into a crossword puzzle. I think she finishes exactly two questions before she falls asleep, head drifting to my shoulder, and then proceeds to snore lightly in my ear for the duration of the flight. I allow it, but only because she reminds me of my late grandmother.

Now, that woman was a saint. At least I know she would have forgiven me when my parents and sisters couldn't. Sure, she would have bashed me upside the head, made me recite Hail Marys until my tongue fell out, and forced me into rehab before I completely ruined my life, but even with her tough love, she would have never disowned me. As horrible as everything turned out, she would have never held me responsible for Beth's death. If only Grandma were still here, things might be different. If only Beth were here, things *would* be different. But neither is, which breaks my heart, so I'm leaving everyone I love behind.

Five hours later, the plane lands. I make my way through the airport, retrieve my bag, and then head to the people mover, which transports me to the car rentals. Moving with the large crowd, I walk inside and stand in the Reliable Car Rental line.

That's when I see the train-wreck bride again. She's in front of me. Somehow she's beaten me here, despite being in the back of the plane, and then I notice a possible answer to how. She has no luggage, just a purse strapped across her chest. The tutu of her dress is uneven and cut shorter in the back, showing her shapely legs. As I'm admiring them, she moves ahead as soon as the clerk waves her forward.

Their conversation starts and I try not to listen, but it's nearly impossible with the girl's voice rising slightly with each new sentence. I lift my gaze from browsing my annoying Facebook feed of friends' babies dressed like sunflowers, pets with handwritten signs proclaiming, "I pooped in Daddy's shoe," and lots of food pics—especially bacon. When I do, I see her leaning all the way over the counter to pull a silvery bendable microphone away from the clerk and to her mouth. She taps the head three times before speaking and it buzzes loudly.

"Attention, attention, all rental car businesses." The sweet impish voice carries through the large room over the intercom, and every traveler or car rental employee stops speaking, their heads turning in her direction.

"Great, thanks," she continues awkwardly. "Anyone here have something cooler to rent me than a mommy sedan or kidnap minivan? Maybe something vintage and cute?" She looks around, waiting for an answer.

I quirk a smile. She's insanely adorable or insanely insane; I'm not sure which. Either way I'm intrigued and unable to look away.

To my surprise—and probably everyone else's—a man at the end of the room waves for her attention. I squint to see the sign above him that reads, CLASSIC AUTO RENTALS. "Awesome. Thanks, everyone." When she pushes the mic back over the counter toward the clerk, it screeches. She turns to leave the line as if she'd just done something normal, completely oblivious to the fact that everyone in the room is still staring at her.

When she passes me, our eyes meet for a millisecond. They're emerald green and sparkling with determination. Her full lips smile again like she did on the plane, sans dripping makeup, but this time her smile is special because it's solely for me—it's gleaming, punctuated with a deep-set scar shaped like a long hook on the line of her jaw.

The girl struts away, tutu and hair bouncing with each step, reminding me of a well-worn porcelain baby doll with spidering cracks over her face and legs. Someone loved her too much, or worse, perhaps abused her.

For her sake, I hope it was the former.

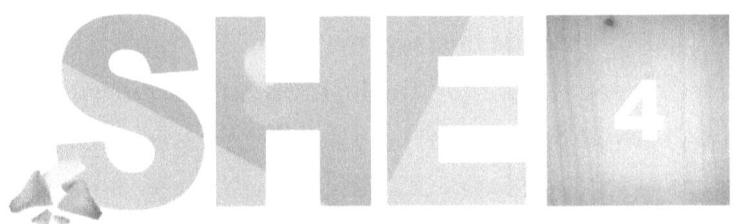

SHE 4

When I slide into the driver's seat of the restored Italian Fiat convertible, I smile. One hand grips the steering wheel while the other slides the key in the ignition. I turn the car on and realize it's been far too long since I was alone and driving myself anywhere. Feeling the car rumble beneath me is my second victory. The first was having the courage to leave.

I look over each shoulder and back out of the parking spot. When I put the car in drive and jam my foot down on the accelerator, I promise myself one thing: This is my new beginning and I won't look into my past with hate any longer, only try to remember the happiness I found there, so I can find it again. It's a stretch of optimism, but in this new place I'm feeling hopeful.

Recklessly, I merge onto Interstate 101, driving north with the convertible top down. After twenty minutes, the boxy skyline of San Francisco appears from the undulating hills that make the city famous. It's as beautiful as I've dreamed about, and as lovely as every photo I've ever seen.

In a last-minute decision met with honking horns and swerving cars, I dart off the highway exit and merge into the chaos of downtown. I didn't expect to want to find a place in the city; I was thinking a road trip was in order. But now that I'm here, I can't resist the idea of seeing San Francisco up close. I cruise and cross many city streets before I see an orange-and-yellow retro neon sign for a hotel opposite the Chinatown Gate, and I quickly maneuver through heavy traffic to pull into the valet lane.

A boy opens my door and says, "Welcome to the Briton Hotel." Despite my appearance, when I halfway expect him to ask me to leave, he hands me a valet ticket instead. The doorman greets me with a wave, and a manager meets me inside. "Checking in today, miss?" No one pays any attention to the way I look. It's a relief because though I wasn't self-conscious when I started this journey, I have been ever since we landed.

"Yes," I say with a nod.

I follow the manager to the counter, where he asks, "May I have the name on the reservation?"

"I don't have a reservation."

"No problem, we do have a few rooms left. How many nights will you be staying with us, and how many in your party?"

I shuffle my feet uncomfortably for a moment. "Just me." I pause at the realization that I'm alone, traveling for the first time and without Bren. I feel myself going to that dark place, just thinking about it. We dreamed about coming to San Francisco—it was one of the top travel destinations on our list—and now that I'm finally here, it's under the worst circumstances.

The man clears his throat, and I erase the picture of Bren's handsome face from my head and respond, trying to take control of my emotions. "I'd like a king bed, non smoking, with a view, for three nights, please."

"We have just the room."

"Perfect." I place my credit card and ID on the counter.

"Great." He takes the card and continues checking me in. "There's a pool on the roof, and we serve complimentary cookies in the lobby at five every evening. We also have complimentary bicycles." He gestures to a pair of beach cruisers sitting by the front door. "Your room is 616." He hands me the room key card.

"May we help you with your luggage?" he asks.

I accept the hotel key and my credit card, then step backward. "No thanks, I left all my baggage behind." He gives me a curious look, but I leave before he can question this and quickly jump into the elevator.

On the sixth floor, my room is large. The top half of the room's walls are wallpapered with pages from famous novels. The lower half is painted a muted apple green. Immediately I walk to the windows and open the blinds, checking my view of the Chinatown Gate. I turn to the bed with a brightly lacquered yellow headboard, and collapse on the mattress.

At home in Baltimore, it would be after dinnertime. And if things had played out the way they were supposed to today, I'd be married by now, eating Chesapeake stuffed chicken at my glittering reception at the Belvedere Hotel, drinking bubbling champagne and break-dancing with the one I love to bad wedding reception music that glorifies chickens.

But here it's barely one o'clock, and all I can focus on is the emptiness in my soul. Depression, anger, regret, guilt—any combination of words you choose to describe my life adds up to the endless tragedy that is now my reality. My stomach rumbles, and I cross my arms over my chest and turn on my side, squeezing my body into a fetal position, crying quiet tears into my pillow.

There are so many things running through my head, a jumbled mess that pushes me farther away from reality. Feeling the shakes rise up through my body like a wave ready to consume me, I quickly reach for my purse, unzip it, and dump the contents on the bed in front of my face. I don't focus on the mess I've just created; it's impossible with the clear rust-colored pill bottle rolling in my direction. It's my necessary bottle of evil. I hate that I am chained to it, but everything inside it will save me. It contains a cocktail of pills to cure my anxiety, insomnia, and other things that led me here. I swipe up the bottle and sit up, unscrew the top like a junkie, and race to the bathroom for a glass of water. By the time I get there, I'm a jittery mess, aching for the release the pills bring.

Somehow the white pills can make all the pain go away, which is an impressive feat considering the size of my problems compared to the size of the pill. Barely able to stand, I swallow one, shut my eyes, and step away from the sink until my back hits the wall. When I open them again, the bathroom mirror reflects my image—a fragmented, stressed-out mess of a girl in a shredded wedding dress who can't get her crap together. She's hit rock bottom, and all she desperately wants to do is climb out of this hole and be happy again.

I make my way back to the bed, crawl under the covers, and cry until the drug kicks in. When it does, I fall asleep for the first time in days.

I awake a few hours later, feeling better than expected. Popping the white pill doesn't make the bad go away, it just makes me not care about what's happened. In theory, it's a great thing until you want to feel again, which I do, and not just the pain. I love the medications for what they do, but hate them for what they steal from me. I know I should be taking them regularly, but I don't want to anymore. More than anything, I want to free myself from them and everything they represent.

Looking to my nightstand, I find a plate of chocolates.

Were they here before? Does it matter? Hunger pangs hit me again, and I lift the plate and settle it on my stomach. ENJOY THESE COMPLIMENTARY SWEETS. SIGNED, THE BRITON. I read the card sitting next to them and then throw it aside.

I take a bite of the first piece of chocolate. When my stomach twists painfully, I realize I can't remember the last time I've eaten. It hasn't mattered until now. I'll give myself ten minutes to lie here and relax, because the next thing I have to do on this adventure is to find a way out of this funk and some new clothes.

When I leave my hotel, I don't head straight for the department stores. Instead, I cross the street, walking through the Chinatown Gate. It's more enticing and mysterious, and when I enter the neighborhood, I'm visually overloaded by the pagoda architecture, the foreign signage, and the festive red lanterns that weave overhead from one side of the road to the other.

I zigzag in and out of several shops, buying useless imported goodies: a pair of satin embroidered slippers, beaded bracelets, a change purse, and a large pack of Twizzlers. Any other time, I wouldn't have allowed myself these things because I was doing the right thing, being responsible and saving for my future.

Fuck the future. The only thing these two years have taught me is to live in the moment. You can't plan for the future. You can't plan anything with life conspiring against you every day. You can only live one minute at a time.

One shop sells what I deem as real clothing, and I try on two pairs of jeans, several T-shirts boasting their love or loss of their heart in San Francisco, along with several other necessities. I try each item on, then hand the mangled wedding dress to the Chinese shop owner from around the makeshift dressing room curtain, and ask her to trash it. I never want to see that thing again.

She complies without comment, then meets me at the cash register. There, I can't resist a pack of women's days-of-the-week underpants and some mini-size travel toiletries. Everything I buy fits into a backpack that I pull from another display.

Once I've paid, I leave the shop and wander across the city. After a long stroll, I make it to the beach to see the Golden Gate Bridge. It's what I've walked all this way for, maybe even what I've traveled all this way for. Who knows why I ended up in San Fran, of all places, but I'm here for some reason. Maybe I'll find what I need to pick up the shattered pieces of my life and mind, and move on.

It's late in the day, and I seat myself on a jagged concrete block to eat a round of sourdough bread I picked up in a cute bakery along the way. With the sun blazing golden in the distance, turning the bridge into a caramel-colored silhouette, the water lapping over the rocks, and seagulls gliding with the breeze that rustles my hair, I feel hope. Real hope. I just have to remember that every-thing that's gone so wrong is inside the stagnant bubble I currently live in. Outside, beyond the clear iridescent orb, the rest of the world makes sense. People are happy, laughing, and in love. I can hope that one day I will have those things, too. As long as I just focus on each moment and what really matters, I know that life can be beautiful again.

After my interview, which I may or may not have blown, I make my way to a nearby park in Little Italy. I felt confident meeting the partners and presenting my portfolio, but when they asked why I wanted to move cross-country to San Francisco, I froze, remembering everything I'm running from. I managed to push past my blunder and speak passionately about the work, but I'm sure they saw the resentment of leaving home in my eyes. Sometimes my past feels like it's stamped on my face for everyone to see.

Though I'm wearing a suit, I collapse on a dirty bench in a park near a large white chapel. The weather is perfect, the sky's a clear blue, and several people lay out, soaking up the sunshine, despite the fact that it's eleven thirty on a workday. All I can think about is that I don't want to go home to Baltimore. I need to find a way to stay, but with no job, the cost of living in San Francisco is prohibitive unless I join the hippie commune at Haight and Ashbury and dedicate my life to street singing and smoking recreationally.

Thinking the possibility might be a doable option, I pull at my tie, loosening it from my neck. That's when the cars waiting at a red light on the nearby street blow their horns. My eyes find the reason and I'm really sorry when they do. At least twenty completely naked dudes riding bicycles circle the park. First they parade their nudity on main roads, weaving around cars, around the square, and then they circle the paths inside the park for an unfortunate closer view. Only in this city of hippies would people clap and wave them on like heroes.

Though I'm trying hard to ignore them, I find myself focused on only one person, all the way in the back of the group, the only girl brave enough to ride with them: the train-wreck bride, wearing only her bra and lime-green panties. I'd recognize her wild dark hair anywhere.

On her approach I stare, shocked that I've seen her again. Our eyes meet and I smile. It's a simple gesture, but this time it wins me something unexpected. She slows her bike, steers in my direction, and rolls to a stop when she reaches me.

"Hi," she says, greeting me like we know each other.

"Hi." I pause to watch her struggle with her bike, which is much too large for her. "Every time I see you, you're wearing something unexpected."

"How many times have you seen me?" The girl dismounts her bike and rests it on its side. She's completely comfortable with her near nudity, and she has reason to be. Every milky curve on her body is perfection.

"Three times."

"Three times!" She leans away to dig into her back-pack, and I see her panties have WEDNESDAY printed on the ass. This girl makes me smile, which is a welcome change from all the drama I've been dealing with.

"Yes, but I think I like this outfit better," I admit as I shamelessly ogle her while she's not looking. That's when I notice the long scar on the inside of her leg, winding its way from her knee and up her thigh.

She turns and seems to notice, then shrugs quickly into a tank top.

"But I think you have on the wrong panties." I point to her perfectly curved ass.

She looks over her shoulder and lifts her butt, looking for proof. "The lame package of undies I bought had two Hump Days and no Mondays. Go figure." She shimmies into a pair of cutoff jeans, buttons them, and sits beside me with her legs bent beneath her. "You look familiar. Have we met?"

"We haven't. I'm—"

"Wait. Don't tell me your name." She cuts me off by pressing a finger over my lips. "Tell me the name you al-ways wished was yours."

My eyes widen at this, and I watch her slowly remove her finger from my mouth, as if she moved it away too quickly, my real name might accidentally slip out. She's definitely insanely insane, and I pause for moment, considering if I really want this conversation to move forward. Who asks for a fake name? I twist uncomfortably, letting my gaze roam around the park, hoping someone might come to rescue me—the naked bike riders? No, I think I'm on my own on this one. So I do what I'm best at, I deflect. "Well, tell me the name you always wanted for yourself."

"That's easy. Shea. At least, that's what I pick this week. Next week, it could be different." She resettles, bringing a knee to her chest. "So, what about you?" She tilts her head.

"Well . . ." I look up and think hard of how to answer, because she's taking this seriously. Though I'm far out of my comfort zone, I answer for no other reason than I'm curious to see where this will go. "I was always fond of the name Hewitt. Spelled h-e-w-i-t-t."

"Like the computer?" She laughs.

"Yeah, I guess so. But what's your real name?"

"Just call me Shea, and I'll call you Hew. You look like a Hew."

"What brings you to San Francisco, Shea?" The question falls out before I realize that this may be dangerous territory. Of course, I'm assuming she traveled here since I saw her on the plane, but I should consider she might actually live here.

Shea drops her chin to her knee, seeming to consider

her words carefully. "Let's just say I'm here on a mission of personal development. You?" She takes a pack of Twizzlers out of her bag and offers one to me. I shake my head. "Sorta the same. I'm here for a job interview." I gesture to my suit.

"How'd it go?" She takes a bite of her candy.

"Honestly, I'm not sure. It could go either way."

"Let me guess what you do for a living." She looks me over, analyzing every detail, as though the angle of my cheek or the pattern on my tie will give her the proper answer. "You're wearing a suit, so you're definitely a business kind of guy, but . . ." She pulls at my collar and her delicate fingers brush against my neck, causing an unexpected rush of heat to spread over my chest that makes me shift in my seat. "You have a tattoo peeking out from under your shirt, and your hair, well, it's kinda . . ." Her words drift off.

"Kinda what?"

"No, no, it's cute—big." She laughs. "And all hipster, it's just kinda . . ." She makes a wavy gesture with her Twizzler and says, "So you're an artsy business guy, which means you're an architect or something."

I stiffen, my brain momentarily freezing, unable to speak from absolute shock. This girl, someone I've never met before and who is this weird, guessed correctly. I wrangle my best poker face, which includes holding my breath behind a stiff mask.

"Or something," I manage to respond, and try to pull myself together. "That's an interesting observation. But if you don't want to know my real name, you probably don't want to know if you're right about my job."

Shea gives me a dazzling smile. "I'm pretty sure I'm right. I'm like one of those people at a carnival who can guess your birthday, weight, and height, but I also specialize in guessing jobs."

"So you're a psychic fortune-telling carny?" I laugh.

"For this week, maybe I am." She stands. "You hungry? Wanna get lunch?"

SHE 6

ew offers me an uncomfortable lopsided grin when I ask him to lunch. I can see the answer *no* in his dark eyes already. Can I blame him? After all, I know there's a good chance he's seen me in my Bridezilla dress, and now half-naked in my special days-of-the-week underpants, while bike riding through the city with a pack of raisin-wrinkled, seventy-plus-year-old hippie nudists.

"I promise, I'm not crazy," I add to make the outing more enticing.

He gives me an appraising look. "Isn't that what crazy people say to convince someone they aren't?"

"Of course, I mean, I've been told I am, but I'm no crazier than anyone else in this town." I point across the park to the naked bike riders, who have settled on the grass to picnic with their bobs and jiggles laid out in the sun for all to see.

"Are we joining them for lunch?" He tilts his head in their direction.

"Only if you want to." I laugh at his expression. The poor guy looks severely pained. "Actually, I've heard there's a great Italian grocery up on Columbus Avenue." I pick up my bike by the handlebars, waiting for an answer.

"But you don't even know me."

"We're all strangers until we meet. Right? Besides, you said you've seen me three times, and I know I've seen you at least once, though I don't remember where. I think that's destiny telling us we need to have lunch." I say it matter-of-factly in hopes this train of thought makes sense.

After a moment of long consideration, he finally says, "Well, when you say it like that, then how can I refuse destiny?"

"Good call, 'cause she can be a real bitch. Trust me."

Hew joins my side as I push my bike across the park. He unknots his necktie, neatly rolls it up and slips it into his jacket, and then unbuttons the top of his shirt, allowing an inch more of his tattoo to show. It's monochromatic and geometric, and I'm more than a little tempted to reach over and touch it the way people touch pregnant women's bellies. But I don't, for fear it would send him running in the other direction.

As we walk, I'm fascinated by the way his dark hair bounces, yet somehow manages to remain perfectly styled. His profile is strong, masculine, and distinctive with a knot in the ridge of his nose, reminding me of a Roman bust. He could be Italian with his tanned complexion.

"Do you always ask strange men to lunch?" He removes his jacket and folds it over his arm, then looks to me with his dark eyes full of expression.

"Only the cute ones." I look up and bat my lashes playfully.

"So this is a pickup?" His lips form another lopsided grin, this one more confident.

"No!" I say too quickly, and immediately feel the hot blush rising in my cheeks. He's cute, hot even. There's absolutely no argument there. "I'm mean, no." I gnaw at my lip because it's true, and hope I didn't give him the wrong idea. "Is that okay? I'm sorry, the truth is that I'm alone and you seem to be alone. Are you alone because you gave me that vibe?"

"The aloneness vibe?" He looks to me in mock horror.

A quick pop of a genuine laugh escapes my lips. It's a nice change from all the days I've spent crying. "Sorry."

"I guess I must since I am, in fact, alone. I thought I'd enjoy the city for a few days after my interview, maybe drive through some of the neighborhoods, see where I might want to live if I get the job. But the truth is that I don't know anyone here."

"Well, now you know me."

We reach the bottom of the first hill that leads to the heart of the Little Italy neighborhood, and Hew offers to push my bike.

"So, what is it you really do for a living, Shea?"

"Right now?"

"Yes, right now. Your job?"

"Well, according to you I'm a fortune-telling carny," I proclaim.

"Is knowing your job not allowed in the rules?"

"There's only one rule, no real names." Keeping things at this level will allow me to have a nice time without getting close. All I need right now is a friend. Even though I'm wishing I didn't choose someone quite so good-looking, because if I'm being honest with myself, a friend is all I can handle.

"It's a strange rule."

"We're just hanging out and having fun, no attachments, no e-mails or texts after whatever this is is over." I roll my hand in the air.

"That's two rules then, and that statement implies that we've started a 'whatever this is.'" Hew flashes me a boyish grin.

"We have. We're friends." I skip into the store marked Sabatino Brothers Deli, leaving him to lock up my bike.

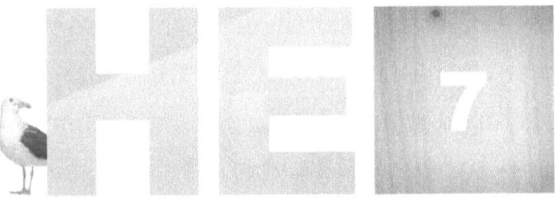

unch is delightfully vague. Shea manages to charm me, despite the fact that she tells me practically nothing concrete about herself. Most of the stories she relays, I'm not sure are true.

She tells me she's painted on the Seine River in Paris like a real artist, rode on a Mardi Gras float in New Orleans, which she may or may not have done topless. But I'm going with topless; I enjoy the visual. She sang karaoke with my favorite football player in a dive bar in Baltimore, even though she admits she can't sing, and only knows what football teams she likes based on the colors of their "outfits." Her favorite movie is a toss-up between *9 to 5* with Dolly Parton and *Xanadu* with Olivia Newton-John, but she's leaning toward *Xanadu* because she loves to roller skate. And she's even taught art to underprivileged kids. Despite my pointed questioning on each topic, which she answers convincingly, but also with a wink, she swears it's all true. Even if it's not, it doesn't matter, because I realize I'm having a great time. We manage to talk about everything useless and nothing specific.

I, however, do tell her the truth, but also with a wink so it's not clear if I'm telling the truth either. It seems we're playing a game—to one-up each other with awesomeness. And when I ramble off the highlight reel of my life, the scenes actually make me appear like a semi-interesting person. Of course I leave out the most recent events that landed me in rehab and jail. But it could have been a lot worse without my great lawyer, time served, good behavior, and an unwavering sense of remorse.

"In my sophomore year in college," I say, "I traveled to Brazil to install solar panels on the rooftops of this little village in the Andes."

"Shut up!" Shea slaps the tabletop with excitement.

"No, really." I lean in and push my empty plate away. "I have to admit that I agreed to do it as a cheap way to see South America, but volunteering my time and having the opportunity to improve an entire community's quality of life was incredibly rewarding." I leave out the fact that I dropped out my senior year and didn't get my architecture degree until this past summer.

"So you're the really nice-guy type." She leans back and crosses her arms. "I don't think I'm that good. I wish I was a better person and did stuff like that."

I want to say, "No, I'm not the good-guy type, I'm the type that doesn't even deserve to be having lunch with a nice girl like you." Instead, I push all those thoughts away. My guilt has been torturing me for long enough.

I'm trying to start fresh here. I deserve a fresh start. Everyone does; even me. "You've taught art to kids. What's not good about that?"

As she shrugs uncomfortably and turns her face away from me, I ask myself if maybe that was a lie. In her skittering gaze, I find scars as deep as the ones on her face and leg. Why can't she be her real self for an honest conversation, tell me her true name or anything else factual about herself? What the hell happened to her back in Maryland?

Shea picks up a paper straw wrapper and winds it into curling spirals as she talks about a shopping trip she took through Chinatown yesterday. I find myself comparing her to my ex-girlfriend, Cara. They're nothing alike. Shea is carefree, magnetic, and seems so hopeful despite whatever she's left behind. Cara, well, she's shallow and reckless, and part of the reason things ended up the way they did. Since she was my sister Beth's best friend, Cara and Beth were immersed in the party world, and like a love-struck idiot who wanted to date Cara, I willingly followed the two of them, tagging along like a little brother.

After a few hours, and in the middle of a conversation about the many uses of the candies Pop Rocks and Mentos in science experiments, which she seems to be an expert on, Shea abruptly stands. "I'm not sure about you, but I've got a raging case of flat ass from sitting so long." She shakes her legs and stretches.

"Why do you think I keep shifting around? My toes have fallen asleep at least ten times since we've been here."

"I guess that means we should walk." She pulls me to my feet and her hair brushes my arms. Leaning on her, I can smell her flowery shampoo. Something in the scent activates my senses, makes my palms sweaty and turns me on.

On wobbly legs, she drags me out of the market and then faces me. "It's been fun. Thanks for keeping me company today." She shrugs into the straps of her backpack and begins walking backward.

"That's it? You're leaving?" I raise my hands in shock, trying to move with her, wanting more time.

"Maybe I'll see you around." She smiles brightly and keeps walking.

"Can I get your number?"

"Remember the rules," she shouts, then spins and marches away.

Like an idiot, I say nothing and watch her leave. Apparently she was serious about the "rules" but I never thought she was. I thought—shit. I don't know what the hell I thought.

Why the hell do I want to see her again? I shouldn't. Obviously she has issues; she's the train-wreck bride, and who knows what she's left in Maryland. And no normal person would play this weird-ass no-name game.

But in this moment, it's definitely not my brain I'm thinking with as I watch her strut away. I look past all the irritating questions, the strange and grandiose stories, and I smile, because I'm imagining the word *Wednesday* bouncing back and forth on her undies as she sways her perfect little ass.

God, she's so fucking crazy cute.

'm speed-walking away from possibly the cutest and
nicest boy in San Francisco as fast as I can so he can't
see that I'm crying. Tears roll down my cheeks, and I gasp
a sob. I promised myself I wouldn't do this, promised myself I wouldn't shed another tear. But when I realized how
much fun I was having, guilt poured over me, reopening
all those raw wounds, leading me into the familiar darkness. I just had to get away.

When I reach the top of Union Street, I'm completely
out of breath and finally empty of tears—for now. Somewhere below, Hew is probably wondering what the heck
just happened, and I don't blame him. It's not his fault
he's a charming guy, that I practically forced him to lunch,
and that I'm completely and undeniably insane.

Not fast enough, I twist out of the straps of my backpack and drop it on a park bench, paw through the contents, urgently searching for my salvation—the bottle of
evil. Just clutching it within my grasp causes a tremor
to roll over my skin, and an uncomfortable layer of cold
sweat to encase my body. I'm Pavlov's dog, salivating
at the sight of the color, shape, and feel of it within my

curled fingers. With quivering hands, I wash down another white pill with a gulp from my water bottle.

I breathe a sigh of relief, knowing the pill will calm my nerves and set my mind free. If only I could escape from it and everything it represents. No matter where I am or how hard I try not to take my meds, my issues will always be in the back of my mind, controlling me, and waiting to creep to the forefront like a heinous monster.

After I regain some sense of myself, my only consolation is that I've made it in time to watch the sunset. I seat myself in front of the base of the high-reaching Coit Tower that looks out over the city. Tonight the sun paints the sky in bright magentas and purples, and the sight makes me even sadder that I can't stay here forever. Eventually, I know I'll have to face my problems, but not yet. I'm not strong enough yet.

My next clear thought. *I forgot my bike.* Ugh!

I rest my head on my knees and sigh. After the sun gives way to twilight, I make my way back down Union Street and return to Little Italy. But when I return to the deli where Hew and I had lunch, my bike is gone. Either he took it or someone else has.

For a second, I wonder how much the hotel will add to my credit card for not returning the bike, but I quickly shake off the thought. It doesn't matter. I have so many problems much larger than this, and a stupid missing bike is the least of them. I wish it were the only one.

When I finally make it back to my hotel, many people are leaving, dressed up and headed out to clubs or fancy dinners. Couples slip into limos and taxis, looking happy and in love. I wish I were doing the same, but instead I'm here in a city I always wanted to visit with Bren, and I'm by myself. Watching the energy of the city, where everyone has someone, even a friend, I've never felt so alone in my life.

"Welcome back." The doorman smiles and opens the door for me to I pass through. I make my way to the front desk.

"How can I help you tonight?" the woman standing behind the counter asks.

"I used one of the free bikes this morning, and while I was out, someone stole it."

"Oh no, I'm sorry to hear that. Can I have your room number?"

"Room 616." I lean on the high counter, dropping my chin into my palms as she types my info into the computer.

"I see you checked out a beach cruiser this morning, but it appears you checked it back in earlier this evening." She looks up from behind a strand of dyed red hair the color of vampire blood, and black Buddy Holly glasses. Everyone here is incredibly fashionable.

"I did?" I stand up taller with a nervous laugh. "I think I would have remembered that."

The girl simply gestures to two bikes that are parked

near the glass front door. "We only have two and they're both here. Perhaps someone brought it back for you? The bikes are marked with the hotel info."

"Um, okay. I guess I have a guardian angel then." *Hew.*

"Can I do anything else for you this evening?"

"No, thanks." I step away.

"Enjoy your evening." She waves as I slip into the nearby elevator.

The door shuts and the mirrored walls reflect my puzzled face. Why do I have to meet such a genuinely sweet and hot guy, when I'm clearly not ready for anything more? I groan and turn my head, lightly banging it against the wall. The elevator dings and the doors part, and I drag myself back into my room.

I lock the door behind me, kick off my satin slippers, and toss my bag on the chair, then collapse on the bed spread-eagle. It's only then that I turn my head to see the bright pink blinking light on the phone, signaling that I have a voice message.

I watch it.

On. Off. On. Off.

With each illumination, my body tenses a little more. I don't want to check it, but I must because that blinking light will haunt me and ruin an entire night of sleep. I've told no one that I'm here. Not even my family. I lean over and lift the receiver, then follow the instructions on the phone.

Though I shouldn't, I hope it's Hew, now that he knows where I'm staying, but I should know better. He doesn't even know my real name. Instead, after pressing a few buttons, to my horror, the voice I'm running away from begins to speak. My throat turns dry as I attempt to swallow.

"Babe, I'm so worried about you. Why the hell are you in San Francisco? Can you please come home so we can work this out? I love you."

His voice activates my anxiety. It courses through my veins, pumping pure adrenaline, an instinctual mechanism gearing me up for a fight. Or flight.

But I've already done that.

I try to calm myself, remembering what is real. He's such a controlling ass, he's probably already tracking my credit card purchases, which is no doubt how he found me in the first place. It's just one of the perks of his government job. He can track my every move like a damn bounty hunter. If I don't return his calls, he'll jump on a plane to come find me to drag me home. Thankfully he left the message just before I walked in the door. So it won't be tonight. It would take over five hours for him to arrive from Maryland.

Relaxing slightly, still under the control of the white pill, I try to examine this problem somewhat rationally. I have some time to rethink and recoup, but tomorrow will have to be my last day here.

I lean over to snatch my bag, unzip it, and remove my

pill bottle and cell phone. Tonight, though, I desperately don't want to need it. My body requires the pink pill, logically I know that, but everything in me likes to forget why. As if it's too painful to remember.

I put the bottle on the desk, willing myself not to take a pill. I don't want to, even though I know I should. Parts of my mind block the reason. But from this side of the wall where it's hidden, I know, can sense, that it's evil and uncontrollable. Recalling this little bit sets me on edge and I drag my hands over my face, digging my nails into my skull and skin. The mental tug-of-war to take or not take the damn pink pill is twisting me into nervous chaos.

Finally I give in. I snatch up the bottle, my hands trembling as I pop the top. My unfocused mind and fingers can't seem to find the correct pill, so I frantically dump them onto the desk. The pills spill everywhere; some tumble to the floor, but I don't care because the pink one rolls free, landing at the edge of the desk, and I drop my head onto the surface, practically kissing the wood as I suck up the hard sphere like a vacuum, swallowing it without water. The fix is quicker.

As the medication settles in, I close my eyes. It creates a mental haze, but one I can still function within. I turn on my cell for the first time in days. Thirty-eight missed calls and more than fifty texts, each pleading for me to call or come home. I immediately delete them, just like I want to delete him from my mind.

've been sitting on the sparkly pea-green vinyl couch at Shea's quirky hotel since five a.m., and have counted the number of oversized sixties-style flowers on the wallpaper over the concierge's desk at least twenty times, each time arriving at a different number. Uncomfortable, I cross my arms over my chest and my eyelids sink, first heavy and then shut.

I didn't sleep last night, thinking about the job interview, my past, the crazy but insanely beautiful girl I met, and my unsure future. That's when the guy behind the manager's desk clears his throat loudly in an attempt to wake me. I ignore him because the staff has been harassing me for hours. I keep insisting I'm waiting for someone, but if Shea doesn't show up soon, they'll be ushering me out the front door.

Someone shakes my shoulder and I startle, suddenly awake and ready to defend my presence again.

"How long have you been here?" Shea surprises me, standing rigid with two little bags strapped over her chest, looking as if she's checking out.

"You're leaving already?" Upset, I struggle to stand and ignore her question.

"Yeah, I was thinking that maybe one night in San Fran was enough." She readjusts her bag, looking strangely uncomfortable, not as carefree as the girl I met yesterday, and I immediately realize why. It's me. I've taken this too far and now she thinks I'm stalking her.

"I'm sorry. I shouldn't have come. Honestly, I had so much fun yesterday that I just thought we could hang out again, and this was the only way I knew how to find you."

"Right, right." She looks around me, acting edgy, as if she's waiting to meet someone.

She told me she was alone yesterday, but I guess that doesn't mean she'll be alone today. I'm such a schmuck for assuming she might want to hang out, too. My excitement deflates. "Listen, it was nice meeting you. You probably have plans today so I'll get going." I shove my hands into my pockets and make a quick exit, wanting to end the awkward encounter.

The doorman pulls open the glass doors and I dart outside and trudge up the hill, along Grant Avenue through the Chinatown Gate, making my way back to my hotel. I need a nap anyway. I'm all the way at the top of the hill when I hear it.

"Hew! Wait!"

Everything about that voice, its soft and honey sweetness, causes me to stop in my tracks and turn to meet it head-on. Shea recklessly runs across the road, avoiding cars like she's in a damn Frogger game, and it's a relief when she meets me safely on the sidewalk.

"I wanted to thank you for returning my bike," she says as she nears.

"Sure."

"You know, we could hang out for today. I really don't have anything else to do."

My eyes widen with shock. "Are you sure? 'Cause I don't want to mess with the rules of the game." I tone it down, trying to play it cool.

"You're not." Her lips quirk as if she sees right through me. "But listen, I had to check out of my hotel, so do you mind if I leave some of my stuff at your place while we're out?" She holds up her small bag and I wonder where the hell the rest of her stuff is, but then remember she didn't have any baggage at the airport. But who travels across the country with almost nothing?

"Well?" She nudges my arm and I snap out of the list of questions that are building about her.

"Yeah, no problem."

"I know it isn't much," I say as we stand in front of the HelgaInga Hotel.

"You think I'm worried about your hotel choice?" She raises an eyebrow and grabs my hand, pulling me up the stairs. Just like yesterday, I'm surprised when she touches me. It's so effortless and natural.

We enter the lobby, if you can call it that, and looking around at the ancient dimly lit place, I admit that I'm a little more than embarrassed to bring her here. The hotel is a grade-A dump and when I made the reservation, I was only thinking I needed a place to crash, not a place to impress a chick.

"You're right." She turns and crosses her arms. "I am worried. You didn't tell me you had a jukebox in your lobby." She practically skips to the dirty thing, squeezed between the 1970s vending machine and dusty, outdated rack of tourist flyers.

"You got any change?" She drops her bags on the floor and holds out her hand. I scramble for a few quarters deep in my pocket and pass them over. She rolls them into the money slot and selects a song. The machine clicks a few times and soon a melody hums, filling the small lobby and awakening the snoozing hotel manager sitting behind a cracked glass window.

She places a hand on each side of the machine and sways her behind in a soulful way as the tune fades in. If I could see it, I know the word *Tuesday* would be swaying with it, and my temperature rises at the thought. The lyrics kick on over the music and she twists to face me while dramatically lip-syncing to "Dancing Queen" by ABBA. I chuckle when she slides her palm over my chest and slinks around me, dancing seductively. When she drags her delicate finger, it leaves a heated trail on my skin. My hands ball at my sides as I try to be chill, but it's difficult with her sprinkling her sexiness all over me.

"Don't act like you don't know the words, too." She grabs my hands, waves them around, beckoning me to dance.

"No, no." I slide back, holding up my palms. "I require many, many drinks before I can submit to that kind of mortification." And I don't do that, not anymore. At least, I try my best not to, but it's an endless battle. That, and I can't take my eyes off her every move—her sparkling eyes, her wild mane, her impossibly thin waist above her curvy behind. Why would I want to dance and miss one moment of her parading around me like a peacock?

When she throws her head back with laughter, I want to melt right onto my knees and worship this girl. There's something about her outlook on life and her magnetic passion that I want to soak up and keep. I want to see life through her eyes, even for just a little bit.

The haunting vocals fade and the song ends.

"Maybe next time," I say, and pick up her things.

"Just remember," she offers seriously. "There may not be a next time."

Shea moves past me and heads for the stairs. I follow, wondering what she means, but then remember that I don't even know her real name. After today, we may never see each other again. For all I know, she could take off in the next minute like she did yesterday, and I still don't understand why. When we reach the top of the first flight, her good mood seems to have returned.

"Which room is yours?"

hen I reach the top floor, I head straight for room 507. The door isn't even locked when I instinctively turn the knob. "You might wanna lock your door," I holler back to Hew and push through. A cloud of musty air hits me, and I scrunch my nose and cough.

Behind me, Hew quickly tromps up the stairs. I spin to see him barge through the door and push past me.

"What's wrong?" I widen my eyes at his reaction.

He drops to his knees, shuffling through his open suitcase like a crazed person, and then jumps up and races to the bathroom, checking his stuff but he doesn't answer.

"Are you okay?" I ask again.

"Someone's been in here!" he yells. "I think I've been robbed!"

"Oh my God, were you robbed?" I step forward, worried, and waiting for him to come out. A moment later, he pops around the corner with that beaming smile of his. "Gotcha!" He winks and points at me. "Just kidding."

I narrow my eyes, pick up a pillow from the unmade bed, and hurl it at his handsome face, but he quickly ducks behind the wall, laughing. The deep rumble is so loud that it resonates in the small room, filling my heart with a genuine smile.

"You jerk! You had me going! I was worried." I giggle as he picks up the pillow and throws it back. It lands squarely in my chest, but he's already hidden back in the bathroom.

"There's no way I'm leaving anything important in this place. Not where anyone can find it," he says in explanation from the other room. "The door's lock was broken when I got here, and all the other rooms were taken."

"Good call." I throw the pillow aside and reach to tug open the curtains as I fight with the instantaneous guilt. I shouldn't have to feel guilty for having a good time. For thinking he's handsome with that dark wavy hair, his warm chocolate eyes, his raspy voice that does something strange to me every time he talks, or for laughing and joking around. I lift my chin and tell myself what I need to—I won't feel guilty anymore. With all I've been through, I shouldn't have to. Now, I just have to try to take my own advice.

"I'll be out in a minute and we can leave," Hew calls out, and shuts the bathroom door.

"Okay." I look around the room, which is pretty awful. A crooked bronze lamp hangs above, surrounded by horrid avocado-colored walls. The room is furnished with old and dented lacquered furniture, and the bed's comforter is brown with a geometric pattern faded from years of washing, or lack of washing. I scrunch my nose at the disturbing thought and reach to open the window. I unlock and lift the frame and lean out into the crisp fall air, taking a deep breath. That's when I notice the metal fire escape. Unable to resist, I crawl out the window and settle on my butt with my back pressed against the wood-slatted wall. I always wanted to live in a building that had a fire escape. It's all so romantic, like in *Breakfast at Tiffany's.*

I lodge my boot against the railing and lean my head back with a sigh, happy to be away from my hotel, where I could potentially be found. If Hew hadn't shown up, I'd be on the road by now. The truth is that I need a plan. With worry-filled sleep last night, I never got around to making one. I have to go off the grid to hide, and the only way to do that is get some cash so my credit cards can't be tracked.

"Shea." Hew leans out. "Aren't you freaked to sit there?" He looks down five stories and shivers.

"Nah, not afraid of heights, though it's not the most stable structure." I kick the railing and it jiggles. "But this is the best part of your room." I gesture to the view of the Golden Gate Bridge in the distance. "You wanna join me?" I slide over a little, but he grabs my arm.

"You're seriously making me nervous. I don't do heights, and I definitely don't do rickety fire escapes."

"Really?" I move to shuffle back to the window and he releases my arm, but instead of climbing back into the hotel room, I stand. "So you wouldn't want me to do this?"

I jump—twice. In response, the entire metal structure gives and bounces with a deep, squeaky moan, sounding like it may detach from the building at any moment. All color drains from Hew's face and he reaches out to me like he wants to save me, but I step just out of arm's reach and jump again, enjoying torturing him a little. I've looked death in the eye once, so nothing about this makes me nervous. I know from experience that you can't control when you go. Destiny does.

"Shea, please, you're going to fall. Be careful."

"It's just payback for making me believe that you got robbed." I do a rep of jumping jacks, and Hew breaks into a perceivable sweat. I laugh manically at his reaction.

"Okay, okay, you got me, evil one. Now come in." He waves me forward.

"Tell you what, how about you get your stuff and we'll leave via the outdoor stairs?" I squat down to meet his gaze.

"How about—" He leans out of the window and looks down again. "No!" He quickly encircles his muscular arms around my knees and back, locking me in a death grip, and pulls me inside the room through the window, far too fast for me to resist. We collapse onto the edge of the bed and slide with a heavy thunk onto the floor, my weight crushing his chest, and both of us laughing hysterically.

"For an architect who should be able to handle heights, you're a wuss!" I try to stand, but he grabs and tickles me as if we've done this a million times before. I find myself attracted to him when I clearly shouldn't be, but everything between us has happened so naturally. I have to wonder if destiny is messing with me again, so to protect my heart and mind, I wiggle out of his grip to stand. Anything to keep the distance, though admittedly, it's not easy.

"If I were you, I wouldn't be caught dead on that floor." I offer him a hand. "I think I saw it moving earlier."

"Nothing can be as bad as the bed. Trust me." Hew clasps his fingers with mine. His touch is warm and comforting, just like the timbre of his voice, and I yank him to stand. When he does, he lands right in my personal space. Close enough to kiss me, and I suck in a breath before stepping back a pace.

"Really? You won't sit out on a fire escape, but you'll sleep in a bed with sheets that probably haven't been changed since the eighties?"

"I have to draw the line somewhere, don't I?" He slips on his jacket. "Let me just grab one thing and we can go."

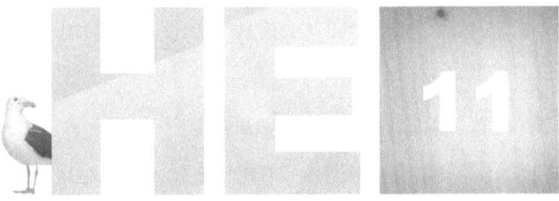

I go to my secret hiding place, kneel onto the cushion, and reach behind the back of the lone armchair. When I checked in and found that my room couldn't be locked, I searched the room for a hiding place. I knew that if anyone came into my room, no one would even bother looking behind this mold-covered thing. I grab my camera and loop the strap around my neck, letting it rest on my chest.

"A camera? You left a professional camera in an unlocked hotel room?" Shea asks.

"Living on the edge."

We leave the room, shutting the door behind us.

"I'm just surprised to see you with it. I didn't figure you for a photographer, too." We shuffle down the stairs.

"Clearly, your freaky carny radar must be off today," I suggest as we reach the lobby.

"You're right, I haven't been feeling myself." She pauses and turns to me. "You know, I took a photography class in high school once, but it was mostly so I could make out with Turner Bishop in the darkroom. He was wicked hot.

A total badass. The kind of guy who ticks off your parents."

"So how'd that work out for you?"

"Not great. Mr. Catalono, our teacher, caught us playing tonsil hockey in the darkroom while Turner massaged my boob under my shirt. It was my first time to second base. Not as great as I thought it would be, but I blame Mr. Catalono for killing the mood."

"The nerve!"

"Right? I know. We spent the better part of the semester in detention, and I never did figure out how those f-stop things worked." She points to my camera. "I don't have the patience to figure out mechanical stuff."

"Once you figure it out, it's not too bad." When we get outside, I lift the camera and remove the lens to snap a quick succession of images. Shea's hair blows in long, soft, undulating waves, just like a Botticelli painting. She turns and looks to me with her beautiful eyes framed with perfectly sculpted dark eyebrows. But it's her lashes that make me want to reach out and touch her creamy face, sprinkled with delicate freckles. Her lashes reach far, black and thick-fringed, intensifying her sparkling green eyes.

When I'm done with my impromptu photo shoot, I look down at my digital screen to see what I've captured. I scroll through each image, but she isn't smiling, only staring right through me. In the deep, churning ocean behind her gaze, I sense all the hurt that led her here, and I desperately want to ask her about the day I saw her on the plane, who she was running from and why. Did he betray her? Did he hit her? But I can't ask, not yet, because when she bares her soul to me, I'll have no choice but to share my story, too.

For the first time since I met her, I understand her need to keep her name secret and respect that. Here, someplace other than at home, we can be who we want, be with who we want, as long as it makes us happy. There's no past today, only this moment together, right now. I may need that as much as she does. We are exactly the same that way.

"I know what will make me feel better." She pushes my camera away, like she's trying to hide what the photos reveal.

"I can honestly say that I'm scared to know." I follow her down the hill. "Let me guess, you want to scale the high support beams of the bridge?"

She laughs. "Not today."

"Well, I have a map we can check out." I stop, pull it from my jeans pocket, and unfold it. Just as I lift the map to reading distance, Shea rips the paper from my hands and tears it into a million little pieces. "Hey!" I try to stop her, but she dodges from side to side and tosses the shreds in the air like confetti. They flitter around in the breeze. Several pieces land in her wild hair.

"Today is not about planning," she says. "Today is about exploring. Today is about adventure and getting lost. We'll be as free as birds." She spreads her arms into the breeze, and I'm not sure if she's putting me on or if this is really how she is.

"Okay. Where do you suggest we go?"

"I have an idea. Surprise me and take me to your favorite spot in the city."

"That's your grand idea?" I ask. "That sounds planned."

"No, then I'll take you to mine. You'll never guess where it is." She bobs with excitement.

"You'll show me yours, if I show you mine?" I wag my eyebrows and give her cute little body a once-over, knowing it will garner a reaction.

She smacks my arm. Exactly what I wanted, anything to make her touch me.

I laugh and continue. "Small problem. I needed the map to get to mine."

"Oh, I bet you do!" This time she looks me up and down and laughs.

"Ha-ha." I bump into her playfully. "I guess I walked into that one."

"You make it too easy." Shea grabs my hand and squeezes. "Seriously, though, that's where the exploring part comes in. If we walk in the right direction, we'll get there eventually, but who knows what we'll see along the way."

"I just hope it's not the bicycling nudists."

"That's exactly what I'm talking about! That was so random and awesome, and when we tell our friends about that, they'll think we're lying." She looks at the next four-way intersection. "So, which way do we go?"

ew shrugs his shoulders and complies with my request to take me to his favorite spot in San Francisco. "It's a pretty far walk from here, or we can take a taxi," he suggests.

"No way! We walk. It's perfect outside. Everyone keeps saying that the weather should be crappy, but I think they're lying. It's been in the seventies and sunny for two days, and I heard it was the same all last week."

I twine my arm with his and he leads me north, up and down several hills lined with beautiful homes. Many people are out walking their fur babies, their real babies, or exercising.

"Oh, I almost forgot," I say. "I need to get some cash. Wait here."

I leave him on a corner and run across the road to a banking machine. I unzip my purse and riffle through for my debit card. When I find it, I insert it into the machine, type in my PIN number, and take out as much cash as they allow—two hundred fifty dollars. This will hold me for a few days; at least I can sleep easy tonight knowing that no one can trace my credit card. I will be safe.

Hew joins my side and gives me a strange look when I quickly roll up all the bills and shove them in my coin purse. "I was completely out of cash," I explain.

"No worries, I've got cash, too," he says, patting his back pocket, and his words catch me off guard. It's something couples say to each other, to let them know they've got the other covered. But he doesn't really even know me, nor do I know him. The thought of him forming an attachment to me leaves me feeling guilty at first, but then happy.

"So, where to?" I ask.

"This way." He leads me to the peak of another hill and at the top, I can see that it leads all the way down to the crystal-blue waters of the South Bay. We don't walk straight down the hill. In the spirit of adventure, Hew zigzags us all over the place, up and down hills, playing the part that I gave him—that of architect.

"San Francisco is a mix of homes and architectural styles. Of course, there are the famous Victorian painted ladies." He gestures to a row of them, all aligned perfectly, but each with their own color scheme.

"They're like my perfect house. Where else would you get away with painting ten different colors on one building? They definitely wouldn't do that at home."

"And where's that?" he asks as he lifts his camera, taking shots of the streetscape.

I catch myself right before screaming out the name of my town. My real town. But the same rules that I gave us yesterday still apply. "I've lived all over, but I'm thinking it may be time for a new home," I lie, and point to one of the painted ladies, a mostly yellow and white one. "Yellow houses are happy houses. That's why I like this one the best. I think I'll move here." I stop at the bottom of its long front stairway.

"Yellow houses are happy houses?" he repeats and turns his attention to me. "Are you sure? Because the psychology of color suggests that a yellow house would make you feel anxious."

"The psychology of color?" I raise my brows and smile. "That sounds official, and very much like an architect."

"Seriously, psychology suggests that colors can make people feel a certain way, like blue or cool colors can make you feel calm. Red rooms can make you feel hungry. That's why interior designers paint red on dining room walls. And yellow walls can make you crazy!" He laughs.

"Yellow equals crazy? If that's true, it certainly explains a lot in my life."

"I'm joking," he says, backtracking. "Reaction to color is subjective. What's perfect for one person is not for another."

"So, which one of these would you pick?"

He walks to each, seeming to consider not only the colors but also all the features. "I pick this one." He stops in front of a mostly lavender house with bright white gingerbread trim.

"Why this one? It's kinda girly for a guy."

"Well, I could tell you it's because purple is the color of introspection, knowledge, and power, which it is, but the real reason I pick this one is because of that." He points to the side yard with an elevated porch. "This one has a Jacuzzi!"

I laugh and push his arm. "I don't think Jacuzzi qualifies as a color."

"But I'm thinking that being in that Jacuzzi after walking up and down all these hills would be more important than house color. I have a feeling I'm going to be hurting later."

"Just think of it this way, this city is a natural Stair-Master. That's why all the people who live here have perfect asses." I point across the street to a man.

"That's what you consider a perfect ass?" This time Hew pushes me and laughs.

The man hobbling away from us and up the hill is at least ninety, and carrying a grocery bag in each hand. His khaki pants drape over the area where there should be a butt, but his body moves straight from slim hips to skinny thighs.

"He has no ass," Hew says with a laugh.

"A concave ass."

"Flat-ass syndrome," he counters.

"The anti-ass," I add, and we laugh harder with each newly made-up term.

"Ass-licking."

"Ass-licking?" I lose it and double over cackling because we're so caught up in ourselves, in our compounding laughter, that everything is much funnier than it should be. To everyone around us, I know we look ridiculous.

"No! No! Lacking, not licking! Ass-laaaacking!" he tries to explain through his happy tears. "If that is the perfect ass, I'm really in trouble." He grabs his own firm butt. "You'll have to let me know if it's any flatter by the time we're done today."

"I'll be sure to let you know."

With those words, we stop and stare at each other with out-of-breath smiles. My cheeks actually hurt from our exchange, and I remember the last time I felt like this. It was with Bren.

Bren and I were making a midnight run to the supermarket; I wanted ice cream and he wanted oranges. He liked his sweets in the healthy form, just one of the many things I used to love about him. He would never eat my ice cream, and I would never eat his fruit. We stood at the bin of oranges, and each time Bren filled the clear plastic bag with oranges, the bottom of the bag would split apart and all the globes would tumble to the floor, rolling everywhere. We tried using new bags, three different times, but each time the fruit fell out of the bottom of the bag for no reason. Our laughing increased with each new attempt. We crawled around the cold terrazzo floor, collecting the oranges, and looked for the hidden cameras we were certain were there, but there were none. The bags were really just faulty.

It was real and uncontrollable laughter, the stupid kind for no good reason, just like this moment between Hew and me. That's when I realize he's snapping more photos of me as I'm lost in this private thought, the part of my relationship with Bren that I want to remember. It's the most recent part, or lack thereof, that I want to forget.

"So, are we close to your spot?" I ask to break him away from his viewfinder. I have the sinking feeling that when he's behind it, looking at me, it reveals everything about my past—my secrets, my real home, my house color, and even my real name. Everything I can't afford for him to know.

"Almost there."

S hea stops in her tracks when we reach the intersection of Baker and Bay Street. Her eyes grow wide and she claps her palms over her mouth and squeals with excitement.

"What is this place? It's like a dream!" She takes off like an uncontrollable child and rushes across the road to the park.

I knew I'd find the Palace of Fine Arts eventually, but I'm half-glad that Shea ripped up my map, making the walk take longer so we could spend more time together, at least until she decides to take off again. I sigh at the thought of her walking away for another time and join her side, determined to make her want to hang out with me as much as I do with her.

"It's called the Palace of Fine Arts, and this is my favorite place in the city."

The grass is perfectly trimmed, sparkling in the afternoon light with a velvety sheen. With the sunny sky, the colors of the garden are blindingly beautiful. At our feet, a black lake shimmers while graceful white swans glide across the surface. But that's not the most beautiful part, it's the actual "palace" that is the gem of this show. The massive Roman-inspired dome and matching high-reaching colonnades are stunning, and their terracotta color complements the cloudless blue backdrop.

If Shea didn't realize before that I'm an architect, she certainly does now. This building is everything I studied in college, every history of art and architecture class that I loved sitting through and dreamed about at night. Even though it's not truly as old or detailed as any ruin in Europe, it's equally as impressive and romantic. It's the idea of it, and I know if I ever said any of that out loud to anyone but Shea, I would be laughed at for the unmanliness of it all.

"Oh my gosh, this might be my new favorite place, too. I never even knew this was here!" She walks to an ornate bench and sits. I follow and drop down beside her, and look out at the scenery.

"I always imagined the dome as a gazebo for King Kong. It's the perfect size, it's so large," I add. "And over there"—I stand and point to an open grassy spot, getting excited about this idea I've had for ages—"I wanted to design an outdoor sculpture of huge white 3-D glasses that sit looking toward the dome. I mean huge—with one red lens and one blue lens." I raise my arms above my head. "Maybe twenty feet wide and seven feet high."

"Why?" She scoots to the end of the bench and leans forward, her eyes wide with interest.

"Because when you look into the glasses toward the palace dome, you would see the Space Invaders coming down from the sky, a black and white old movie-style Godzilla getting ready to crush the dome with a slap of his giant tail, and over there, King Kong fighting him off to save his giant gazebo!"

Shea leaps from the bench and claps. "I love the idea! Impressively creative, and it would be the coolest sculpture ever! I'd visit here every day just to look through the lenses and see all that."

"Really?"

"Yes."

"It's the first time I've ever told anyone about it. Don't go stealing the idea," I warn her. "You could be a famous sculptor, for all I know, related to Da Vinci or something."

"I'll try not to, but it'll be hard. Uncle Da Vinci is my hero." Shea looks away and says, "I love this place. It reminds me of a garden for a Roman queen or something. It's honestly the prettiest thing I've ever seen. Thank you." She reaches out and grabs my hand, threading her fingers through mine. "Thank you for bringing me here. It's magnificent." She bites her lip the way chicks do when they're flirting. Or it could be me hoping that she's flirting, making me want to kiss those plump lips.

With that look on her face, I can't concentrate on the architecture or my grand sculpture idea, because she's more beautiful than anything here. Yes, she's touched me before, but not like this. This is different, and I sense that the scales are tipping in my favor—I hope. The truth is, I want to be more than friends with this girl, no matter what's happened to her in Maryland and who is waiting for her there. It's not fair, but I'm too into her to turn back now. I'll do whatever it takes to get her to agree to another day with me.

We meander through the path in the park, a loop that circles the lake, then weave under the tall colonnades and into the massive dome. We're unable to walk completely inside when we arrive, because it's roped off today for a private wedding.

The bride's large white dress reminds me of the one Shea wore on the first day I saw her, and standing next to the bride is a groom in a tuxedo. Both are smiling, clutching each other's hands for dear life as they repeat their vows before a minister and a small wedding party.

Shea stiffens and her face contorts, like someone who's seen a car accident take place right before her eyes. Her expression fills with horror and her lips begin trembling, and that's when the tears begin. I put my arm around her back and pull her close, wishing I could take away whatever pain her fiancé caused her. But she jerks away and her entire body convulses. Pulling away turns into running away, and she's pushed past several groups of tourists before my brain can even register to chase after her.

SHE 14

ew stops following me when I run into an empty ladies' room at the Palace of the Arts park. I stumble in, finding my way to the sink to hold myself upright, before I work myself into a panicked frenzy that will cause me to pass out. I've slipped into the silent darkness before; it could easily happen again.

My head pounds, sweat runs down my back, and dots form in front of my eyes just as I unscrew my pill bottle. With shaking hands, I grab one white pill and place it eagerly on my tongue, chasing it with a gulp of freezing water from the faucet. Cold water dribbles over my cheeks and chin, dripping down onto my shirt as I slurp it like an animal, and I collapse to the wet tiled floor, weeping.

It only takes a few minutes for the drug to kick in, and to save me from myself and my tragic endless tears.

"Shea?"

Hew peeks his head around the corner and his eyes widen when he sees me in my state of grief. I didn't want him to find me this way. I don't want to share this part of my life with him; I want to hide it away from the world.

God only knows how tired I am of people knowing everything about me and all the horrible details. I just want to be alone to cry my eyes out in my own space, and get over things in my own time. And when my mind and soul are ready, carve out those little pieces of happiness, one chip at a time, like some large sculpture. Maybe even a Roman one.

I look up to Hew. Eventually, with enough chips, shavings, and dust, my picture of happiness will appear. I have to keep believing that and hoping for it, because if I don't, then what else is there to live for?

He comes to my side and hugs me. I've received many hugs and words of comfort, but not from someone I don't truly know. He hugs me and he has no idea why, and when he does, it's different from the others. Maybe because there's no judgment behind it, or no reason other than he's a good guy and wants to make the hurt go away. He's reassuring and so different from the isolation and loneliness that I've been feeling, that I want to melt into every curve of his body, forget my past, and live in this fake little world with him. One where someone thinks I'm perfect.

"Let me help you from the floor," he whispers, then locks his arms under my bent elbows and gently lifts me to stand. One of his large hands splays across my back, and the other cradles my head into his broad chest.

My nose nestles within the small *V* opening of his

button-down shirt, right at the clavicle. His skin is warm, intoxicating, the scent of brown sugar and leather. I inhale and my shoulders relax their tenseness, then I sigh a breath of release. I'm not sure if it's the drug or Hew, but one of them or possibly both of them is my sanity.

"Let's go outside." He leads me into the sunshine and to an empty patch of grass. "Let's sit."

I move with him, still huddled in his embrace, and we slowly lower to the ground. Unlike everyone else, he never asks me why I cry, why I freaked out; he just lets me be, lets me work out this pain on my own. He rocks me while humming a soothing melody.

We sit for at least an hour, and then he does what everyone else before him has done. He ruins everything.

"Please tell me what happened to you," I plead. "I saw you on the plane from Baltimore, saw you in your shredded wedding dress. Please tell me so I can try to help you in some way. I feel useless not knowing." Even though I don't know this girl well, I feel an intense need to protect her.

Shea stiffens under my embrace and pulls away so our eyes are level. At first I think she's going to open up and finally share something true about her life, but her words aren't the ones I want to hear.

"I can't. I just can't."

She stands, collects her handbag, and takes off, striding as fast as she can across the park to the nearest street.

"Shea! Come back!" I leap to chase after her again, maneuvering the camera from where it's been resting on my back to my front, where I can hold it in my hand. I can't stand the thought of not knowing if I'll ever see her again, like I felt when she walked away from me yesterday. The moment she left, a heaviness settled in my chest, and I ached for more. I have to see her again. I grab her arm just as she's about to step into the open back door of a taxi.

"Don't leave, please. I'm sorry I said the wrong thing. I just want to help."

"You can't help. That's the problem, no one can help!"

She jerks away, and regretfully, I let her go again. Her expression conveys her feelings more than her words. This girl is broken. But who am I to think that I can fix her? I may be just as broken or worse, though, for some reason I would give anything in the world to try to make her better.

The door slams, severing me from the best thing that's happened to me in years, and my shoulders slump in defeat.

"Fuck!" I scream so loudly that the people around me cringe. They're looking at me in a way I don't want to be looked at. I screwed up royally. I should have known; we made a promise on the first day not to be ourselves, to be the best version of ourselves. But when I saw her crying that way, so helpless, the way I've cried a million times before, I couldn't help myself.

The yellow cab speeds up the hill and I watch it for as long as I can, until it turns the corner, disappearing forever, just like Shea.

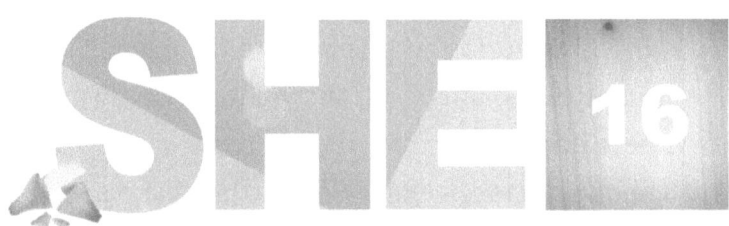

For some reason, despite my anger, I can't help but turn to look at Hew through the back window as the taxi drives away. It's the second time this week a yellow cab has been my getaway car from a guy. The difference is that this one doesn't deserve my outbursts. Hew is better than anything I left behind at home. I already know it, despite knowing nothing about him. He treats me with respect; he opens doors for me, makes me laugh, and comforts me when I cry. He owes me nothing, yet gives me everything in return.

Even from a few blocks away, I can see him throwing a fit, arms flailing and camera swaying around his neck. Somehow, when I try to get away from the drama, I seem to invite it back into my heart easily, again and again. Romance is so complex for me.

I turn to ask the driver, "Can you please take me to Washington Street?"

He nods in the mirror.

I want to weep again but the drug has taken that part of me away, lifted me up on a cloud, distracting me from the pain in my heart and taken me to the edge. It's surprising that I had enough spit and vinegar to jump up and leave Hew, despite the muck the pill creates in my mind. It just shows the resolve I have for letting that part of my past go. Maybe I need to let everything go.

The taxi driver stops and I pay him, jump out, and run into Hew's hotel. Five floors later I'm breaking into his room to grab my small bag of things. I pick them up from a chair and shrug into the straps, then stop to look around, thinking I must say something, to give him some kind of explanation.

I walk into the bathroom and grab a small bar of soap next to the sink. With it gripped in my hand, I write the word "sorry" in swirly letters on the mirror, as if the beauty of each stroke and curve will somehow make my actions explainable. It's all I can do, the only truthful bit of myself I can offer because there's hardly any truth left.

I step away to leave, shut the room door behind me, and gallop down the stairs. I need to leave before he returns. If he's determined, which I think he is, he'll try to catch up with me here.

When I make it back outside, I'm a little sad when Hew is nowhere to be found; that's how messed up I am. I want a new friend, but I don't want to tell them anything real about myself and I want them around, even when I push them away. My brain is a twisted wreckage. I consider my problem might be the loneliness I've felt for so long, looking for something that isn't there anymore, and I just need to learn to depend on myself and not others. If I can learn to be alone then maybe, eventually, I'll be okay again.

I amble down the hill and toward the tall buildings of downtown. I haven't really visited that area yet and I need to find a hotel for the night, someplace to sleep off this mental haze.

I meander past the high-rises, weave around the vintage streetcars, and stop when I come across a large hotel that faces the water and the Ferry Building. I don't even bother going back for my car at my old hotel; I'll return there to pick it up from the valet tomorrow so I can start my road trip.

Here, the hotel is corporate and modern. Inside I'm met with a large circular sculpture that appears to be rotating, though it's not. Or maybe it's rotating in my head because of the drugs; sometimes it's hard to tell reality from fantasy. In the massive atrium, a large crowd gathers—people dining, families chatting, and couples and singles meeting at the bar for drinks. With all the noise that they create, I feel myself disintegrating into the chaos.

Twenty minutes later I'm in a new room facing the water and though the view is picture-perfect, I'm more interested in sleep and revisiting my actions in the last several hours than in soaking in the sunset.

I drop into bed and hug several of the feathery-soft pillows. In my mind, I replay the events of the afternoon. I remember the way Hew made wild gestures with his hands, barely able to contain his excitement about his sculpture idea in the park. There was so much passion that I easily fell into the moment along with him, and saw every detail he envisioned through my own eyes. It was a cool idea, yes, but it was so much more than that. I felt connected to him, felt the way he loved something that was not even there yet, how he loved the idea of something—the hope of something.

Throughout the day he was charming, funny, and intelligent. It's been so long since someone talked to me about something other that my problems that I've forgotten what a real conversation feels like, one where you don't know the outline of the speech already because the details don't consume your life.

Then seeing the wedding ruined our perfect day, taking me back to why I ran away in the first place. My stomach cramps with a sharp pain, and the dark hopelessness creeps over my skin, soaking into every pore.

I do what I need to in times like these: I take another pill, a blue one this time. I need to sleep and wipe the gray slate in my mind completely clean so I can swirl for hours on a fluffy cloud, and release my soul to the evil in the bottle.

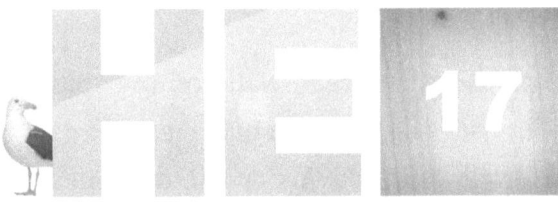

S hea has taken all her things from my room. When I returned, I prayed they would still be here, to give me a little hope that I might see her again. I came back as quickly as I could, but my taxi got tied up in traffic from road construction. The driver should have known better; it's her job to know which streets to use, but instead, she used the opportunity to raise her rate and show me her spiral book of autographs that she's collected from transporting celebrities around town.

I kick the pillow across the floor, the same one that Shea launched at my face when I first brought her here and pretended that I had been robbed. I spin in a circle, taking in everything; looking for what, I don't know. Maybe I'm looking for myself. I've been so calm and collected since I got out of jail and deep into rehab, easily telling myself that I'm miraculously a new person, that I don't do the reckless things I used to, like letting that dickhead beat me to shit three times.

But since meeting Shea, I feel again. Feel everything that I've been trying to repress since I forged into unfamiliar territory.

Screw this.

I punch the puke-green wall and the spidering pain over my knuckles feels good. My fist leaves a gaping crack in the drywall and it dawns on me that Shea has left a crack in my carefully constructed facade, one that can't easily be fixed or removed. I don't want to remove it. I want to rip it open and see where it leads.

Because I can, I do it. I push into the crack and the drywall pieces fall inside the hollow between the walls. I'm not sure what I expected to find. It's empty and dark inside, the same way I feel, and the only thing I want to do is find a place to drink it away.

It's been over twenty-four months since I've had one single drop or hit. And keeping myself in check is easily the hardest thing I've ever had to do. It's not like I just magically decided to stop drinking, and after a few weeks or even months the urge went away. No, addiction is a constant battle. When I see someone buzzed out of their mind, I don't feel bad for them, I feel envious. It's a sickness, and I crave it even though I know it will hurt me or even kill me.

Like I've taught myself to do in reaction to the weak times like these, I speak to myself from my good half. Some people would call it the voice of reason; I call it my don't-fuck-up voice.

The voice says, "But this girl is better than any liquor that's ever touched your lips, and you want more." For once the voice is right, and I'm eager to listen.

Because of the ruckus I've made, the person staying in the room next door bangs on the wall. Or maybe it's coming from below? I don't know or care and direct my energy into bed, while fighting my urge to seek out the nearest whiskey, rubbing alcohol, or NyQuil bottle. It's sad what I'll settle for.

If I can force myself to sleep, I know I can find salvation in the arms of a dream featuring Shea. Somehow, despite the fact that I'm fighting this with every quaking nerve in my body, the thought of her saves me. She is my sanity.

SHE 18

Dim light bleeds into my room through the sheers covering the windows. I roll within my blanket to check the time. I've slept late because of the sleeping pill. If I don't leave soon, the hotel may charge for another night. Almost faster than humanly possible, I shower and dress. In front of the mirror, I pull my wet hair into a loose low braid. My hair has grown so long that it hangs down my back, wetting the fabric of my long-sleeved shirt. One thing I've been dying to do is cut it shorter again and change the color, like the old happier and normal me. I can't help but think that it will help. Maybe I'll finally do it on this trip.

I pay my bill, check out, and step outside. Today is finally cloudy, the weather you would expect from San Francisco. The gloominess and gray streetscapes match my mood and the dark circles under my eyes. I came here to start over mentally, but have only managed to make my only friend in the world right now hate me.

Several blocks of walking up a hill, I finally reach the valet at the Briton Hotel. It only takes two minutes before I hear my name. "Shea!" I recognize the voice before I see the person.

Hew charges down the street, arms pumping like a crazed octopus as the camera strapped over his shoulder swings wildly. Normally I would smile at the sight but instead, I ignore him, embarrassed about how I acted yesterday. These last two days I've tried to pass myself off as someone who doesn't have a care in the world, but that's so far from the truth, and he knows it now.

I hand my valet ticket to the boy, and he takes off running down the street to retrieve my car from a nearby garage.

"What are you doing?" Hew asks as he finally reaches me.

"Leaving. What I should have done yesterday." I press my lips together as I grip the straps of my backpack.

"You broke your promise to me, you know."

"I don't make promises—ever." Not anymore, not ever again.

"You said you'd show me your favorite spot in the city and you never did. I stayed up all night thinking about it." He continues as if he'd never asked me about what happened in Maryland, as if I didn't run off on him like a crazed idiot—twice. "Can you imagine losing sleep over something like that? It's the worst."

"You're really reaching," I say with a sigh. "You sound ridiculous." I cross my arms over my chest and frown at him.

"It's important to me," he says, sounding sincere.

My rented Fiat appears and the valet jumps out of the driver's seat as he hands me my bill. I hand over all the cash I have left, except for some loose change that I drop into my jeans pocket. San Francisco is expensive, and I already need more money.

"Thanks, miss." The boy looks thrilled with my tip.

"What are we doing here?" I turn to Hew after I drop my backpack in the trunk of the car.

"I'm just asking for one more day. That's it. Besides, you owe me."

I stall, saying slowly, "I don't know. I don't think it's a good idea."

I'm half facing Hew and half facing the glass-plated hotel entrance when I see him—Bren's older brother, Luke. He's found me. Or at least, he's traced me to this hotel. He stands tall and arrogant at the front desk, talking to the red-haired concierge wearing a pink top, the same girl I had to tell about the missing bike.

He slips her some cash. My only guess is that he's trying to bribe her for more information. More information about me. My heart rate amps up and I do all I can to focus on him. I can't see if she accepts but she's not talking, only he is. That's not a good sign, especially with his gift of charming girls, usually out of their panties.

Every atom in my body wants to explode. Luke found me. He came looking for me so he can take me back home. He doesn't care that I don't want to be with him, and that the love of my life was Bren and always will be. Luke only wants what his brother had, wants to steal me away to make me his trophy, among ten million other complications. I break out in a cold, nervous sweat.

Panicking, I look at my car, at the clogged street traffic, and then at Hew. I make a quick decision. "You sold me, let's go," I say, and Hew's eyes light up with happiness. God, if he only knew.

I quickly grab his arm and usher him away. If Luke finds me with Hew, Luke will kill him. Luke will freak out the way he always does, hit Hew, then hit me. These scars didn't appear from thin air. I curse my soul for ever allowing myself to get wrapped up with that man.

The valet chases after us. "Miss, what about your car?"

"I changed my mind," I say quickly. "Can you store it until later?"

"Sure." He rips off a pink ticket and I swipe it from his hand, then shove it deep into my pocket.

By the time Luke struts out of the hotel doors, I'm hustling Hew into the corner café. Just inside, we're literally ten feet away, only separated from him by the large glass window, but it's close enough that I can practically see the heated waves of anger swirling off Luke's skin. If he were weather, he'd be a hurricane—a category-five asshole, destroying everything in his path.

The truth is that I can't blame Luke for everything because I made the decision to walk into the storm and stand there like an idiot, allowing him to beat me and pulverize my soul until I was nothing. Yes, I was desperate and messed up at the time, but it's still no excuse for everything that happened between us. I should have known better. I should have found my way out sooner.

"What are you doing?" Hew asks in a confused huff.

"I need food." I pretend to mull over the bakery counter options, trying to control my reaction to the person I hate, standing far too close. I hope I can distract Hew because I can't, under any circumstances, allow my two current worlds to collide. My legs begin to shake. I strain to lock them tight, fighting the reaction.

"I'm hungry, too," Hew says, "but I was thinking that if I happened to catch up with you, I could treat you to lunch. You know, to apologize for . . ." His words drift off and he digs his hands into his pockets.

"Um," I say noncommittally as I squat eye-level with the lower rack of the counter, not to view the pastries but to relieve my unsure limbs. My head swims with my wobbly movements, and I'm unable to focus on Hew's apology.

With blurry eyes, I watch Luke. He brushes his sandy hair out of his eyes and drops his hands on his narrow hips, scanning the faces of pedestrians that walk past him. When he does, he looks almost identical to Bren, so similar physically yet with such different personalities. My heart aches, pounding at my rib cage at the sight.

"Shea, are you okay?"

"Yeah, I'm just thinking." *Stalling.* I grab the glass counter to steady myself, then close my eyes and swallow, feeling every pore heat to a boil.

Finally Luke marches down the street into the valley of high-rises. I stand, still on edge when he finally disappears from sight, but unfortunately, not from my mind. I let out a shaky breath, but I'm too late to control the panic building within me. *Luke's here. Luke's here!* I bite the inside of my cheek and turn away from Hew.

"I'll be right back." I rush away from him before he can respond, quickly bounding into the restroom. Locked inside the narrow space, I lean over the sink, my arms and legs shaking. I let out a gasp of a sob and flex my fingers open and closed repeatedly, trying to pump reality back into my body. *I'm okay. I'm okay.*

Reaching for the faucet, I release a stream of freezing water, bend over and splash my face several times, then roll a wad of toilet paper around my hand to dry my skin and hands, but it's useless. I know I need a pill. I don't want to need it, but I do. Before I fall into the black pit of hyperanxiety, I quickly swallow another pink one. God knows, I desperately want to flush them all down the toilet, but I know that won't do me any good. Right now, it would only make things far worse, and I hate myself for being so powerless.

Ten minutes later, and still looking like a wreck from

my ordeal, I return to Hew. I need to make things right with him. He's a good guy and I owe him at least one more day. With everything I've gone through, I owe myself one more good day, too.

Shea is acting strange. Well, stranger than usual. When she's in the restroom, I survey the patrons of the French café, trying to assess what has set her off again, but there are no brides or wedding parties in sight. I can honestly say that no girl has ever made me work so hard to see her. But I also know that if I can win her over, she'll be worth the wait. I'm mesmerized by her glow, even the small spark that she's shared, and I can only imagine the fire that lies beneath.

She appears at my side, looking a little off and staring out the window. I place my hand on her shoulder for comfort, careful not to ask anything that might send her darting in the other direction. At my touch, the tension in her muscles subsides and her body relaxes, as if something has set her free.

"Shea?"

"I was going to head off on my road trip, but I like your idea. Let's do it," she says, returning to a glimmer of her "normal" self.

I beam at her, happy to have one more day. "Where

should we go?" I gesture toward the exit and we head out the door.

"I think we should start where we left off yesterday, before I made a complete ass-hat of myself," she says as she turns and begins to walk down the hill. "I was having fun with you, and I'm sorry I freaked out."

"We'll never talk about it again." I've learned my lesson, and even better, my words win me something more important—one of her beautiful smiles.

"But let's restart San Francisco style." Her eyes light up, and she adjusts her purse on her shoulder.

"What's that mean?"

"You'll see."

First, Shea makes another stop at a bank, but this time she skips the ATM and goes inside to the teller, presumably to withdraw more money. I wonder how in the hell she spent the roll of cash she withdrew yesterday. Judging from the wad she shoved in her purse, there was at least two hundred dollars. But I dismiss all the questions when she returns and guides me through Union Square. There she buys a floppy hat with a large brim, and a pair of mirrored aviator sunglasses from a street vendor.

"You realize it's cloudy today, right?"

"I know," she says, completely unconcerned as she settles the hat on her head and slides the glasses in place. She proceeds to roll her braid into a knot and shoves it under her hat. By the time she's done, she looks like an incognito movie star, dressed in a bohemian way that makes it look as if she doesn't care about the way she looks, but her attire still screams *stylish*, regardless.

We walk a few blocks down Powell Street and soon, Shea has us in line for the master of all tourist traps, the San Francisco Cable Car System, or the trolley. The line, though long, moves quickly and when we reach the front, we luck out and snag some of the best seats on the car.

I sit on the wooden bench, facing outward, while Shea insists on perching on the running board and clutching one of the outer brass poles. The conductor takes our tickets and the gripman dramatically opens and closes the large clutch. When it catches the cable running beneath us at street level, a jolting series of jerks lurches the trolley forward.

Our ride is a graceful glide punctuated by rumbling bumps, similar to that of a wooden roller coaster, which elicits giggles from the tourists who are riding. The car makes its way up the hill, stopping several times along the way at crossroads that level out.

I lift my camera and take a few snapshots of the antique car, its mechanical workings, the gripman and conductor, and then of Shea. My photo trails always lead to her beautiful face. She's carefully watching scenery as we pass, and when we teeter over the crest of the highest hill, she whoops with excitement as the trolley races down the other side and makes a sharp turn that nearly sideswipes three cars, and threatens to run over several pedestrians.

"How many photos have you taken on this trip?" she asks as she grips the pole tighter and leans in.

I shrug and consider. "Maybe three hundred or so."

"Three hundred!"

"About. Why?"

"Do you ever think about all the random people you capture in the background of your photos?"

"Not really."

"Well, think about it. We're touring around this huge city. How many people do you think have caught us in their photos? Over a few days, it's probably hundreds, and after traveling a lifetime, it could be millions."

"It's impossible to know."

"I bet some brilliant scientist, some geek extraordinaire, has discovered some complex equation to figure it out."

"Maybe you've been holding out on me and you're the geek extraordinaire."

She laughs. "If I can't figure out a camera, I certainly can't figure out that."

"That reminds me. I think it's my turn to guess what you do for a living."

"You'll never guess. Not in a gazillion years."

"I accept the challenge." I look her over, considering every inch of her body as if something she's wearing will give some indication of her job. I try not to let my gaze linger in any one spot, but I take my time, which I can honestly say that I don't do often. I'm the type to plunge into everything without thinking. Or, that was the old me, anyway. But it's the new me, controlled by that don't-fuck-up voice who reminds me, *Take your time on the good stuff.* And the old me agrees that Shea is definitely the good stuff.

"Come up with anything yet?"

"Still processing the possibilities," I say, but I think she knows what I'm doing, but she doesn't seem to mind. I'm about to say something witty enough for our regular banter, but the truth is that I don't want to answer. I want to keep the free pass to look at her anytime I damn well please, when really, I just want to memorize every freckle and every curve, even if it's just for one more day.

"Well?" Shea asks, pressing for an answer.

"I've decided to withhold my observations until a later date."

"Ha! Which means you've got nothing!"

I bob my head, neither agreeing nor disagreeing. After all, I don't claim freaky carny fame like Shea does. But when I do guess, I need her to be as impressed and stunned with the truth of my words as I was with hers. And though she believes she's been hiding behind her half truths, winks, or just full-out lies, what she's really been doing is slowly painting a picture of herself for me, one that will give me a clear impression of who she truly is. "We'll see."

"In that case, I win!" She smiles triumphantly.

"For now. I'll allow it."

When the train halts at a final stop a few blocks from Fisherman's Wharf, Shea jumps off. "Come on, this is it."

"This is your favorite spot?"

"This is just the first stop in a series, so prepare yourself." She grabs my hand, locking our arms, and eases her body close to mine the way I love.

"I'm scared," I say jokingly.

"You should be."

We stroll into the wharf area but quickly work our way out, distancing ourselves from the tourists. Several blocks west, Shea parades us in front of a row of old cheesy souvenir shops where she points out the classy array of T-shirts—cartoon squirrels with surfboards asking if you touched his nuts; the classic stick-man/woman, man/man, but no woman/woman sex-position shirt; and a shirt that claims happily, "I pooped today." Thankfully, she buys none of these gems and we move on.

"There it is!" She points in the direction of another building.

"A store?"

"No, not the store. This." She stops in front of a wooden penny-pressing machine.

"I think I have to call foul on this, Miss What-ever-your-last-name-is." I pause because it's so strange that we've spent all this time together, that I'm this infatuated with her awkward sincerity, and I still don't know her name. "This penny machine can't be your favorite place in the city because it is, in fact, a thing, not a place." I lean on the case, draping my arm across the top.

"Calm down, thing police, it's just something I love to do when I travel. Find a small token." She digs through her pockets and comes up with two quarters and one penny.

"So this thing takes fifty cents and gives you back one illegally defaced penny?"

"I don't know if defacing money is really illegal or not," she says. "I see dollar bills with websites written on them all the time. How come those people don't get in trouble? And why would this machine exist if every time someone used it, they would get fined by the government?"

"Or maybe all penny-pressing machines are government owned and it's their get-rich-quick scheme to get us out of national debt."

"How very conspiracy theory of you." She laughs. "Well, in that case, I'm just being a patriot and doing my part." She leans in to consider her penny-design options. "Which one do you think I should pick? They all say Fisherman's Wharf, San Francisco, but we can choose from a crab, the bridge, a sailboat, or a trolley."

"Trolley," we say at the same time.

"Great minds." Shea taps her head, but I don't think she realizes how alike we are. With the unanimous vote, she rotates the crank to the trolley image and then drops her money into the machine. She rotates the handle, using all her strength as the revolution grinds the penny through the gears and cranks. The resulting coin spits out into a silver cup, making a high-pitched *ting, ting* sound.

She leans over to grab it and holds it up between two fingers. "Hew, I give you ultimate flat-assness. This is what you should be aspiring to."

I turn my back to her and pull my pants tight over my backside, then flex my muscles. "Any flatter today?" I look over my shoulder for her reaction.

"Hmm." She moves in close and slowly slides her hand over my ass, feeling me up as if she's examining the goods, which causes me to flex more. Each stroke causes a twitch in the front of my pants that I try to will away. The truth is, she doesn't have to do much to get that reaction. Just the right look will set me off.

"Let me see what we have here." She cups my left butt cheek and squeezes, then gives it a quick double slap. "I'm afraid not, bubble-butt," she whispers in my ear. The heat from her breath sends tingles down my arm.

"Are you sure you don't want to check again?" God, I hope she does.

"Maybe later." She blushes, which makes me think I deserve a rating better than "bubble-butt."

"Any ideas about what I can do to help out my poor cheeks?" I say flirtatiously.

"Feng Shui Tacos!" she screams and points across the road.

"Somehow I don't think that Feng Shui Tacos is the answer to flat-assery," Hew says, seemingly sad that our playful ass touching stopped.

I am, too, but I have to be careful. Part of me feels I can't let this go where it seems to be going. But my other half wants to touch him, laugh with him, and have a good time. Being with Hew is too easy. Teetering on the edge of a decision, I go for the diversion—food. The highlighter-yellow food truck sits across the road. My tummy rumbles at the spicy scent that saturates the air.

"So, how do you think one feng shuis their food?" I ask him as we mosey toward it. "You are the resident architect, after all."

"Quite easily. You arrange your food in a harmonizing manner, preparing them with the five elements," he offers in a somewhat academic tone.

"Let's see if you're right." We step to the front of the truck. There, next to the logo, in thick black hand-painted lettering is the mantra of the Feng Shui Taco: HAPPY KITCHEN – HAPPY FOOD – BALANCING THE FIVE ELE-

MENTS OF TASTE.

"Ding, ding, ding. You win the prize, Mr. Whatever-your-last-name-is!" I clap my hands and whoop, simulating the roaring crowd of a TV game show.

"Why, thank you. What is it that I win?"

"A Nun Chuck Chicken, avocado, tomato, won-ton, secret spicy cream dressing, on a sesame-seed wheat taco!" I read from the menu.

"I've always wanted one of those!"

"Great, we'll take two." I step to the counter and order.

The truck owner takes my money and a few moments later, hands over two cardboard boxes of food. As it turns out, the Nun Chuck Chicken Taco is pretty good, and Hew and I eat as we stroll along the waterfront, stopping several times to bat away the seagulls that seem to threaten our lives simply because we're holding food.

"The seagulls must have tried the Nun Chuck Chicken and know it's worth the fight." I wave my arm at a one-legged bird that dive-bombs me from above.

"They are kind of vicious!" Hew waves away two predators as we duck into the alcove of a marina shop to try to finish our meals in peace.

"But isn't it weird that seagulls want to eat chicken? Seems all cannibally or something." I take the last bite of my taco and lick my fingers.

"The Cannibal Seagulls of Fisherman's Wharf? Sounds like a B movie horror flick."

"Only if the seagulls were mutant-size, brain-eating zombie birds. Maybe they could help King Kong beat off Godzilla in your sculpture?"

"I'd pay money to see that one—maybe." He chuckles. "We could make the film together. You can do everything on your phone now. There are apps for everything, probably even for moviemaking."

"It's a deal!" Hew finishes his food and throws the box in a nearby trash can. The twenty or so mutant, brain-eating zombie birds that followed us quickly dive-bomb the trash can, fighting over what's left, and we use the diversion to make a quick getaway.

The sun manages to fight its way in front of the crowd of gray clouds so that I don't look like a complete idiot wearing sunglasses. Of course, I'm hiding from Luke, but I realize the chances of him finding me in this large city are slim. Though the fact that Hew keeps finding me gives me reason to think that it's not impossible if someone is determined enough. The thought causes a shiver of anxiety but I fight the fear, trying to remain in this moment.

Several blocks later near the Aquatic Park, I drag Hew onto a new trolley, but this time we sit next to each other, squished between two railings.

"So, what do you do with all your flattened pennies that you've collected?" he asks.

"I've always wanted to make a bracelet out of them, like a charm bracelet, but I haven't had the time. For now they sit in an old cigar box on my dresser."

"How many do you have?"

I hold up the one penny, considering if I should tell him the truth, that this is the only one, that there aren't others because I really haven't been anywhere or done anything in my life. Yes, I've been everywhere and done everything in my daydreams, made pin boards and collaged journals of photos of every place I've wanted to go, do, or see, but I've never done anything for real. Bren and I were going to travel the world together after college. We never got around to it.

"I've got so many I can't count." I lie instead; it's so much prettier than the truth.

"And here I always thought they should get rid of pennies completely. They seem kind of useless to me." Hew takes my flat penny and holds it close to his face, inspecting the design.

"That's why I love the thought of reusing them. Everyone deserves to become something new—to have a second chance. Even a little old dirty penny." I want so badly to believe that it's true.

"Is this the part where you tell me you have a butterfly tattoo tramp-stamped on your backside because it symbolizes renewal?"

"Don't make fun. And yes, I have one for that exact reason." I laugh.

"You don't."

I nod my head, egging him on.

"Seriously? Where? I don't believe you." He teasingly lifts the edge of my shirt, and I fight him off with playful swats to the head and arm.

"You'll never know."

Everyone around us on the trolley is giving us that eye roll, "get-a-room" look, but I don't care. With Hew here, I'm happy to be laughing and smiling. Happy to just be happy. I think that's why I keep giving in to him and hanging out. I can feel myself drifting closer to my normal self, like the bad minutes in my day are slowly being captured, kicked in the ass, and defeated by the good minutes.

Before I realize it, we're almost back to where we started, close to Chinatown. "Let's get off at the next stop."

We jump off the trolley at the California and Powell Street stop and make our way down the hill.

"Should I even ask if we're there yet?"

"Almost, I promise."

"Why does it look like we've made a complete circle?"

"We have. If I would have walked you to my favorite place in the city from where we started, our adventure would have been over in fifteen minutes."

For the first time since we met, Hew grabs my hand. Yes, we've held hands or locked arms, but I always initiated it. I've been touchy and affectionate with him, probably in a way that I shouldn't have been since I only proclaimed us just friends, but everything between us since the moment we met has fallen into place so naturally, like we were meant to meet. The truth is that, messed up or not, I can't help flirting with him because, well, with his thick dark hair, warm eyes, and deep, raspy voice and genuine kindness, I find him incredibly attractive and charming. Anytime he elicits a giggle from me, I feel myself falling for him a little more. All the things that should make me run the other way, but I can't seem to.

I don't pull away. I allow the closeness, even though it means something more than it has every minute before now. To me, to him, or both. The good minutes are winning, and I turn my face away from him to hide my smile. My hearts beats faster at the thought of my little crush.

In Chinatown we stop for another pressed penny, this time the impression is of the Chinatown Gate. So now I officially have two. Ninety-eight more or so to go, and my lie won't be a lie any longer. One hundred seems like it may be an acceptable too-many-to-count number. Now if I can just make every other lie I've told Hew in the last few days into the truth.

I stop and sniff the air, mostly for the benefit of driving Hew crazy, but that's part of the fun between us. "You can smell the sweetness of my favorite spot from here."

"Smell it?" He sniffs, too.

I pull him down a narrow alley of fire escapes and intricate Chinese signs to the propped-open double doors of a small factory.

"Ta-da! I give you my favorite place in the city."

"The fortune cookie factory." He nods. "I definitely approve."

We step in and are immediately greeted by an over-zealous Chinese manager. "Welcome to the our fortune cookie factory. Please come closer." He gently pushes us in the direction of the busy factory workers. The room is narrow and mostly taken over by the enormous cookie-making machine. A conveyor belt of mini flatirons, like waffle makers, produce flat, round, caramel-colored disks. The workers remove one at a time, place a paper fortune in the middle, expertly fold the cookies in half, and then bend them over a silver rod to create the unique shape.

Hew, of course, is already snapping pictures of everything and everyone in the room. As he does, I drop a large tip in the workers' bucket, whose sign reads, FIFTY CENTS PER PHOTO. Ten dollars probably won't be enough for the damage he's doing.

"Fresh cookies." The manager hands us fresh, unfolded cookies, warm from the conveyor belt.

"Thank you. They smell delicious!" I take a bite and the cookie melts in my mouth.

"So good." Hew finally stops his picture-snapping for the treat.

"Can I buy a bag?" I point to the rack of them on the wall.

"Of course. Would you like plain, chocolate, mixed, or plain with dirty fortunes?" The manager lifts his eyebrows playfully, looking between Hew and me.

I look to Hew. "Well?"

"Do you really have to ask? I think it's clear which ones we should buy."

"You're such a boy!" I laugh. "How about one plain and one dirty?" Which makes the manager giggle, too. I pay him and he drops them into a reused plastic grocery bag, then hands me my change.

Hew and I walk out, and I turn to face him. "So now that you've seen my spot, our day seems to be over."

In the back of my mind, I've been dreading this moment all day. The moment when I would be confronted with Shea telling me she's going to be leaving me for the third time, or maybe it's been more times. I've already lost count.

"I think we should break the rules and plan to meet each other," I offer and dig my hands into my pockets, knowing her response already. That heaviness in my chest creeps back, waiting for her response.

"We can't keep meeting like this and flirting. The truth is that I like you. Probably more than I should, and more than in a friendly way," she admits, her face flushing into a beautiful lively shade.

I'm certain they're the few truthful words that she has allowed to pass her defenses, and her perfect pouty lips— ones that I've been dying to kiss for days. I lift my arms, lacing my fingers behind my head and walk in a circle, thinking of a way that I can stop this, something that will change her mind, and I spout off the first thing I can think of.

"Okay. I have a proposition for you." I stop in front of her.

"I'm listening," she says as she loops the bag of fortune cookies around her wrist.

"What if we leave it to destiny. The bitch is in charge anyway, right?"

"She is." Shea rocks back on her heels and smirks, and I know I have a chance because she's still standing here.

"So, hear me out." I push my camera strap around my shoulder to my back, and begin to gesture with my hands. "You're leaving to go on your road trip, right?"

She nods.

"I was going to use my car to drive around and see more of the city, but I'd much rather spend my time left with you."

Shea rolls her hand in the air as if to say, "Get to the point."

"We'll leave each other now and meet up again in two hours, after I return my car to the nearest rental facility."

"That's not fate or destiny, that's planning," she points out.

"I wasn't done. Here's the destiny part. We have two meeting places—one at your favorite place, right here, and one at mine, across town. You drive to one of those spots with the intention of picking me up. If we separately choose the same place to meet, then that's destiny telling us we should hang out for a few more days. If not, we move on with our lives like we never met."

Shea doesn't answer right away, which is a good sign

that she's considering the proposition. I'm on edge, body rigid and barely breathing until she tweaks her lips back and forth and finally responds.

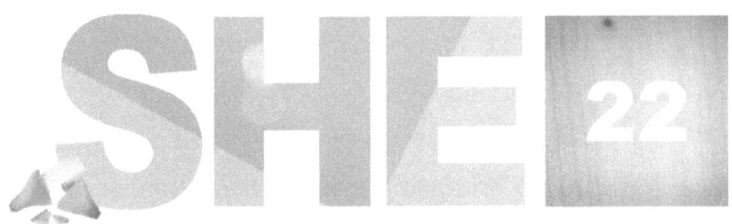

"You've got yourself a deal." I know I shouldn't accept, but I can't help myself because the truth is that I want the chance to see Hew again. "Should we spit in our hands and shake on it or something?" I laugh.

"Let's not and say we did." Hew crinkles his brow.

It seems weird to walk away from each other without so much as a hug, though I know I've been the first to walk away every single time. This time, though, there's a real possibility that I may not see him again. And even if it was true every other time before, I hadn't taken the time to think it over. Those other times, I had left under duress. But this proposal is as frightening to me as it is a relief, which is why his offer is so enticing. I don't have to make the big decision here; destiny will make it for me, just like she has with everything else in my life. I've learned there is only so much I can control anyway.

"So, in two hours, I'm picking you up in one of two spots?" I slowly step away in the general direction of my car. Hew does the same but in the opposite direction. The pulling tension between us stretches like a rubber band pulled to the limit that at any moment could snap and break us apart forever, and it leaves my stomach unsettled and my heart sad.

"Yes." He settles his camera in his hand, and lifts the viewfinder to his squinting eye to take a final shot, like he doesn't have enough photos of the girl-with-the-fake-name already. I remove my glasses and hat, revealing myself to him, and allow my hair to fall loose out of my braid. The shutter snaps, and I imagine this photo as a good-bye kiss, and for the first time, I offer a small smile for one of his photos. He can add me to the millions of other people he took photos of these past few days. After today, I may just be someone in the background among the crowd.

"So, I'll see you if I see you?" I clutch the rim of my hat, stepping away.

Hew nods with sad eyes, turns like he can't take any more, and finally walks away. When he turns the corner, melding into the tourists a hundred feet away, I sigh with confused relief, but immediately sense his absence, which instantly makes me long to be with him again.

"You like him," a voice calls from the fortune cookie factory. The manager stands at the entrance with his arms crossed, and he nods with a knowing smile. He must have been watching and listening all this time.

"No. I mean, yes. The truth is I do—a lot—but I can't." I look around, searching for the correct words and settle on, "It's complicated."

"Not complicated. Only you make it complicated. Life

is simple. He likes you and you like him. My mother used to say coffee and love taste best when hot."

"Is that some kind of Chinese proverb or something?"

"No, Ethiopian."

"But I was supposed to be married a few days ago. To someone else."

"But you didn't?"

"No." I shake my head and look down, ashamed for how everything has played out.

"Then there's no complication. There is a reason you're here and not where you planned to be. It's simple," he says so matter-of-factly that I want to believe him. That Hew and I met for a reason. That this whatever-it-is relationship is leading somewhere important. The shop owner diverts his attention, greeting a group of Dutch tourist who meander into his shop, and I'm left with my thoughts.

I admit that I tend to make things complicated for myself and consider if this is the real issue. But the question is: Can I shove all the drama aside and jump headfirst into a lake of happiness? Would it, could it be that simple? I've dipped a toe in, feeling the warmth, and I know I want to submerge completely into Hew. When I don't think too hard about it, of course.

My heart says yes, but only because it's clearly a stupid heart. If it weren't, I wouldn't be here now. But everything else—my head, my past, my scars, my discarded mangled wedding dress in some San Francisco dumpster, and the thought of Bren and Luke—yell a resounding, "No!"

I'm locked in a mental struggle when long fingers grip my arm tightly, nails digging into my skin. Wincing at the pain, I spin to find Luke staring down at me with furious, stormy blue eyes.

I stop breathing. Involuntarily my body begins to convulse. He's hunted me down. Of course, I should have known he would, but most importantly, I should have left as soon as I realized he was here. Stupid, stupid me.

"What the hell are you doing? Do you know what I had to do to find you?"

He doesn't even bother with pleasantries. Did I expect him to? Everything from the beginning has been about him, but back then I was too naive to spot his overbearing narcissism.

Words of response struggle in my mouth, slip back down my throat, choking me. I jerk and struggle to get away, but he only clenches my arm tighter.

"It's so like you to take off across the country and then stand here like you have nothing to say," he says through gritted teeth.

Finally I manage to twist free. "I have nothing else to say except take a fucking hint. I don't want to be around you!" I push him back. "I flew across the country to get away from you. Don't actions speak louder than words?"

Then he laughs low with that cockiness that gives me the shivers, sending my body into a sweaty, nervous mess. "When will you get it, babe? You can't run from me, just like you can't run from your past. You chose me over Bren, and now we're stuck together forever. I never let anything I want go and you know that."

He smiles in a way that reminds me of Bren. It used to make my heart melt, but now it only turns my stomach in a gale of acidy waves. Luke thinks he owns me. He's always treated me this way. In the beginning it was endearing and attentive, but it quickly escalated into a need to control, manipulate, and sometimes, on those extra-special moments, I earned a heavy-handed slap across the jaw and or the random scar that I'd like to forget.

"Like hell we are!" I take off running, practically knocking down an elderly group of Chinese men who are doing little to help my situation. They don't even look at me—or at Luke—and our violent exchange. I drop my new flamingo-colored hat and shiny sunglasses, but manage to cling to my purse and fortune cookies. The bags bob in time with the rapid stomping of my fleeting feet.

Turning the corner onto the busy main street, I slip because I'm wearing the imported silk slippers; they weren't meant for epic chases on foot. Luke uses it to his advantage to close the distance between us and as he does, my heart punches at my chest with anxiety and I pump my arms harder at my sides. The more I've found my independence and tried to pull away, the more he's tried to cling to me, intensifying our meetings. I kick off the shoes and take flight again in my bare feet. My heels, pads, and toes grip the concrete, each hurried step feels like running on sandpaper, each hard breath a slice of a razor.

"Help! Someone call the police!" I point back to Luke as I run past a group of tourists, but they appear dazed at my request. I don't stop to explain, I keep moving; my getaway is the only thing that will keep me safe. The next time he hits me, I may not wake up. I weave around cars, street vendors, down alleys, and behind dumpsters. I've been through this neighborhood several times already, so I need to use this advantage because Luke has long legs, endurance, and strength on his side. And knowing him as well as I know myself, he wouldn't come all this way just to let me get away now. He won't willingly ever let me go.

My saving grace appears in the form of the shop I bought clothes from on my first day. The shop owner's eyes widen as I near. Somehow, I'm sure her face mirrors my own—panic.

"Please help me!" I grab her small pale hands and plead, and look over my shoulder, sucking in ragged breaths. Luke hasn't spotted me yet, his gaze searches farther down the road, where I should be at this point.

She nods her head without questioning me or looking for the danger, and quickly pulls me inside. "Go hide behind the counter," she urges. On hands and knees, I make my way around the counter as she drops the metal gate to the front of her shop and locks it, severing us from the sounds of the passing cars, the tourists snapping photos, and most importantly, Luke.

I'm pressed against a wall between a trash bin and several cardboard boxes of merchandise, hyperventilating as my muscles quake. Compressing myself into a tight ball, I try to calm myself. I drop my head to my knees and cry hysterically because I know that everything that has happened has been my fault. Everything from that first night years ago changed my life in a way I could no longer control.

"Can I call someone for you?"

A hand gently presses on my shoulder. I jolt and look up to see the shop owner practically in tears herself.

I shake my head and wipe my damp face. "No. Thank you. For helping me. Thank you." Each word fights to leave my quivering mouth. I whimper at how close I came to losing myself again and close my eyes, wishing for everything to be better.

I wish for Hew.

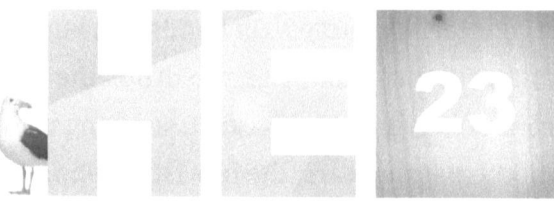

ow that I'm standing in front of the Palace of Fine Arts, I'm certain I should have chosen the fortune cookie factory. But I was stupid enough to not only agree to this fifty-fifty chance meeting, but to also come up with the idea. Knowing what I know of Shea, this was the best chance I had for another day.

But as I glance at my watch, twenty minutes past the time we agreed to meet, I'm nervous that I made the wrong decision all the way around. I should have taken her in my arms and kissed her the way I wanted and told her the truth—that I didn't want to be away from her another second, even if it would have caused her to run in the other direction. If we have no other truths between us at this point, at least then she would have known my truth.

I pace to the corner, thinking of her and all her kooky ways—her sweetness, her insanity—when added up, they equal an undeniably inspiring charisma, like pure sunshine, even when she's crying. She's the only girl I've ever met that the sun seems to follow, tethered like a balloon, always warming the space around her. And for someone who's been left in the darkness so long, the warmth of her bright light feels so good, like radiant beams that I could lay out under and soak up forever.

But even the sun burns, I remind myself as the seconds close in on forty-five minutes after our predetermined meeting time. With a deep sigh, I mentally give up on ever seeing her again and drag my suitcase to the edge of the park, lay it on its side, and sit down next to it to look out at the palace dome, and the families and tourists enjoying it.

Shea's not coming; not to this location. I chose unwisely, or she chickened out and chose not to drive to either spot. Either way, I feel a little lost when the real sun dips behind the clouds, painting the sky in an array of pastels. Somehow it's symbolic of losing my sunshine. Just as the last bit of the blazing orb kisses the arc of the palace dome, a car's horn blares behind me.

"Hew! Let's get going. We're losing the light!"

I whip my head so quickly in the voice's direction that my neck may crack. At the curb of the nearest street, Shea waves to me from a vintage cream-colored Italian Fiat convertible.

I stand immediately and stare, beyond shocked that's she's here, that I waited, that she showed, that destiny worked in my favor—our favor. Maybe she's not a bitch, after all. A huge smile splits my face and I charge her, dragging my suitcase and duffel bag behind me.

"I think our appointment was for an hour ago, Miss Whatever-your-name-is." I throw my bags in the trunk and slam it shut, then quickly jump into the passenger seat. When I shut the door, Shea is tying her hair into a low loose bun. With her hair pulled from her face, her scar is more prominent. And it's all I can do not to reach out and trace it, to try to rub it away.

"Sorry I'm late, hit a little traffic. I figured that if it were destiny, you'd still be here. And you are." She finishes fussing with her hair and rewards me with a crooked smile, though looking a little disheveled.

"I am." I stretch my arm over the back of her seat, anxious to be stuck anywhere with this girl. "So, where to next? Your favorite part of California?"

SHE 24

When Hew jumps into the passenger seat, a relief I haven't felt in years sweeps over me. Somehow, by managing to escape Luke and finding Hew here waiting for me, despite being late, I've decided that things will be better from here on out. At least I'll take the happiness wherever I can find it. Whether it's laughing with the almost-complete stranger next to me, or with someone that I know. What difference does it really make if I'm happy? I want the good minutes of the day to take over the bad in this fight, so who cares how it happens, or who I'm with as long as I cultivate smiles when urged in that direction.

I stayed at Pearl's shop in Chinatown longer than I wanted. That was her name, Pearl, which matched her perfectly with her white hair that seemed iridescent in color, and her skin, pale gray and rough like the outside of a dry oyster shell. After I had calmed somewhat, she guided me to her apartment above her shop and force-fed me hot green tea and something called *tang er duo*. And though she spoke to me in Chinese the entire time, with her elderly mother nodding and pointing a crooked finger at me while we sat in their cramped kitchen, its walls papered with tiny flowers, I complied because I hadn't gotten myself together emotionally yet.

But when I finally did, I did so without the use of medication, which in itself was an challenging feat. I held it together because I couldn't allow myself to drift away into never-care-land when I needed to be able to drive a car to pick up Hew. After that I needed to see him, be near him, and feel the security that he gives me.

So now here I am, still running away from my past for a second time, but this time with a friend. Someone I want to be more than a friend for as long as it makes us happy, no matter the consequence and the guilt. I deserve to be happy.

Making my getaway, I slam my foot on the gas and merge onto Highway 101, heading north. After traveling across the stunningly red Golden Gate Bridge and onto the winding highway between the mountains, I find a comfortable spot in traffic and glance over at Hew. He's smiling. Not a big, toothy smile, but a cheeky one. Like the kind when you're zoning out and thinking of something and you just smile unknowingly. It's adorable. His thick hair flops back in forth in the wind, and he runs his fingers through it a several times. I don't think it's to make his hair look better, but more like a quirk or habit. After a few strokes, he settles back into his seat, his strong arms relaxed, lean thighs and legs stretched out. His head tips to one side and he glances back at me from under his dark eyelashes, and when he flashes me this sexy look he does incredibly well, I absolutely dissolve. I don't even think he's trying. God help me when he does.

"What?" he asks.

I shake my head. "Nothing," I say as a heavy heat rises up from my stomach and through my chest to my neck, then floods my cheeks, because I realize that he just caught me checking him out. To divert his attention, I reach behind Hew's seat while trying to stay in my lane, and grab a plastic bag and quickly drop it in his lap. "Can you open these for me?"

"Sure." He smirks and unties the plastic supermarket bag to reveal two smaller clear bags of fortune cookies. "Which would you like to try—the plain old regular, boring fortunes, or the super-awesome and sure-to-be-hysterical dirty fortunes?"

I laugh. "Let's go with . . ." I drag out my words as long as I can like a game show host because I can tell by the waggy-eyebrow-teenage-boy look that he's giving me between glancing at him and the highway that he wants to open the dirty fortunes—of course. "The normal, plain old, boring fortunes."

"Boo!" he says with a whine. "I have a better idea." He opens each small bag and dumps the contents of both into the larger supermarket bag. He then twists the top, leaving a bit of air inside, and jumbles the plain and dirty fortunes around. "We'll mix them up! A little bit of sweet, like you. And a little bit of dirty, like me." He lowers his voice seductively.

"I'm all for equal fortune-cookie rights." Our little banter makes me sing inside. My smile is possibly bigger than my face right now.

"Besides, I thought the dirty ones would make the drive more interesting. Who knows how long we'll drive with you at the wheel."

"Yeah, I think we can drive to Alaska from here, or the tip of South America if I turn around and go the other direction. I've always wanted to see Cape Horn, or is it Cape Fear?"

"Cape Fear is a movie and Cape Horn is technically an island at the end of Chile, so unless your Fiat can drive underwater, 007-style, like in those commercials, I think that might present a problem. We can, however, drive to Ushuaia, Argentina, which is considered the southern-most city in the world."

"Smarty-pants. How could you possibly know all that?"

"Because I've always loved Martin Scorsese films, and I grew up obsessed with maps. Some boys played cops and robbers, I played nerd. I even made my mom cover the walls in my bedroom with maps." Hew twists open the bag and takes out one fortune cookie, which he hands to me with instructions. "Remember to read your fortune and yell 'in bed' afterward."

"Okay." I laugh, then take a bite, breaking the hard shell between my teeth. Half the cookie crumbles in my mouth, and my moist tongue captures the dry paper inside. I grab the small slip, which feels foreign in my mouth, and pull it out. Between juggling the steering wheel and navigating traffic, I read what's inside. "You are very talented."

"In bed!" Hew screams.

"Right, I forgot. In bed!" I scream back over the racing wind of the convertible.

I look over to Hew, who is looking at me with a boyish grin, and I nearly die.

"Good in bed, huh?" he asks.

"Fortune cookies do know best."

I finish my cookie and Hew takes one for himself, which he lodges between his teeth and bites. The cookie breaks with a crunch, and he pulls out his small white paper and reads, "Accept your imperfections."

"In bed!" we scream together.

"How do I get imperfections in bed and you get you're talented in bed?" Hew guffaws.

"Don't worry, I'll teach you everything I know." I reach for his knee and squeeze. Though all these little flirtatious innuendos started out as a joke, they are slowly holding more weight as we get to know each other. And

I can't deny that there is pure electricity between us. It causes me to shiver and I pull away. Hew is like a flower to a bee, and my body is buzzing.

Hew hands me a new cookie and we do it all over again several times. It doesn't matter what we're doing, we always find a way to make things fun. And plowing through a bag of fortune cookies while racing down the highway at seventy is more fun than I imagined.

I steer off the highway, taking an exit, and pull into a gas station.

"You need gas?"

"Nah, I'm parched from all the fortune cookies and no water." I pull into a space and park, facing a Quicky Mart. We run inside and separate to load up on goodies. After I've grabbed an armful of Funyuns, water, Mountain Dew, Twinkies, and a reload of Twizzlers, I walk up to the cashier and drop everything on the counter. Hew joins me and adds a supersized beef jerky, a bag of pretzels, and a Coke.

Hew scans my pile and gives me a quizzical look. "How the hell does someone who looks as sexy as you eat all that garbage?"

"I'm a trash compactor of junk food. What can I say? It's a trait I'm quite proud of." I flip my hair with a wave of my hand.

"Can I also get one random Mega Millions ticket?" Hew asks the clerk as he removes his wallet.

The cashier nods, hands him a ticket, and rings us up. Hew pays, and we leave with a bagful of goodies.

"You realize that you have a better chance of physically sprouting wings and becoming a zombie brain-eating seagull of San Francisco than winning the lottery, right?" I ask.

"Shea, you of all people should understand."

"I should?" I open the car door and slide inside. Hew settles in the passenger seat, slams his door, digs through the bag, then hands me a bottle of water.

"You're the queen of adventure, so you should know that I didn't buy this ticket because I think I have a chance of winning. I bought it to have the right to dream about the 150-million-dollar jackpot, and what I would do with all the money."

"The right to dream?" I laugh. "You don't have the right to dream without buying a one-dollar ticket?" I unscrew the top of the bottle and take a swig of water. Though I'm questioning Hew, I realize that there are many things in my life that made me feel like I didn't have the right to dream. Luke being just one of them.

"Sometimes I need a little help. Even just spending the dollar loosens up the dream muscles, gets me thinking creatively." Hew stretches his long neck and rotates his shoulders as if he's warming up for a basketball game, and suddenly my mouth goes dry watching him. I take another gulp of water.

I laugh nervously. "And what would you do with your dream money?"

Hew blows out a long breath. "For one, since I'm an architect," he winks, "I'd have to build you a new dream home. A bright yellow one that will make you crazy-anxious."

"Oh yeah, don't forget the hot tub." I smirk. I love how he's still playing along with the job I gave him several days ago. "And where would you build this magnificent domain?"

"Not sure. But I think we should start looking for the perfect spot on our road trip. We may have 150 million bucks to spend in the next few days. So we should make an effort to dream a lot." He waves the ticket in my face and then slides it into his wallet.

"Keep dreaming, big boy."

"I intend to." He gives me a smoldering look, suggesting he's thinking about more than money. It's the kind that suggests that I *am* his dream.

hea stabs the key into the ignition and turns on the car, but she's mostly been turning me on with her sexy cuteness. For some reason, I'm all about her strange and mysterious ways.

Within a few minutes we're back on the highway. The interesting thing about California is that every thirty minutes the terrain changes. Just driving north out of the city, we've passed over the cerulean water of the San Francisco Bay, through the mountains, the high rolling hills covered with long brown grass, and then smaller hills with green farm-type grass. Each area is so distinctive, you would never know how close together they are. But as the evening turns quickly into deep night, Shea announces, "I think we're almost there!"

Sometime later, the car rolls to a stop and she turns off the engine. Without opening my eyes, I hear her unbuckling her seat belt, and she leans close and strokes my arm from shoulder to elbow. Her touch warms my skin in the chilly fall air, causing pinpricking hairs to rise at attention, among other things. I restrain a smirk, not letting on that I'm awake, so that she'll continue.

"We're here," she whispers, but I have no idea where here is. I've had my eyes closed for the last twenty minutes, listening to the music as we drove through the countryside. Every so often I stole a peek to study her shape in the night. Long tendrils of dark hair escaped her bun, coiling in the wind, while the stars looked down on her with an extra-special sparkle, just like the sun. While she thought I was sleeping, I watched her silently lip-synch every song on the radio, grooving in her seat, arms rolling and hips swaying to the beat. I bit my lip, holding back laughter when she enthusiastically rocked out with an invisible microphone, singing "Lady Marmalade," the Christina Aguilera version.

Shea's adorable, sexy, and someone I never want to stop stealing looks of. There should be a rule against falling for someone so quickly, but how can you tell your heart and dick to get a grip when they seem to beat to their own rhythm (not "Lady Marmalade," thank God, but still). And the truth is that I'm not exactly fighting it. I'm inviting it.

I open my eyes at her seductive voice, and she's still close. Her breath warms my cheeks and dries my lips, making me lick them. Our gazes lock, and it's all slow motion and breathless. Looking into her eyes under the lamp of the quiet street, I get a clear view of their striking jade color. Immediately, I want to seduce her and press my lips on her ear, breathe hot and seductive air down her neck, plant soft kisses on her pronounced clavicles to drive her crazy, and finally mix her warm, soft lips with mine, and so much more.

The thought of her beneath me makes me adjust in my seat. But I know I can't go there. Not yet. I've come this far, and I need to be patient. I want every sexy part of her, but only when the time is right—her body, her mind, and her truths, every single one, no matter what they are. I suck in a ragged horny breath, trying to control my thoughts, and she smiles, like she knows her proximity affects me. This girl is seriously messing with me. She leans away, and I stretch my arms high in the air, looking around, trying to focus on anything but her in a desperate attempt to make the hard need in my pants relax.

We're on a neighborhood street of little slat-sided bungalows with golden light illuminating front bay windows and country porches. The only sounds are the crickets who haven't yet died for the season, or maybe they never die in California, and a distant highway that I can't see.

"Where are we?"

"Yountville."

"Why did you choose this place?"

"Because it's just outside Napa and when we were driving through, it reminded me of Tuscany, Italy. So obviously I had to stop."

"Italy in North America," my sister called it after she and her husband got back from their honeymoon. But Layne didn't talk about the wine with me like she did with everyone else in the family. Singing the praises of the fruit and body of a great glass of cab isn't at the top of an alcoholic's dream discussion. Even though wine wasn't my poison, it still doesn't stop me from salivating at the thought of what it would do in my bloodstream, loosen me up, guarantee me a good time. I've always been the party drunk, no drama needed, just fun.

Even now, over two years completely sober, I still want it, just from thinking about it. I suck at my cheek and realize that alcohol and Shea have something in common. I desperately want both, but I can't seem to have either.

"Hew?" Shea looks at me in question, like she may have been talking to me all this time.

"Sorry, just zoned out there for a sec. Always wanted to visit after my sister told me how much she loved it on her honeymoon." Which is actually true. I always did, just given the circumstances, I didn't. No point in tempting the bull with a red muleta.

Leaving the tension behind, we exit the car and grab our bags from the trunk. Then I close the fabric convertible top and lock it shut. At the sidewalk, I can see a small blue neon sign that reads VACANCY in the window of the multistoried stone cottage, which is covered with thick winding vines. Shea walks along the rose-lined path, up a stair to the main door. We have to knock because it's getting late, and this is a private bed and breakfast.

A young guy, who looks like he might be in high school, answers. "Hello there. How can I help you tonight, do you have a reservation?" He opens the door completely.

"We don't." Shea takes the lead. "But I see you have a vacancy." She points to the window.

"We just had a cancellation. Come in." He waves for us to follow and guides us into a small back room. "You're kinda the luckiest people on the planet right now. This is the only room left in a twenty-mile radius."

"Why?" I ask.

"The Harvest Festival. Wine connoisseurs, locals, tourists, media, they're all here. It's a big deal. You didn't come for it, then?"

"No." I shake my head. "Did you know anything about it?" I ask Shea.

"I saw some signs on the way here, but I didn't know it was anything big. We must be lucky." She perks up with excitement, and I perk up that she just referred to us as *we*. "Do we buy tickets for it or something?"

"The street festival starts tomorrow, and is up in the next town, Saint Helena. That's free during the day, and all the wineries have their own swanky parties every night, but I think they're all sold out."

"I have a feeling that won't stop you, will it?" I instinctively slide an arm around Shea's tiny waist, pulling her close and whispering in a conspiratorial manner.

"It usually doesn't," she says.

"Can I get your ID and credit card?" the boy asks.

Shea and I awkwardly glance at each other. To take out either card would reveal our real names, and it seems that even now when we're about to share one room, our game is still on.

"How about I take care of this one?" I offer.

"Are you sure? I have cash." She places her purse on the counter.

"I'm sure, but you're gonna have to go in the other room if we're going to continue playing by the rules." I half hope that she'll give up.

"Okay. Thanks." She squeezes my arm, collects her bags, and saunters into the next room, a large common area with a stone fireplace, sofas, and a dining table.

After she leaves, I remove my credit card and ID from my wallet and hand them to the boy, who is eyeing me suspiciously. "Don't ask," I tell him with a slight smile.

I figure if I make a joke he will let our strange conversation go, and thankfully, he does. He finishes checking me in and points us in the direction of our room, then returns to studying the thick textbook on his desk.

Shea and I walk back through the cottage, which is decorated in what my middle sister, Ashley, would call "shabby chic," with her fancy interior design degree from MICA.

We drag our bags up the creaky stairs of the old home and find our way through the dark hallway to room five. She leans close to the doorknob and fiddles with the key. "It doesn't want to open," she says, sounding frustrated after a moment of jiggling the loose metal handle. The sound rattles not only the wooden door, but also echoes off the surrounding walls of the rickety old home.

"Shh, we have to be quiet. I think everyone is asleep already," I offer in hushed tones near her ear, and place a hand on her forearm. She shivers, and the sensation seems to run over her skin. I'm finding pleasure in torturing her the way she does me. Just enough to get her thinking that she may want more.

"It's not even nine yet."

"Trust me," I say. "In this place, I bet we're the youngest people. Here, let me try."

I take the key and we trade positions. I lean in and slide it into the keyhole, but once it's inside, it won't turn. It's really and truly stuck. I wiggle it, shaking the door the same way Shea did, and she shushes me like I did with her, and giggles as if to say, "I told you so."

This continues for a few moments, but I'm too far in not to get this damn thing open. It's the whole principal of the thing. I'm a guy. I push my shoulder into the door and finally, with the right amount of pressure, something catches in the lock. The door flies open and I lose my balance and tumble into the room, crashing onto the floor with a huge thump. "Uhh!"

This time Shea is not the only one who's laughing. I let loose an uncontrolled crow, and it's anything but quiet. That's when we're rewarded with several strong bangs on the wall from the adjoining bedroom. This, of course, makes us laugh even louder, but we hold our hands over our mouths, trying to be quiet.

"I guess you were right," Shea says as she regains control of herself and helps me up from the floor.

I stand and drag my bags into the room, then shut the door behind us. The room is really small, maybe ten by twelve feet. The outer walls are old stone, and there's barely a place to stick my luggage, but I find a spot in a low niche. There's also a bathroom and shower stall, but together they are as small as a closet.

Shea's already found the best part of the small room, a set of narrow French doors that lead out onto a second-floor veranda. It's private and all ours.

She walks outside and I follow. I think at this point, I would follow her anywhere.

SHE 26

"It's so beautiful." Looking out into the darkness, we see there's a low mountain ridge. Behind it, on the other side, glows a gradient light that runs the length of it, silhouetting the rolling and jagged shapes of the peaks. A city sits on the other side, but from here it's only represented in light, not buildings or the chaos of people and traffic.

Hew joins my side. "Wow. Nice job." He pushes two reclining lounge chairs together, sits, and then pats the seat next to him.

"Hold on a second." Wanting to make everything perfect, I hurry back inside and gather a few items: a quilt folded over the back of a chair, a bottle of complimentary wine (it's Napa Valley, after all), a corkscrew, two plastic wineglasses, and the rest of the fortune cookies. With everything carefully balanced, I walk back out onto the terrace. Hew grabs the quilt, and I settle everything else on a small round metal table.

He's watching my every move like he normally does, but this time there's a certain intensity that I don't understand. His gaze follows me as I quietly walk to his side and retrieve the quilt, unfold it and shake it out, then drop it over his body, spreading it like I'm making a bed, and then I return to my side to open the bottle of wine.

"You like wine?" I ask.

He doesn't answer right away. Instead his jaw tightens and his gaze flicks away, but then he finally says, "I do."

A few minutes later, we each have a plastic wineglass, and I settle into the lounger next to him.

"Here's to dreaming." He lifts his glass and toasts, but his grasp seems shaky.

"To dreaming." I clink my glass with his and as I sip, he places his aside.

"It's bad luck not to sip after a toast."

"I know, but I'd rather drink you in," he says jokingly, and nuzzles into my shoulder. It's playful and sweet, and I just may let him.

"While you were gathering your tools here, I was thinking that with our lottery winnings, I could build you a house in the valley with this incredible view. Just think of doing this every night on your own private veranda." He leans closer to me at the last part, and his breath is warm on my neck.

I think he realizes this turns me on, and I sigh inside. Could this guy be any more romantic?

"With a Jacuzzi," I insist.

"Of course."

"I could totally handle that." I reach for the fortune

cookies and offer one to Hew, but he shakes his head, so I remove a few and pile them in my lap as we snuggle close.

"Fortune cookies and red wine?" he asks.

"Actually, it's the perfect combination. The slightly sweet wafer with the wine." I break off a piece of cookie and eat it, then sip the wine. "I think I'll try to start a new trend."

"When we win the lottery, you can use your half to travel the world, promoting the combination."

"That's a great idea!" I say, playing along. "I could do chocolate-covered fortune cookies and wine, too. Ohh," I say dramatically, thinking of the possibility. "That would be so good. I'm dying just thinking about it."

"You can call it the Napa Valley Wine and Fortune Cookie Company."

"Yes! I'll sell gift baskets full of the stuff. Can you design a retail space, too, or do you only design houses?" I crunch a mouthful of cookies while talking.

"I'm multitalented." He strokes my arm, practically giving me a heart attack. I hold my breath at his touch, because I can only imagine how talented he is. With his lips, his hands, his fingers.

Hew turns on his side, facing me, giving me that smoldering sexy look of his. The one that makes me want to throw myself at him. I put my wine and cookies aside and turn to him, and huddle under our blanket. Now face-to-face, we smile at each other, and with a fluttering heart, I examine the Roman god who is looking back at me.

Our intensified breathing warms the space between us. I smell sex on his breath, or maybe it's mine. Either way, I sense the pheromones pumping. It may be the glass of wine I just downed lowering my inhibitions, but Hew has never looked as devilish as he does right now with his messy, wind-blown hair, thick dark stubble, strong chin, and full lips. My gaze lands in that last spot for a moment longer than it should, and there's an intense urge to press my lips to his, to relieve the wanting ache building within me.

I take my time, wanting to extend all these intense feelings, but most importantly wanting to make the right decisions. I reach out one finger and gently touch the spot right below his ear. He stiffens just slightly but relaxes as I drag my fingertip down the long slope of his neck, follow the shape of the collar, and land at the tattoo right above his collarbone. Stopping there, I mindlessly trace the edge of the black design.

Hew doesn't protest or move, he only watches me memorizing him. There's an undeniable thickness surrounding us, and whatever it's made of—desire, loneliness, or restlessness—it's an aphrodisiac urging me to do things I hadn't intended when we originally met.

With new bravery, I slowly unbutton the rest of his shirt to where it meets the waist of his pants. Once open, I push the fabric over and off his shoulder, until it rumples on his back and bunches at his elbows, revealing the entire tattoo. Hew's chest breaks out in a flurry of tingled flesh and aroused nipples as they meet the chilly air. I know what it's doing to him because I'm feeling every bit as excited. I gently glide my palms along his defined pecs, and he leans his head back, closes his eyes, and sucks on his lower lip in response.

I stare at those lips, plump, wet, and warm, and I want to bite them. I move my body closer, capturing the heat between us. My eyes are at the same level of his tattoo now. It's triangular in shape, fitting perfectly in the natural triangle created by his collarbone, neck, and shoulder, like it slid into place and lodged there, forever trapped by the rigid shelf of his bone. I make another round with my hands over the tattoo and his chest. My heart skips a beat because for the first time, I realize that I want him. Something in me needs him.

Taking my time to consider this new intense emotion, I trace the tattoo, a simple three-pointed Celtic knot entwining a single blooming rose. The artwork is beautiful.

"Does it mean something special?" I whisper.

"It's a trinity knot." His gaze meets mine as his words roll through the air, caressing my face. "It means many things to different people, but to me it means life, death, and rebirth."

"That hints at a serious back story." I smirk seductively.

Hew nods and swallows, seemingly out of nervousness. "You have no idea." He looks into the distance and I feel him drifting from me, so I leave it alone. We aren't here to tell those secrets. But it's the first time that I realize that he may have his own complex past. Part of me wishes I could share my real story with him, too, but if he knew how screwed up I really am, I suspect he never would have even had lunch with me on that first day.

Hew grabs my hand in his, like he can't take any more of that discussion. His skin is rough and warm, and his heated energy seems to flow out from him and into me. He lifts my hand to his perfect lips and gently kisses my palm. At the point of contact, a shot of lust races through my body, and I physically jolt with delight. He pulls away and I clamp my hand closed, as if I can capture the sensation.

I roll into him so that I'm facing away. I don't know where this is going, but I need it to last as long as possible. My shoulders, back, behind, and legs snug into his every angle. He slides his impossibly long arms around my waist, pressing his palm into my stomach to pull me closer, and then places his chin in the arc of my neck where it fits perfectly, like curving pieces of a puzzle.

His breath is even warmer than his body, and with every rise and fall of his chest against my back, I'm acutely aware of the magnetic attraction between us. When the heat from his lips spills like a waterfall over my neck and chest, a wildfire of electricity races down my arms, hips, and legs. And just when the sensation consumes my entire body, my toes curl and my muscles clench as I try to contain my excitement.

Hew must notice because he hugs me in response. At the moment my energy leaves me, it seems to seep into him. I know because I feel his skin prickle, small hairs rising with excitement, just like mine.

Somehow we're connected. Truly connected, and I don't know how or why. We don't say anything, we only continue to explore each other's body by shifting, rubbing, and pressing. I slide the pads of my feet up and down his shins, and in response, Hew slowly drags his palm along the curve of my hip and thigh, intensifying our encounter. I rub my back into his chest, and in response, Hew brushes his rough stubble over my cheek. I reach back and rake my fingers through his thick hair and gently tug, and he moans with delight and answers me by cupping and massaging my breasts, and sliding his palms down the center of my abs.

Every movement we share creates a wild, animalistic friction. Fabric shifts on fabric, skin brushes against skin, and every sensual touch ignites an intense fire that connects us. It's passionate and erotic, but we go no further; we never even kiss. We don't need to. We start our own kind of blazing bonfire. We're kissing and licking with our entire bodies, our breath, and our eyes.

We're playing a new game where Hew is in charge.

I place my trust in him, something I've never done with anyone else, or even myself. Everything I left behind is so far away, and with Hew, it doesn't seem important anymore. So I just give in.

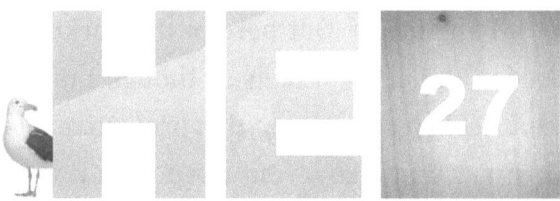

I'm a horny teenager all over again. The intensity of this unorthodox make-out session could ruin me to this girl forever. We're doing nothing but touching, but every movement seems to mean everything. Every part of my body wants her, but I decided on the car ride here that I would only go where Shea prompted, do what she's comfortable with. And though I'm tempted to slide one hand up her shirt to caress the skin of her breasts and lightly pinch her nipples and sneak the other down her pants, to massage the sweet spot between her legs with my fingertips, I hold back on those and many other urges. I don't want to ruin the perfection of finally feeling her sexy body against mine. This moment is a victory in itself.

When we're only holding each other tightly, all of Shea's muscles relax, probably from exhaustion and, I suspect, too much wine, and she falls asleep in my embrace. Seeing her like this—vulnerable and real—I realize that I more than "like" her, but there are no exact words for what I feel.

I pull her close, as though I can hide her away and

keep her all for myself. Out here in the darkness and in the middle of the night, it feels as though I may actually have a chance. I've never been this protective of any girl. It's an instinct that rises from deep within that I can't explain. I try to relax and sleep, too, but my mind leaps forward into any future that we may have, and the road is blocked by all the issues from my past. I'm certain that she'll want nothing to do with me when she knows my awful truth.

And that truth is that I'm so unworthy of her playful spirit, her perfection, her hot body. Despite this, I can't help myself from wanting to wake her and finally kiss her, continue where we left off and keep going until I've made her mine and she's made me hers, but I hold back.

I've been running away from the guilt of what I've done, and it's not easy to forget. Nor is it something I want to forget because if I do, it's as though I've forgiven myself, and I never will. The bottom line is that I don't deserve Shea. Even as I held that wineglass in my hand earlier and toasted with her, my mouth watered, my hand became shaky, and my body was instantly covered with nervous sweat. Alcohol hasn't been that close to my eager lips in ages, and I desperately want to give in. It was all I could do to control my reaction in front of her so she wouldn't see what a weak fuck I really am.

Even from here in the moonlight, I can see the outline of the wine bottle. It tempts me, like the seductive curve of Shea's hips. I catch a faint whiff of grape on the night breeze, and cringe as the scent activates the demon inside that seems impossible to quell. I pray to be free every single day, but I know it's a useless and stupid wish.

I look down at her, breathing peacefully, and run my hand lightly around the halo of her mussed hair. I think she could be my salvation from all my struggles if she allows it. And in that thought, I realize that everything hinges on this crazy girl, and the unbelievable part is that I'm comfortable with that.

I sigh and give up thinking in constant racetracks that take me back to the same issue over and over again. Releasing her from my embrace, I slide out from under the blanket and stand and stretch. I move beside her and gather her in my arms, sliding my hands behind her knees and back, and easily lift her. The blanket drapes over the curves of her body and she moans, waking slightly, and tucks her head into the curve of my chest. I carry her inside and place her on the bed.

"Come to bed," she says, her voice raspy with sleep, and she reaches out, beckoning me.

"Anything you want." I answer by sliding in beside her.

"Ahhhhhhhhh! Oh my God! Oh my God!"

My eyes open wide. I shoot straight up and immediately jump out of bed, my heart beating fast because of

Shea's scream.

She frantically flaps her arms, yelping and hopping around, and it feels like complete chaos because my brain has yet to catch up with my instantly awakened body.

It takes a moment to realize what's happening. She's fighting off a fluttering bird. A big, fat fucking bird.

Get the bird out of here. I pick up a pillow and wave it through the air, trying to guide the frantic creature out the French doors, which I apparently left open last night. Wings flapping loudly, the bird flies away into the blinding sunlight.

Breathing heavily from the excitement, I turn and walk back into the bedroom. Four loud bangs rattle the wall between us and the next room. I look at Shea and she looks at me, and we begin to giggle like we did last night. The action immediately relieves the frightening tension, helping my heart rate return to normal.

"I think our neighbors hate us," I say.

"But they didn't wake up to a bird nesting in their hair."

I snort. "In your hair?"

"Yes," she says, still catching her breath and crosses a hand over her heart. "Holy crap, that scared me! Those little bitches!" She looks out the open door and purses her lips, fists clenched at her side, and takes off running out onto the veranda. With pointed fingers, she's attacking a flock of birds that have camped out on our terrace, devouring the contents of her leftover fortune cookies. She shoos them away, arms waving and legs kicking the air. I want to capture it in a photo, but I can't look away for fear of missing something.

I rub my chin, watching her, realizing I feel exactly the same as the first time I saw her in the airport. She's so fucking crazy-cute.

"Thanks to the birds, I guess we can buy more dirty fortunes." I playfully waggle my eyebrows.

"Maybe." She purses her lips. Her shoulders and legs turn inward, as if she's suddenly turned shy. Sometime overnight, she must have shimmied out of her jeans shorts, and I'm sincerely sad that I wasn't responsible. Now she's standing in front of me, all bare legs and sexy in her days-of-the-week underpants, making my dick twinge with excitement as I remember last night. Apparently she does, too, because her cheeks burn a rosy shade to match the large graphic heart on her oversized T-shirt, hanging off one shoulder that reads, I LEFT MY <3 IN SAN FRANCISCO.

I wish to God she would just leave that heart with me. Or just give herself to me, because I'm totally captivated.

"Morning," she offers timidly.

"Afternoon is more like it." I walk to her and capture her in an embrace. The most significant part is that she allows it, because part of me worried that she wouldn't even be here when I woke up. This is progress.

"There's something about you that birds love," I say, and she laughs into my chest, her body rising and falling quickly. She leans away and looks up at me.

"I think they're your cannibal zombie seagull minions. They're just following their master around."

"You caught me," I say with mock seriousness. "It was their mission to confiscate the boring fortune cookies and they succeeded. I'll pay them handsomely in beer and pretzels."

"Is that the key to bribing them? I thought it would be bird brains or something zombie-ish."

"They're vegetarian zombies."

"Of course they are." Shea pulls away from me and I instantly miss her. She spreads out her arms, soaking up the sun rays. "It's such a pretty day. What should we do?"

"Anything you want, sunshine."

H ew takes a shower and gets ready, and then it's my turn. I lug my things into the bathroom and shut the door behind me. After I dump my toiletries onto the vanity I take a long moment, wondering if I should take my medication, just in case my illness finds me again. If I had to guess, the chances of wandering into a wedding or a similarly upsetting situation in Napa Valley is high. Even just thinking of the possibility makes my shoulders tense.

I unscrew the top, remove a pill, and drop it on my tongue, but I don't swallow. I want to be better than these things, not be chained to the pills like a tortured prisoner. For once, I want to be in control.

I spit the pill back out into my hand, toss it in the toilet, and flush. Unsure if I'm doing the right thing, I cross my arms, holding myself together as I watch it swirl around the bowl and plunge into the hole.

Then I close the commode top and sit down, raking my fingernails over my arms and rock back and forth.

Things have been going so well since we left the city,

that I can't imagine Luke ever finding me here. There's no way for him to track me, and the thought immediately causes me to relax. A part of me, though it's dangerous to think this way, feels like I've finally escaped him, and I have Hew to thank for that. With him by my side I feel stronger, and though it worries me to death, I'm doing my best not to be scared anymore. I can do so much more without fear. I want to kick fear in the ass and make it my bitch.

I think I can do this. I need to do this. Leaning on my knees, I run my hand over my face. With a deep breath, I slap my thighs and stand up straight, mustering my girl power, and gaze at my reflection in the mirror. The day I arrived in California seems so far away. I'm already feeling stronger. My coloring is healthier, and my smile somehow brighter.

The truth is that I—feel—good.

I think of last night again, remembering how hot it was just to touch each other. If Hew and I had kept going, I surely would have spontaneously combusted into a hot, fiery mess. Despite the fact that I want to do it all over again, right now, I do my best to concentrate and continue with my regular routine: shower, teeth, face, hair.

I reach for the hair dryer, plug it in, and turn it on. As I yank at the cord to remove a kink from it, I accidentally knock my open pill bottle over. It falls on its side, pills spilling out and rolling as if in slow motion down the curve of the sink, then dropping from view into the yawning chasm of the open drain.

"No!" I scream as if it will make a difference. I catch a total of three sleeping pills, losing all the white and dreaded pink pills. I yelp with concern and fall to the floor on my knees with the last of them in my hand, cursing because I can't get any more without a new prescription, and the last thing I'm going to do is call my doctor for one of those.

Destiny, you bitch.

Hew knocks on the bathroom door. "You okay?"

"Yeah." My response is small and I know it doesn't sound convincing. It's shaky and unsure, which is exactly how I feel. I suck the inside of my cheek and tighten my arms around my body. What will I do if I break down again? Can I talk myself through the anxiety like I did at Pearl's in Chinatown? The answer is that I don't know. That was partly a fluke, something I hadn't been able to do—ever. But if I'm to continue on my little road trip, I'll have to be in charge of my own body.

I inhale a long breath through my nose, summoning the parts of me that are right to overpower the bad.

I can do this.

I can do this.

Eventually I emerge from the bathroom clean and

dressed. Hew looks me over, probably sensing the slight distress in my eyes. How could he not suspect that something's happened, and it has everything to do with the noise I made while was in there. He stands and I dig my hands into my pockets, waiting for him to ask me what's wrong.

"Everything good?"

"Yeah, let's go explore!" I perk up when he lets it slide, but I think he's starting to realize when my enthusiasm is real and when it's not.

He grabs his wallet, room key, and camera, and I wander into the bathroom for my purse. Then we lock our room and head outside.

The wine festival is in the next town, and Hew drives. Outside the city of Saint Helena, cars park along the side of the interstate, so we do the same and walk, following the crowds to the main street. It's closed off for pedestrians and lined with tents selling hand-painted wineglasses, wine stoppers, wine holders, and wine decanters, as well as Bedazzled wine shirts, scarves, and hats, and any other wine-themed item you can possibly imagine. There are food vendors, other shops, children's activities, farm animals, bounce houses and, of course, lots of flowing wine.

"This would be the perfect place to sell your Napa Valley wine and fortune cookies," Hew suggests.

"You're joking, but I'm seriously considering it. If

you're going to build me a house here, then I'm going to need a job, too.

"So true, Miss whatever-your-name-is."

We knock around the quaint town for a few hours, watching a people parade, a kid parade, and then an animal parade. The last is the most exciting, including everything from house pets to farm animals to the random beasties, all wearing wine-related costumes. My favorite is a camel encased with a bunch of round purple pillows, representing a bunch of grapes. The sign hanging around her neck reads, My name is HUMPOPOTAMUS. I decide in that moment that I must have my own Humpy for my Napa home, which of course, Hew argues with.

Humpy ends the parade and I follow behind her, hoping for a better view.

"Look!" I become distracted and run to a vendor who is selling temporary tattoos. "I think I should get one. What did you say I probably have on my back? A butterfly?"

"I was joking." He leans on the display.

"But I think it's perfect." I decide it's exactly how I feel when I'm with Hew, free and beautiful, and most importantly, renewed.

I scan my options and decide on a plain black outline of a monarch butterfly with its wings spread wide. Though, to my despair, I have to wait in line behind four children who are being temporarily tattooed with Sponge Bob, Spiderman, and two Dora the Explorers. When it's my turn, I sit down in the chair and lift the shirt from my back, explaining to the tattoo artist where I would like the image to be. She nods and immediately gets to work, cleaning the spot and applying the transfer image.

"Are you sure you want to go through with this?" Hew asks. "It's a very serious commitment."

"I think you should get a matching tramp stamp. But for a boy it would have to be called something else."

"A douche mark?" He laughs and shakes his head. "Not a chance."

When I've officially been "butterflied," I stand and look in the mirror. "I love it!"

"Would you ever get a real one?" With his finger, Hew traces the shape on my lower back. I close my eyes, coming undone with every stroke.

"Never." I swallow, trying to form words to answer, but it's hard when he's distracting me like this. "I'm deathly afraid of needles, hospitals, or anything medical related."

When he stops, I open my eyes and pull myself together. I tie the hem of my shirt in a low knot, the same way that Hew ties me in knots. I leave it on one side so that it shows my midriff and new awesome fake ink. With him I feel sexy.

"Why?"

"It's one of those stories you don't want to know." As I say the words, the scars on my face, head, and legs throb in unison.

Hew gives me a quick glance and I realize that I've let my guard down and said something truly real about myself without planning it. Yes, I dropped in truthful little details here and there, but I embellished them with unrecognizable nonsense. And nothing was ever said without serious consideration. I've become so relaxed around him that I've forgotten myself.

I'm waiting for him to ask me for further details, but he doesn't. He lets it go, just like this morning. Instead, he wraps his arm around my back, pulling me close like he's protecting me from whatever I may be hiding. He doesn't know it, but the closer we become, the more that seems plausible.

After I've run off on him so many times, it's possible that Hew learned his lesson, and for whatever reason, and despite my obvious tall tales, he continues to want to be around me. And more than ever, I want to be around him.

A clown that was part of the parade walks past us with a bunch of cotton-candy-colored balloons. They bob around, hitting me in the face, but through them, between their smooth curves, I see a face—the one that I've been running from—and my heart absolutely stops.

Shea tenses at my side and bats away several pink balloons. When one pops, scaring everyone around us, the clown holding them turns to her and says, "Watch it, lady!" He gives her an annoyed expression before stomping away.

I'm expecting a cute comeback, something worthy of Shea's good humor, but instead I look down to find her squatting on the ground, shoulders hunched over and body shaking.

"What's wrong?" I bend over.

"We need to leave. Right now." Her face settles into a scared mask. One I recognize from the other times that she ran off on me. Worried, I grab her arm, twining it with mine, immediately anchoring myself to her. She's not going anywhere without me. I'm not letting this girl go. I haven't even learned her real name yet.

"Did I say something wrong?" I held my tongue this morning when something happened in the bathroom. I even held it when I wanted to ask her about the hospital thing.

Apparently, she's too upset to respond to my question.

Instead, she seems to frantically scan the faces of every-one as they pass. Kids, adults, it doesn't matter. Each per-son looking down at her sends her into a spastic panic, and she clutches me tighter.

"Did you see someone you know?" It's the only expla-nation. I glance around now, too, searching for anyone looking at her.

"Just please." Shea breathes heavily and doubles over. At any moment she looks like she'll hyperventilate or puke. I hope to God it's neither. "Get me back to the hotel," she pleads.

I nod, wrap my arm around her shoulders, and we stand. I guide her out of the festival. When we're several blocks away from the party, I rub her back, doing my best to soothe her, but she keeps her face turned into my chest, like she's hiding.

But hiding from whom?

When we arrive back at the B&B, I jump out of the car, run across the sidewalk, push through the front door, and race up the stairs to our room. But when I realize that I've forgotten my room key, I lose my wits, shake the knob, and bang on the door like it will some-how magically open.

Hew runs up the stairs to my aid. "Hold on. I got it," he says in his calm voice, which I have come to know well, but this time it won't help me. As soon as the door creaks open an inch, I push through and dodge into the bath-room, slamming the door behind me.

Frantic, I pace the bathroom. Three steps, turn. Three steps, turn. How did Luke find me here? I should have known he would; he always does. There is no way to get away from him, and the thought of being hunted by him poisons my mind. Thank God he didn't see me. I pull my hair and scream, and then think of Hew in the next room.

I stop, trying desperately to control myself, which leaves me shaking where I stand. I bite my nails, bite my fingers, bite my hands. Nothing works. The only thing I can think to do to save myself is to turn on the shower and step into the freezing stream. So I do, fully clothed. I want it to wash Luke away. Wash everything in my past away, even if it means I'll forget Bren. I press my back against the tiled wall and slide to the shower floor, landing on my butt. From the new position, the water pelts my face but it seems to calm my anxiety. I curl myself into a tiny ball, wishing, like I have so many times before, to fold in on myself until I'm so small that I become nothing.

Hew knocks on the bathroom door. "Shea, are you okay? I'm really worried."

"Yeah." Even though I'm mumbling, my voice echoes in the tiny shower stall.

"Okay." He doesn't press for more info. That's how good he is, how much he respects me, and I know it's not really fair that I keep doing this to him without telling him why. Can I tell him? Will it all really matter when our whatever-this-is fling is over? He still doesn't know my name. I'm positive because I have taken every precaution to make sure he doesn't find out.

Water pours over my skin until it shrivels into the likeness of a chilled prune. Hew does check on me a few times, each time I think to confirm that I'm still alive, but for the most part, he leaves me be. That's a good thing because I need to get myself in check before I face him.

Finally calmed, I drag myself out of the shower and stand, dripping on the floor mat, and open the door. It swings open and Hew jumps up from the bed where he's been waiting and rushes in.

"Did someone hurt you, Shea?"

I shake my head. It's not the truth, but it doesn't matter.

"Are you cold?"

I nod, but Hew is already pulling a towel from the rack. He drops it around my back like the comfort and protection he always tries to show me, and hugs me close. In this moment, I want to stay wrapped up in him forever. Somehow, I always feel better with him at my side.

"We need to get you out of these wet clothes. You're shaking like a leaf."

He must take my silence as assent because he sets the towel aside and grabs my shirt from the hem and begins to lift it. "Raise your arms," he says, and I comply. He peels the shirt from my body and the air hits my skin, freezing me further, and pricking every inch with goose bumps. He throws the drenched shirt into the sink and then turns back to me. His hands slide to my cutoffs. His fingers twist at the button until it pops free, and then he tugs on the zipper, dragging it open. My wet and heavy jeans fall to the floor at my ankles, and I lean on him as I step out of them.

He wraps the large towel around my body, starting at my chest. I grab it and turn away from him. "Help me with my bra."

I look at his reaction in the mirror. He stares at my

bare back for a moment as though he, too, is undecided, but then does as I asked, gently, slowly. The clasp releases, freeing my restraints. Now I'm only wearing my Thursdays.

This is a test. For me. For him. To know what it feels like to be with someone other than my Bren. To be in control and to defy Luke. To move on. To do something for myself.

At the thought, my shaking subsides. I don't have a panic attack. I don't feel guilty. I don't feel like I need to run away. I only know I need to leave everything behind to be here with him, right now.

These feelings have grown stronger in the last days, but the sense of comfort and intense attraction is the same that I have felt in every intimate moment with Hew from the beginning. I'm drawn to his strange familiarity. I care for him. It's easy to tell he cares for me, too.

I let everything that I've been fighting against happen. My body's physical reaction is stronger than my mind, and I turn to him and twine my arms around his neck, dropping my towel on the floor. And finally, after all this time, I press my lips and body to his. He tastes like the candy he was eating at the fair, sweet like caramel, and salty. I swipe my tongue across the inside of his mouth, wanting more, and he growls.

Hew is as hungry for me as I am for him and he reaches over my shoulders, down my back, pulling me to him. He thumbs the elastic of my panties, pulling and stretching, sending a fire of desire racing across my skin, over my quivering stomach muscles, and dropping south to that spot between my legs. The throb there begs to connect with the one pressing on me from his pants, and I forcefully push him backward and into the bedroom. When we can't walk anymore, we fall onto the bed.

I land on top of him, sit up, and straddle him, locking his lean torso between my thighs. Looking down at his handsome face, that sexy grin leaves me feeling in control, the one thing in my life that I'm desperate for. It fuels me to press forward. I tug at his shirt, flipping it over his head, pulling it free and toss it across the room. I lean over and trace the deep lines of his hard abs with my tongue, as well as the curved hip flexor muscle that forms a *V*, pointing directly into his pants.

We slide farther onto the bed by rolling, twisting, and turning with each other. My kisses are frantic, nipping and playful, but somewhere along the way, his kisses turn tender. When the difference between our intentions becomes agonizingly apparent, I pull away to question him.

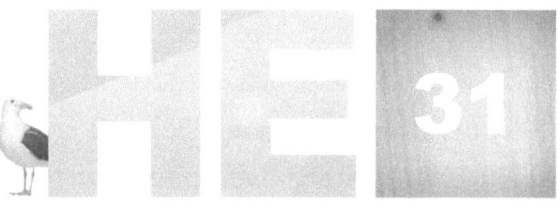

have wanted this to happen for days, hours, minutes, and seconds. I can't even count the number of times I've seen her naked in my mind, when I saw her nearly naked on the bike the first time, and my wet dreams. And now here she is, on top of me, squeezing me between her legs, licking my body, and even more beautiful, more perfect than I ever imagined. Jesus.

But something has happened to Shea. She changed her mind in the shower and I don't know why. My brain is fighting a death match with my dick. It wants to allow this kissing, touching, and—oh God—playful biting to continue. I don't want my brain to care why everything has changed all of a sudden, but it does. Or maybe that's the don't-fuck-up voice, telling me to do the right thing.

I slow us down, transitioning from hot and heavy to gentle and sweet kisses, and she notices. She pulls away and tethers her emerald gaze to mine.

"What's wrong? You don't want to?"

"Of course I do. Can't you tell?"

"I can, actually." She looks to my nether region and smiles. "So, what?"

I sigh and rub my hands over her back. I'm not sure if my concerns will win me points or cause her to run in the other direction. Everything with Shea is a crapshoot. "I want you. But I don't want it to be in reaction to whatever just happened to you out there at the festival, or in that shower. I want everything to be perfect when we do this, and I'm worried about you."

She immediately rolls off and I think this is it. It's over. "You're such a fucking chick," she says, surprising me. She laughs, pulling the sheet over her perfect breasts.

"Maybe. But it's only because I care about you." I sit up.

"I know." Her gaze falls to the floor. "And I appreciate that. A bad person would take advantage of this situation." She points her foot and draws a circle on the carpet with her big toe.

"I did something terrible back in Maryland." Her words fall out so effortlessly that I try not to react. "I cheated on my boyfriend, my fiancé, actually." She looks up from under her lashes but she doesn't blink, signaling that she may or may not be telling the truth. Somewhere over the last few days, the lines between truth and reality have blurred.

"Okay." I shift where I am. I didn't exactly see that coming. In my mind, I imagined something in reverse, where Shea was the victim.

"With his brother," she adds.

"Wow." She's caught me off guard, and I don't know

what the hell to say.

"Yeah, I suck."

"No, you don't."

"I do, and I know it."

I rub her arm, trying to comfort her. I know there must be a reason.

"Anyway, ever since I ran away from the ginormous mess that I created, the brother has been looking for me." And here is the reason. The brother. "Is that who you saw at the festival?"

She nods. "And in San Francisco, on the morning of the day that we visited the fortune cookie factory. That's the only reason I agreed to go with you. I was hiding from him. He's been tracking me since I left him."

"And I thought it was because of my charming personality." I try to keep the tone lighthearted, even though everything she's telling me is upsetting. Thinking back on our time together, I remember how she wore a hat and sunglasses and tied up her hair, even though it was cloudy. How she freaked out at the sight of a wedding, and her appearance the first time I saw her on the plane. All of her strange choices now make sense.

"That too, obviously." She reaches out and grabs my hand. "The thing is that this brother is kind of a bad guy." She pauses, seeming to look for the proper words. "We'll just say that he needs a gigantic douche mark on his lower back to warn away other girls."

"Did he hurt you?" I ask the question again, focusing on her scars. The hook on her face, the long, ragged line running up the inside of her leg, and other small chips and dents marring her soft skin. Could he have done that to her?

She doesn't answer this time, but her silence is enough of an answer for me. I tense, my blood heating at the thought. The anger I've been trying to suppress and control bubbles to the surface, ready to kill someone for hurting this beautiful creature.

"So do you think I'm a good person now?"

This question disarms me, and I feel every bit of the pain I can see in the pools of her eyes. I've been there, too. Neither of us is perfect. We've just been playing the part for days, actors in a perfect play, trying desperately to run away from our pasts. Getting lost with a stranger.

"As far as I'm concerned, there was nothing before I met you. I only know this version of you, and this is the version I'm falling for."

Shea is in my arms in seconds. We're not just holding each other but pressing out all the bad, letting it seep from us, and allowing it to disintegrate in the air, leaving room for only the good within our embrace. With everything that we have with each other, I think there is no room for anything negative. Not anymore.

We reposition on the bed and take up where we left off the night before, just spooning, no kissing, only chatting,

MICHELLE WARREN

but still without sex, and every second that she doesn't run away from me is a victory. It's only been a few days since she broke down crying at the sight of a wedding, and a few more since I saw her in a trashed wedding dress at the airport. I'm honestly not sure how long I can make this last, but I'll take everything that I can.

We decide to stay for one more night after tonight, and then move on to the next place—wherever that may be— on Saturday morning.

Shea falls asleep in my arms. And with my insomnia, my brain won't shut off. My flight back home is for Sunday, and I'm undecided if I should cancel, call in to work and stay with her, or get back to the reality of trying to find a new job in San Francisco. I can't stay at my sister Ashley's house in Maryland any longer. She and her husband don't want their twenty-six-year-old fuck-up little brother there forever, and I certainly don't want to be there either, under the current circumstances.

I wonder if BCT got back to me about the job. They said they'd be contacting me at the end of the week, either way. I reach for my phone on the bedside table. I've neglected it with all that's been going on. There are no voice messages but when I check my e-mail, I see that Bob Clayton, the partner at BCT, wrote me earlier today. They want a second interview, and I'm one of three final candidates. I obviously didn't screw up as much as I thought, and I want to whoop with excitement, but keep my enthusiasm inside. They want to meet again this Monday, so now I know I need to stay in the area and change my flight, but I also need to get us back to San Francisco.

I'm not sure how this will go over with Shea. Our relationship is carefully balanced at the edge of a knife, and one slip may sever our connection. So I need a backup plan. I need to figure out some way to break her rules, to learn her real name and contact info, so that when she runs off again, I'll be able to find her. Even though I know she's having fun now, I know it's only a matter of time before I somehow mess things up, or say or do the wrong thing. I always manage to. Unfortunately, though, she's blissfully and thankfully unaware of the fact that it's my MO.

Maybe I can find her purse, slip into the bathroom, and read her license while she's sleeping? I could now if my arm wasn't pinned under her neck. I wiggle it, thinking I can tug away, but she only turns completely, facing me, and tosses her arms around my stomach, latching on. I frown. Now there's no chance of that happening. I'll have to be sneaky tomorrow, maybe when she's in the shower.

This train of thought has me thinking about looking at her license and seeing her real name for the first time. What will it be? At the least, it will be strange to call her anything else. She'll always be my Shea. I guess possible name options in my head, like counting sheep, until I fall asleep.

SHE 32

I wake up bright eyed, feeling wonderful for being wrapped around Hew. I take a moment to think about what happened yesterday. One: I almost slept with him, and despite his chivalry and my mostly clear head, I still want to. Two: he told me he's falling for me, which leaves me feeling giddy with happiness. And three: I'm not exactly sure where I channeled my bravery, but I feel a sense of relief at telling him at least part of the story. I decide quickly that these are all good things, and though I'm concerned about Luke, I do feel safe here with Hew.

I roll out of bed, stretch my arms, and head straight for the sunshine. The French doors creak as I pull them open, allowing the light to flood the room.

Hew stirs and moans.

"How can every day be so stunning?" I suck in a deep breath and scratch my head of tangled hair, then look over my shoulder.

Hew grabs a pillow and shoves it on his face to block the light. "Argh! It's too early." He rolls over, pulling the fluffy white duvet with him.

I can't resist teasing him to get up, so I pad across the

floor and leap onto the squeaky mattress. He doesn't respond so I lift the bedding, peering at him in his pillow cave.

He snaps it shut and I quickly pull it off of him when he protests.

"You have to get up. We've got a big day ahead of us." I lean in to place a sweet kiss on his lips. When I pull away, he lifts his head, trying to move with me to steal another.

"You'll be the death of me, woman. I'm exhausted."

"This is our last full day here," I remind him. "I want to get out and see everything!"

For the first time in a long time, I'm not worried about Luke. I know that if he manages to find me again, Hew will be my rock, and I'll stand up to him and end this once and for all. The only thing I want to worry about right now is the person next to me, who has done everything for me, even though he knows nothing about me. I draw swirling designs with the tip of my finger over his bare chest.

"Fine." He moans. "But you get ready first so I can sleep longer."

I jump up with more energy than I've had in months and gather my things, then duck into the bathroom. Hew is already wrapped back into the blankets, eyes closed and body relaxed when I shut the door. I follow my regular routine, getting showered and dressed, stopping to stare at the three pills left in my bottle of evil. I let out a shaky breath, knowing that the sleeping pills won't help me during the day. It doesn't matter what's left. I don't want to be on meds; I'd rather feel every moment with Hew with a clear head.

Forty minutes later I finish and find Hew snoring lightly with his mouth hanging open. With him cuddled up with a pillow, he's adorable, even though he's drooling like a leaky faucet. I bite my finger, holding back a snicker. Seeing him so tired, I feel bad about waking him, so I slip out of the room and jog down the stairs to the common area to grab us some food.

hen the room door closes behind Shea, I sit straight up in bed. I wipe the drool from my face with the back of my hand and listen to her footfalls as she bounces down the stairs to the first floor. Not knowing how much time I have, I break away from the twisted sheets and scour the messy room for her handbag.

I find it on the vanity in the bathroom. But right before I tug at the zipper, there's a moment of hesitation on my part. Learning her name will break the rules of the foundation on which our friendship is built, the voice inside warns. I fight back. This game has gone on long enough. I'm doing it for any chance of a future that we may have. One I hope to have.

I take a deep breath and tell my don't-fuck-up voice to shut up. I don't want to lose her. With one hand inside, I rummage around, pulling out a lip gloss, some loose Twizzlers, a change purse containing a disturbingly large amount of cash, and a pill bottle, but no wallet. But the bottle may be enough. I bring it to my eyes and try to decipher the label. It's torn and ripped in all the important spots except two. There's an *S* in her name. First, last, or middle, I'm not sure which. Either way, the information is useless. The only identifier is the name of her hometown—Davidsonville, Maryland. Just a fifteen-minute drive from mine.

"Damn it!"

There's a knock at the door and my heart drops out of my chest, leaving me chilled with anxiety.

Shea's back.

Faster than should be possible, I shovel all the items back into her purse, zip it, and throw it back on the vanity.

She knocks again, a little harder this time.

I run for the door, but go back to adjust the strap of the purse so it looks similar to when I found it. I run back to the door, take a deep breath, drop my shoulders, muss my hair, and squeeze my eyes together like I've just woken up, then calmly open the door.

ith several muffins stacked in a napkin, I stop to chat with the woman behind the front desk.

"How can I help you today?"

"When we checked in, we were told about some parties held by the wineries. Do you have any info about them?"

"I can give you a few flyers, but I believe most of them have been sold out." She lays out a series of fancy-looking invitations. Some have gorgeous photos. One in particular captures my attention.

"Whoa, what's this one?" I point with my elbow.

"That's the Coppalina estate. Fabulous restored buildings, world-class wines, and an unforgettable party. I know the tickets are sold out for the party, but you may be able to visit the property and pay for a tour of the chateau, the infinity caves, and vineyards." She slips the brochure and invitation between two of my free fingers, and I pinch it securely. "Can I call and make a reservation for you?"

"That's okay, but thank you. I'll chat about it with my friend first." I make my way back to our room and knock on the door with my elbow.

It takes several moments, but Hew finally opens it. His hair stands straight up, his lips are pouty and eyes sleepy. He scratches his ass and steps aside for me to enter.

"I can't believe I didn't hear you leave," he says and yawns.

"I thought I'd let you sleep." I drop the flyers and muffins on the dresser. "Brought you some food in case you're hungry."

"Thanks." He shuts the door and staggers over to give me a kiss on the cheek. He picks up a corn muffin and drops into a chair, his long legs extended. He lifts the muffin to his face, smells it, and peels back the paper wrapper. Then, with one enormous bite, he devours the entire thing.

"Impressive and gross." I scrunch up my face.

He finishes chewing, cornbread crumbs sprinkling over his bare chest. "Big mouth. You know what that's for?" He wags his eyebrows and brushes his hands over his pecs, wiping away the leftovers.

"Sloppy kisses?" I tease, but his are anything but. They're perfect, romantic, sensual, and as I have found out—any-day-of-the-week panty melting. I clench my gut, feeling the familiar heat rise through my body. If I don't get out of this room with him sitting here in his sexy boxer briefs, looking up at me with those eyes, we will never leave.

"You know you like them," he says in defense of himself, and grabs another muffin from the dresser.

I look down, feeling shy because it's true. Lost in a daydream, I drag my finger along the edge of the dresser and pick up the invitation, and then fan myself with it, as if it will help. I segue into something new—a distraction.

"The reception lady gave me the info on some winery parties tonight. I really want to go to this one." I hold up the flyer, pointing out the photos.

"Looks fancy and expensive," Hew says with a mouth full of food.

"It's my treat. Just think of it as our first date."

"First date?" He raises an eyebrow. "What about the rules?" He reaches for an open bottle of water and takes a swig.

"They still apply. Let's just have fun."

"Don't we always?"

Hew rises from his seat and plants a sweet and non-sloppy kiss on my cheek as he passes. I slump into his chair, picking at a chocolate chip muffin while he showers and dresses. When he emerges from the bath, he still looks tired but better than earlier.

"You didn't sleep well, did you?" I sense it. There's a new stress hidden behind his eyes.

"Sometimes I can't turn off my brain." He slips his feet into his flip-flops.

"It's a good thing. Means you're alive."

"You always find the silver lining, don't you?"

Hew grabs his wallet, room key, and camera, and I wander into the bathroom for my purse. Then we lock our room and head downstairs.

In the main living area with the large dining table, they are just cleaning up from the complimentary breakfast, but I've already formulated a plan of adventure for today, one that will hopefully impress Shea.

"Wait here a sec. I'll be right back."

"Sure," she says, and drops into a wingback chair next to the window, then picks up a magazine.

I make my way to the back of the house, where I find a small industrial kitchen. I peek my head through the open doors. "Afternoon," I say to the man prepping food at a stainless-steel counter.

"I wanted to surprise my girlfriend and take her out on a picnic." I pause at my choice of words, wondering what Shea would say to that. "Is there any way I could order some sandwiches?"

"Of course." The man sets down his knife, removes his gloves, and hands me a menu hanging from a nail on the wall. "Choose whatever you'd like."

"Thanks." I peruse the options, settling on several items, including dessert and drinks. After relaying my order to the chef, I return to Shea.

When I walk in, she's standing next to the main dining table, removing a tall vase of sunflowers, and then proceeds to pull the long tablecloth toward her, bundling it at her chest.

"What are you doing?" I stop in my tracks.

"Borrowing this." She continues on her quest.

"What?" I laugh. "No, I don't think that's a good idea."

She walks close, speaking low. "Okay, I didn't want to tell you this, but I kinda have a thing for pretty fabric. It's a sick obsession, really. I collect all kinds of vintage-fabric-related items. And this is the prettiest pattern of teal cabbage roses on fabric I have ever seen."

"Really? You collect lots of things, don't you?" I think of her pressed penny collection. I look down at her, looking up at me like she's almost asking me permission to "borrow" it, and she flutters her eyelashes a few times and I realize she's putting me on.

I've learned her tell, broken the Shea code, and she doesn't even know it. So I play along and grab her hand. "Release the tablecloth, Miss Whatever-your-name-is." I speak like a police officer and wink. "When we win the lotto, I'll buy you rooms full of beautiful fabric, all with this exact same pattern."

"Really. And what shall I buy you?"

I inspect the room for some bauble worthy of a pretend heist. "That." I point to the painting above the stone fireplace. It's a vibrant oil landscape of the valley with long rows of grapevines drenched in the golden evening light. The colors remind me of a Maxfield Parrish painting. I walk to it.

"Why this?" she asks.

"So it will always remind me of my time here with you."

"We haven't even started yet." She lifts up on her tiptoes and plants a heated kiss on my ear. With her this close, I imagine her lips cracking into a smile before she spins and walks away. The little tease always knows how to leave me hot and bothered.

Just when I'm about to take her by the arm and spin her back around to kiss her the way we did yesterday, the chef walks into the room, ruining the moment.

"Sir, I have your order."

I keep my eyes on Shea until he hands me a large bag. "Thank you so much."

The chef nods and leaves.

"What's this?" Shea peeks into the bag.

"It's a surprise." I swipe it away, happy to have my own secret.

"Have you been scheming without me?" She bats her long eyelashes.

"You'll see." I lead her out the front door to the side yard. There, stacked against a tall white picket fence, are several bicycles.

"In honor of the day we met, I thought we could take the bikes out on a picnic and explore." I hold up the bag of lunch.

"Naked bike riding?" Shea looks hopeful.

"Negative. I'd never be able to live up to your previous biker clan." *And I'm not as brave as you.*

Shea laughs. "Oh, I think you definitely could." Her gaze explores my body as she bites her finger. She's killing me.

She pulls out a bike for herself, picking the lemon-yellow one. And in keeping with our designated color scheme, I pull out the purple one and drop the bag of food into the front basket. I pull my backpack over my shoulders and steady myself on the seat, then push off.

We ride out onto the neighborhood street and I take the lead. The town is small but I don't bother seeing the sights; I head straight for the country. I want Shea all to myself.

ew and I ride on a long stretch of country road. I balance the bike between my legs while pedaling, let go of the handles, then spread my arms wide, tilting my face to the beaming sunshine and close my eyes. In my mind, I'm the happiest I've been in ages. It's happening. The good minutes in the day are taking over the bad.

"This is the life! Woohoo!" Hew screams.

"Woohoo!" I scream, too, and open my eyes.

Hew weaves his bike from one side of the road to the other. To the right and left of us are a million rows of grapevines. At the far end of the rows, rolling mountains shoot high where they're met with a sky the color of bluebird eggs.

This day is perfection.

We ride for a several miles, keeping pace with each other, and stop on occasion for Hew to take photos. There are many opportunities, especially when we meander onto a dirt road and encounter red barns, white barns, barns that are falling apart or ones that already have, cows, llamas, chickens, and goats. Then we arrive at a field, where Hew pauses again.

"What's wrong?" I roll up next to him and stop.

"It's time for you to get revenge." He gestures to a field of low grass where hundreds of birds are grazing peacefully.

"Oh my gosh, you're a genius!" I set my jaw and remount my bike, then aim my front tire for those little bastards. "Fortune cookie stealers!" I yell as if it's my battle cry, and pedal as fast as I can through the flock. The bike rattles beneath me, bumping over holes and tufts of grass until I reach them. In a wild frenzy, they take off in a white wave of fluttering wings and cackles, flying away, dotting the blue sky. After I've scared off every bird in sight, I ride back to Hew, who has been snapping photos of me all this time.

"That'll teach them," I say.

"You've literally scared the bird shit out of every flying zombie beast in this county." He points to my bike, which has been christened in several white gooey blobs. Thank goodness they missed me.

"Ew. Gross."

"You sure taught them!" He laughs.

"I've heard that it's good luck," I say, and count them. "Looks like I have triple luck here."

"Always trying to see the sunshine, aren't you?"

Hew waves me on and I follow him until we arrive at a clearing with a large shade tree at a river's edge. I drop my bike on its side and walk to the water. In this area, the

Napa River gathers in a wide and deep pool of clear water. Hew stands under the tree and removes his camera
from his backpack, then sets it aside. Then he takes out a
rolled-up white sheet.

"And you yelled at me for trying to steal a tablecloth."

"It's a sheet from our room. The difference is I'm actually going to return it." He flips it into the air and I grab
the edges. Together we pull the fabric flat and place it on
the ground. I plop down and Hew joins me, then sets the
bag of food between us.

"You wouldn't have stolen that tablecloth anyway."

"Ha!" Even though it's true, I've never stolen anything
in my life. I've been a decent person by all normal stan-
dards, but it doesn't mean that I wouldn't, at least in my
mind I think I could. Would that change who I am?

"You wouldn't because you're a good person. I can
tell."

"Things aren't always black and white. It wouldn't
make me a bad person if I took it, I would still be the
same. Even good people make mistakes."

"Even though you know the difference between right
and wrong, you still would do it?" he asks doubtfully.

"Maybe it would make me happy."

"Maybe, but you might die of guilt. And where does it
stop? First you take a pretty tablecloth, then the pretty
table, then a pretty camel named Humpapotamus, and
before you know it, you're running your own theft ring of

circus animals."

He's joking, of course, but I sense a serious tone.

"How do you know I don't already? Maybe it's my real job," I say as I unpack the lunch bag. "Have you ever stolen anything?" I pop a strawberry into my mouth.

Hew rocks back on his haunches and takes a swig from a water bottle. "Yes," he admits and looks down.

I sit up straight at his answer. "Care to elaborate?" I push a wrapped sandwich in his direction.

"No." He takes another drink of water, looking uncomfortable.

I let it go, even though I don't want to. I've let many things go in the last few days, and I wonder how long we can spend this much time together and not really share those things about ourselves that make us partly who we are. People aren't just made of rainbows and sugary-sweet candy, though I wish that were the case. Half of who we are is written by our mistakes, mishaps, and imperfections.

"Can I tell you how starved I am?" Changing the subject, I open my sandwich and settle my back against the wide trunk of the shade tree.

We eat in silence. Hew devours his sandwich while I work on the fruit and a few bites of my own sandwich, when he finally says, "What if I told you that I stole a car?"

"What?" I stare at him.

"Would you still think I'm a good person?"

Hew's eyes won't leave mine, and he's not winking at me in the way we do when we're telling our playful fibs. Not that he did that as much as I did. And from his expression, I think he's not only telling me the truth but also testing my response. It's easy to see that he's nervous about what I'll say.

"Of course I do."

"I could be a serial killer and you wouldn't know it," he jokes and relaxes back, staring off at the mountains.

"I could say the same to you." I turn toward him.

He shakes his head and sets his jaw.

"Look." I move closer and place my hand on his shoulder. "We obviously both have our pasts, but that's not important right now. I don't have to know every bad thing you ever did in your life to know that you're a good guy now. People change, grow up, get smarter, move on. In ten years I could be completely different, but I'll never be the person I was yesterday, or even this morning. I don't want to be. I want to try to be better with each second I'm alive."

Hew still doesn't say anything. Like before, he's drifting off to that place in his past where he possibly stole a car and did who knows what else. I want to erase that hurt, soothe the frown between his eyes, and the ache in his heart. I've been there, too, known plenty of my own heartache. I know he has a good soul; I can see the regret in his eyes, in everything that we've shared. He can't hide his true self, even behind a fake name or any other silly thing we make up in our little world. So I do the only thing I can to change the trajectory of this moment; I abruptly stand.

This fails to get his attention, so I begin to strip. I kick off my shoes and set them aside. When I peel off my shirt and it hits the grass, I do have his attention. He isn't someplace else anymore. He's right here with me and fully focused on my hands as I unzip my cutoffs and they slide off my hips, falling to my ankles. I step one foot out and then the other, then launch the shorts straight up into the air with the tip of my toe. At about ten feet up, the shorts begin their descent and land on Hew's head.

He smiles through the leg hole and I turn and flash him my backside, wearing my Friday panties. They're the yellow ones, printed with swirling rainbows.

"Your mopey stormy talk brought out the rainbows." I shake my ass and then take off running. At the edge, I leap into the deep, swirling water of the river. It's chilly as it splashes around me, and I sink underneath to dunk my head. When I pop up and clear my eyes, Hew is now standing under the tree staring at me.

"Come on!" I yell and wave. "The water feels fantastic." I float around, flapping my arms.

Hew turns away and I think he's still upset, but then he flips his T-shirt inside out and over his head and I get a full view of his wide shoulders and lean muscles, and the dimples at the bottom of his back. God help me! Every inch is strong and defined, and that ache I felt yesterday is tingling in my Fridays again. Hew throws the shirt aside, and it lands in the branch of a tree.

He looks over his shoulder and smiles. I scream for him like a horny housewife at a strip club. He said he doesn't dance unless he's trashed, but I think I see him wiggle his hips when he unzips his jeans and bends all the way over, pushing them to his ankles. He's wearing his boxer briefs. Dark blue ones.

Hew turns, taking his time, allowing me to ogle him. I can see every curve and line of him, even beneath his trunks. His size is large, outlined in the shadows. Desire consumes me as I drink all of him in. He races forward and when he reaches the edge of the river, he leaps, doing a cannonball into the water.

I open my eyes underwater and swim until I find Shea's smooth, shapely legs, then pull her under. Before she submerges, I hear her scream. She playfully fights with me until I release her and we bob above together, wrapped in each other's arms.

"Glad you decided to join me." She shifts closer.

"You shouldn't swim after eating. I came to save you."

That tension is back. The one where we're having difficulty breathing the same thick air with our chests heaving like one of those damn romance novels my sisters read. I focus on her, caressing her chin with my palm and stroking her cheek with my thumb. "Every second I'm with you, I feel like a better person. You make me believe it's possible that I can move on from every mistake I've ever made and live in your world."

Shea inhales a quick breath, her gaze sealed to mine. I gently drag my thumb over the corner of her peach lips and she dips her chin and kisses my palm. Her cheek slides into the cup of my hand as she looks up at me from under her long, wet lashes, head tilted. Her wide eyes are beautiful, and as vibrant a green as the grapevine leaves in sunlight. I can't take any more of being careful around her. I want her. Not just for now, but for always.

My lips come down on hers and immediately our bodies arch into each other. Like flipping a switch, every emotion that I've been holding back releases into this kiss, urging my lips to work over hers in a panic of passion. Her chin, her neck, her shoulder, and back to her lips again. And the most astonishing part is that she's kissing me back. She's allowing it. She wants this as badly as I do. Her hands work over my chest, my shoulders, and tangle into my hair. Each touch sends me further into a race to make her mine. With heavy breaths, she nips at my lip with her teeth, and I lose it and grab her ass, lifting her. Her legs wrap around my hips, locking behind me so I can press my dick against her. I slide my hands over her skin and into her panties, looking for the treasure at the end of her rainbows.

"What the hell do you think you're doing? Get out of there!" a man shouts.

We disconnect and whip our heads around in the direction the voice. It's a police officer, standing behind his open cruiser door on the opposite bank of the river. When I see his uniform, my heart stops. The last thing I need is a run-in with the cops.

"No swimming here, this water runs into the reservoir. Can't you read the damn signs?" He waves to one near him. It's clear as day and I missed it.

Shea and I look at each other again and we cover our mirroring smiles. Despite being scared shitless, I can't help it. I feel like a sixteen-year-old who's just been caught by his parents with his pants down, making out with his girl. We quickly drag ourselves out of the water, dripping wet, and run for our bikes. I grab my backpack and shrug it on, then toss my camera into the bike's basket. Shea grabs everything else and jumps on her bike and takes off. I hop on my bike and pedal quickly to catch her. We're a half a mile away from the cop when we break out laughing hysterically, still half-naked.

"We just got busted by the cops!" she says.

"We suck at being good." It's like we're partners in crime.

She looks me up and down, raising her eyebrows when she stops to look at my trunks. "Welcome to Naked Biker Gang."

"Do I measure up?"

"Ha! I'll let you know." She blows me a kiss and leans into her handles, grits her teeth, and pedals faster, taking off.

Our getaway has transitioned into a race. And being the competitive person that I am, I can't let her win. I lean into the breeze and chase her. A few moments later I sail past, giving her a victorious face.

"Race to the Jacuzzi!" she yells, pressing hard to take

the lead. We're neck and neck for about a mile, and then we both seem to run out of steam. We've ridden farther than I realized. Our racing turns into meandering and joking, stealing smiles and waving at passing cars that honk for our partial nudity, until we return to the bed and breakfast. We drop our bikes in the side yard, and I grab her and kiss her the way I did in the river. I've been craving her since then, since the beginning when we first met. Her tongue teases mine, and her hands rub over my chest and down my back. She pulls away and begins stepping backward, beckoning for me to follow.

"Why do I feel like you're playing hard to get?"

"Because I am." Shea grins and with that response, I tackle her, lifting and tossing her over my shoulder. Her knees kick at my chest and her elbows beat on my back.

"Put me down!" She giggles, but then she starts to play dirty. "I'll give you a wedgie!" She tugs at the waistband of my briefs, threatening me.

"Argh! You're killing me, woman!" But I don't give in, I nudge open the tall fence door with my knee and walk into the backyard, where there is an in-ground pool and Jacuzzi.

"Fine, you get it!" She pulls the elastic hard, lodging the fabric between my ass cheeks and I scream, drop our belongings in the grass, and reach up to tickle her. She loses it, squirming and yelping, which causes her to laugh harder.

"Stop. Stop!" she squeals.

I do and I lower her so that we're face-to-face, her arms draped around my neck, and we kiss again.

Out of the corner of my eye, I notice we're not alone, and take in all the people I didn't realize were in the pool area. Some are lying out in the sun, sipping wine or reading books. Collectively, they look over and frown. We're being loud and obnoxious, so I pull away, allowing her to slide to the ground. She flips her messy hair over her shoulder, coming down off our make-out high, and takes in the scene, too.

"Oops." She hides her face in my chest and snorts.

I lean down to her. "Let's be on our best behavior. Try the good thing."

Shea nods, accepting the challenge. We collect our mess from the ground, lift our chins, straighten our postures, and walk across the pool deck as though we're actually wearing bathing suits.

We drop our items off on two lounge chairs and make our way to the Jacuzzi. We slip into the hot water and take our place next to each other, positioned so we're looking out over everyone.

SHE 38

"Of everyone here, who do you think is our crappy neighbor?" I whisper to Hew, needing a distraction so I can keep my hands off him. Hew looks over, seeing right through me, then grabs my hand and places it on his knee. I smile and lean in close.

"If they're here, they're probably figuring that we are."

"Probably."

"Based on the number of rooms in the B&B, there's a fifty-percent chance that they're here. That's if they haven't checked out yet."

I look at each couple, considering if they could be the one who had knocked on our wall when Hew and I couldn't stop laughing. We didn't mean to be loud. Both times were accidents.

"What about couple number one?" I nod to the farthest. They are sitting at a bistro table, probably in their midthirties, playing with their phones.

"Hmm, I don't think it's them."

"How can you tell?"

"They've got bags the size of Texas under their eyes,

they're sucking down wine like this is their last day of vacation, and most importantly, they're the right age to have a couple of screaming kids at home, which explains the first two items. I bet what we did wouldn't even faze them."

Hew slides his arm around my shoulder, pulling me closer, and I snuggle into the curve of his body feeling safe and brave, allowing my hand to explore his lower half below the bubbling water.

"I think you have some freaky carny gifts of your own." I look around to find the next couple. "What about them?" I jut my chin to a fifty-something couple lying back on two loungers. The lady is short, heavy, and wearing a T-shirt Bedazzled with wineglasses, and her nose is pressed into a dirty book. Her husband's hairy chest and rounded tummy are bright red from a raging sunburn. His head is hidden underneath a fishing hat, covering his closed eyes.

I turn to face Hew so he has to look over my shoulder. His gaze jumps to me before it returns to them.

"How can I concentrate on bad neighbors when you're here tormenting me with those magic hands?"

"If you wow me with your talents, maybe I'll wow you with mine."

He smirks. "Challenge accepted." His gaze goes back to the couple, and I continue to stroke his thighs, his hard abs, his chest and hips, being strategic about accidentally brushing over his shaft, knowing it will drive him even crazier.

He continues his observation with great difficulty. "The woman's not the type to complain. She's sweet and often likes to see problems from someone else's point of view. But," Hew pauses, "the man most definitely is a complainer, loses his temper easily, even though he's a nice guy when you get to know him."

"How did you decide that? You're like Sherlock Holmes or something."

"Nah, just guessing on that one. They remind me of people in my family."

Hew continues to talk, doing his best to concentrate on our conversation, but every so often his eyes become hooded and his body sinks a little deeper under the water, giving me more area to massage.

"And what about that last couple?" They're sitting closest, and the woman is typing on her laptop while the husband is talking on the phone.

"Hmmm. She's definitely a strong contender, based on the sideways glances she's giving her husband. She's working on vacation, and the way her shoulders bunch up by her ears, I'm guessing she's a little uptight."

The man laughs loudly, and the woman leans over to swat him on the knee, shushing him.

"I think we have a big wiener," I say and finally allow my hand to go there, rubbing the thickness beneath his boxer briefs. "The question is, what shall we do with this info?" I bite my lip, feeling naughty.

"Shea, what happened to being a better person?"

"I said I'd try, I didn't say it wasn't a challenge."

Hew sinks a little and moves closer, speaking in a low, seductive voice. "What did you have in mind?"

"Something mind-blowing," I say teasingly.

"You're going to be the death of me, woman." He pulls me in for a hot and wet kiss as I continue secretly stroking him.

I'm not sure how it happens, but one minute we're in the Jacuzzi and the next we're in our room. Our foreplay has gone on for long enough, and the more time I spend with him, laughing, allowing him to amplify my good traits and enforcing the old, stronger me to come alive again, the more I desperately need to feel us connect on a different level.

Hew kicks the door closed with his foot and I pull down his dripping underwear, finally setting him free. Every part of his tanned and toned body is perfect, with angles and planes that I need to attack.

Our hands are all over each other's bodies. We've been flirting, making suggestive remarks, and playfully touching for days. Now I realize that all of it was merely pieces of the sex bomb that's about to detonate all over this room.

Hew presses his erection against me, and I reach up

on tiptoe in a desperate attempt to move it closer to the throb building in my panties. His hands slide down my sides and his fingers plunge beneath the fabric, dislodging my panties from my hips and rolling them down until they stop at the top of my thighs. Air rushes between my legs, cooling the wetness between them, and instantly I want to lift myself to feel him there.

I moan with pleasure, or maybe in release for finally being in this moment. This beautiful person tumbled into my life and I have no idea why, but there must be a reason. He's been the clarity I've needed and I know that when I give myself to him, he will treat my gift with respect, with care, in the same way he's treated me, even though he doesn't even know my name.

Hew drops to his knees and breathes hot air into my sex as he twists his fingers into my Fridays, dragging them over my thighs until they release their wet grip and drop to the floor.

When the heat from his mouth swirls between my legs, my eyes roll back in my head and I grasp the thick hair of his head. As I massage the strands between my fingers, he brushes the soft stubble on his face on either thigh, and I feel myself opening for him on so many levels.

He stands and meets my gaze, breathing that same sweet heat all over my face, my neck, and my entire body clenches as he kisses me everywhere. His hands drift to my ass, where he effortlessly lifts and settles me on top of the low dresser. I'm tilted back against the wall, completely focused on Hew's sexiness as he seduces me with every move he makes. He slips a single fingertip under the strap of my wet bra, where he rubs the silk up and down, and then slowly drags it off my shoulder. He leans close, and the skin where the strap used to sit receives one soft, wet kiss. The other side receives the same attention, but that shoulder receives two kisses. When he skims his hands around my back and releases the clasp, he dives in for three sensual kisses at my collarbone. I arch my chest toward him, enjoying all the sensual attention.

Hew is worshipping me, building me up slowly, taking his time. His lips meander down my body, lingering over sensitive parts. He cups one breast, and his teeth grazes over my hard nipple. His strong hands palm the outline of my hips, my thighs, my stomach, like he's shaping each curve of my body out of soft clay.

At each new spot, tingles race over my sensitive skin, awakening an animalistic craving that causes my hips to buck to be as close to him as possible. But there's only one spot I need him to touch more than anything else, and as he works his way down, he finally does what I'm dying for him to. He touches the throbbing area with his thumb, drawing slow, languid circles, intensifying my lust. My legs spread, inviting him as my head falls to the side and I breathe heavily, threading my fingers through his hair, guiding him. As he dips down, his hot breath and tongue join the party, though he needs no direction. Each stroke is focused and rhythmic. My body churns beneath him, followed by a drawn-out chorus of primal moans, climaxing as he orally drives me into absolute delirium.

He barely allows me to recover before rolling on a condom and taking me again, filling me completely and fusing us together. My body clenches, legs locked around his torso, begging him to pull closer and deeper. He hasn't even begun to move inside me yet, and I think I may explode if he doesn't move right now.

"Please, Hew," I purr, wanting him to begin the wild friction, but he already knows what I need. He picks me up again with ease and gently lays me on the edge of the bed. With me supported, he stands on the floor, deep within me, then pulls away slowly. The motion causes my breath to release but as he plunges in, I suck in a sigh of bliss as our bodies mold to each other in slow, steady, undulating movements.

When he presses his thumb against that spot again, gently working me in two ways, I come undone, heart fluttering, heat activating every nerve. His touch builds the intense pressure inside, making me greedy for more. I lift up to tug on his hips, forcing him to move faster as I moan and pant to our beautiful rhythm. The more I constrict, the more tension compounds. My body tightens and muscles threaten to rip at the moment I climax again.

Pleasure pulses from my orgasm, sending him over the edge, too. In a waterfall of shuddering movements, he fills me with warmth and love.

I reach for his face as his glittering eyes watch me, and he kisses my palm. In this moment, I realize we're finally sharing the most truthful thing that two people can share, and I think he feels it, too.

We're lying in bed, tangled in the sheets, recovering. Shea is draped over my chest, drawing hearts on my skin with her fingertip.

"There's no place I'd rather be right now," she whispers, and I understand exactly what she means.

"In this moment I feel like a good person with the right person," I tell her. All the bad in my life led me to her, which makes me think that I can live with the past if she is my future.

She readjusts on top of me so that her beautiful naked body is pressed against me and kisses her sweet lips to mine. When I grip the back of her neck, her wild hair falls forward around me, and I feel complete.

But it doesn't last long; she becomes distracted by the chatter in the hallway outside our room and pulls away. A door opens and closes. The TV pops on in the room next door. We can hear the light murmur. Our crappy neighbors have returned.

"Are you ready to learn your second lesson in revenge?" she asks with a glint of mischief in her eyes. With our lovemaking, I've already forgotten about the plan to get back at them.

"What'd you have in mind?" I ask as I look up at her.

She lifts herself up and leans in, placing another kiss on my lips.

"Round two?" I offer, and slide my arms around her impossibly tiny waist, gripping her curvy hips as she sweeps her tongue in my mouth.

"Follow my lead," she says, dragging her naked body seductively across my chest. She presses up on her hands and stands above me, looking down. I'm not sure what's she's doing, but it sends my mind racing. I flash her an amused expression.

"What are you up to, Miss Whatever-your-name-is?" I grab each of her ankles and slide my palms around her silky legs.

In response, she bangs the wall with the palm of her hand and at the same time yells, "Ahh!" She tilts her head back and moans loudly with pleasure, then looks down and smiles at me.

"You wouldn't." I'm horrified and intrigued all at once. "Oh, yes!" She jumps on the bed and my hands release. She bangs and moans again, but this time with more fervor.

I can't believe what I'm about to do. I look up at Shea, at her mouth open and moaning with self-induced, fabricated sexual pleasure, and I laugh to myself. This girl is totally insane, and I can't help loving everything about her.

I sit up and stand next to her, balancing myself. Once

there, we bounce on the mattress together, moan together, and bang on the walls together. But we do it right, starting slow to create realism, and then progress into a natural rhythm that after several minutes turns into a loud symphony of heavy breathing and lustful ecstasy.

Shea channels her best Meg Ryan. "Yes, yes, yes!" She growls from the back of her throat. And I use the standard, "Oh God! Right there! Yeah, baby!" We build ourselves up into a heightened frenzy and finally when our moaning, banging, and screaming meld together in a flurry of sexual chaos, we fake climax together. It's as exhilarating and exhausting and it has totally turned me on, more than ready for the real thing again.

I have a sneaking suspicion that we won't hear from our neighbors again anytime soon. I drop to my butt and bounce on the bed. Shea does the same, but when she does, she bounces off the side and rolls over the edge, hitting the floor and laughing. I roll over the side, following her, landing nearby. "One little monkey jumps in bed. She rolled out and broke her head."

"Ha!" She laughs, still out of breath, cheeks red from exertion, and she's beautiful. "You have no idea."

"I think that was the best pseudo sex I ever had," I joke. It's true but I want more, and I don't want to stop there; I want to make everyone in this hotel hear us. Make them all jealous.

"We did it." She raises her hand to me for a high five.

"Seems weird to high-five after an orgasm of that magnitude." I slap her hand with mine and grasp it, bringing it to my lips for a kiss, hoping to transition the moment into something more.

"What would you suggest?" Shea rolls on her side and rests her head on her hand, smirking with those bitable lips.

"Real sex," I say, and she complies.

As I brush out my wet hair after a shower with Hew, he steps up behind me, wrapping his long arms around my waist. "I think we're running late for our date at the party." He kisses my neck.

"I don't know if I want to go now. I don't really have anything nice to wear, anyway," I say, frowning at the thought of being at that nice party in cutoffs. They'd throw us out in seconds.

"I can fix that."

"You can?" I turn to Hew with a puzzled look.

"Wait here."

Hew quickly slides his pants on, shrugs into a T-shirt, grabs his wallet and key, and right before he runs out the door, he says, "Please don't go anywhere."

He races out of the room and I have no idea where. I have no intention of leaving him. How can I when I feel this way? When he makes me believe that I can fight my demons and live in our perfect world together?

When he returns thirty minutes later, I'm lying on the bed with blown-dry hair, still naked but wrapped in a towel. He shuts the room door and places a large white bag on the bed.

"I need you to stand," he says.

I slide over the duvet and stand.

"Do you trust me?" he asks.

"Yes." How can I answer anything else when he has trusted me from the beginning, even when I asked him to lunch without telling him my real name. When he showed me his favorite places, told me his secret dreams, and we created an entire world of make-believe together. He never questioned me and I never questioned him. Trust is the one thing we've had since the beginning.

"Drop your towel."

I do it without hesitation. It falls to the floor around my feet, revealing all of me to him.

With a dropped jaw, Hew looks me over. Even after today, after he's seen all of me, I blush as he takes his time. "Shea, you're absolutely stunning." It takes some time, but he finally breaks his gaze and digs into his bag. First he removes a pair of new baby-blue lace panties. He rips the tags off with his teeth and I laugh.

"You animal."

He roars playfully and drops to his knees. He places the panties on the floor and I step into them. Slowly he drags them up my legs, leaving a trail of goose bumps behind them. When he pushes the panties in place, snug on my hips, he lodges each hand on my back, pulling himself to my waist. There, starting from one hip bone, he drags his wet lips all the way to the other, kissing and caressing. I thread my fingers through his hair, massaging his head as I tilt my head back and moan with pleasure, slipping into ecstasy at being near him this way. He grips me tighter, forcing me to feel every movement of his face on my body.

When he releases me and turns back to the bag, I can't wait for him to return. This time he does with a matching bra. I have no idea how he knows my bra size, but when he stands and slowly drags the straps over my arms, little hairs stand at attention, and heat races up my limbs. Hew touching me is sexy. But somehow, Hew dressing me is even sexier.

He moves behind me, sprinkling my neck and shoulders with warm kisses as he feels his way around my bra. He massages my breasts before moving the bra into place, and latches the clasp.

He returns to the bag twice more. The third time he removes a pair of glittery silver sandals, then goes back to his knees and slides my feet in securely while rubbing my ankles. The fourth time he returns with a pair of shimmery silver earrings. He slides them into my pierced ears. They make a low, tinkling noise when I move, like miniature wind chimes.

"Almost done." He finally takes out the tablecloth. The one that I lied and told him I wanted to *borrow* from the B&B.

"You took it!"

"I purchased it," he says, correcting me.

"Liar." He winks, so I'm unsure. "What's that for?"

"Why, my dear Scarlett, I thought I'd make you a dress out of a tablecloth," he says in a Southern accent.

"I suppose that's better than curtains."

"It will be. I promise."

Hew allows the fabric to fall long and straight, then drapes me in the folds. I have no idea what he's doing but he seems to, so I just trust him like I have from the beginning. He twists, turns, and ties me into that cabbage-rose-covered linen and when he's done, he pushes me in front of a mirror.

"Where in the world did you learn how to do this? It's so beautiful!" Shea exclaims.

"I have three older sisters. Spent the better part of my childhood engaged in any girly activity you could think of."

"Aw, you poor thing."

"My sister Beth, who is closest in age to me, wanted to be a fashion designer when she was little. She would wrap herself in covers, in linens, or any other piece of fabric she could find, playing a model on a runway. I learned a few tricks from her. Anyway, after she dressed herself and my two other sisters, I pretended to take photos of them walking the catwalk with an empty macaroni-and-cheese box that I cut a viewfinder into." I play with a coil of Shea's hair, rubbing the strands between my fingers, and smile at the memory.

"Really?"

I wink to this and she leaves it alone, even though it's true. Beth never lived out her dream, just another thing my family blames me for.

"I have to admit that I was a little worried when you

referenced *Gone with The Wind*."

"Blame that on my sisters, too. Let's just say they kept me in touch with my feminine side. Shall I sing the words to the songs of *Grease*?"

"You *are* the one that I want." She wags her eyebrows and grabs my hand. "This could be the best first date ever." Shea pulls me into a hug. "Thank you for this." Then she steps back and looks down at herself, and just by the expression on her face, I can tell she finally sees herself the way I see her—beautiful.

"So tell me," I ask. "What party are we crashing?"

"You know me so well!"

Shea has done a complete turnaround. Yesterday she was locked in the bathroom, having an anxiety attack. I'm not complaining about the change, of course, but it does make me worry about that ass-hat she's running from, if there's more to the story that I should know. And I'm concerned about the fiancé she left behind and how that affects us. For now, at least, I just need to be happy she's opening up.

"So do I get to dress you now?" She bites her tongue. She's back to her playful ways, and she does help me dress, though it's more of a sprint than a stroll because we're running late. I wear my gray interview suit, sans jacket, but with a plaid bow tie and suspenders. The blue and gray in my tie matches the colors in Shea's dress. When we walk out the front door of the B&B, Shea picks a white rose from the garden and pushes it through the buttonhole on my shirt.

I leave my camera behind. I want to live in the moment of every second of the night, to commit our first official date to memory, taking photos in my mind instead of with my camera.

I drive and Shea navigates. She directs me to park behind the Coppalina estate, and hide the car in a grouping of dense trees.

"Are you sure about this?" I eye her.

"We're just crashing a party, not robbing someone."

"We can try to be better people tomorrow, I suppose."

"Just relax and have fun."

We exit the car and she grabs my hand, guiding me through the trees and a corner of a vineyard, and to the back of a large restored chateau. From a line of high box hedges, we emerge to the party.

The outdoor affair is elegant and beautiful. Large round lightbulbs are strung everywhere, twinkling in the dying light. Partygoers dance on the stone patio to a five-piece jazz band. White lace covers dining tables adorned with flower arrangements. And then there is a buffet crowded with ice sculptures, food, and chocolate fountains, and strategically placed bars serving lots of alcohol. Even the people are beautiful, and I can't believe that we sneaked in this easily.

"You're a genius." I lean over and kiss her temple.

"I know," she says cheekily as she throws her shoulders back.

We mingle. Shea grabs a glass of wine. I stick with a soda, and tell her it's mixed with rum. I want to tell her the truth, but today is not the day to ruin all that we've built up. We snack on hors d'oeuvres while we meet people, important people from all over the world. We should stick out like sore thumbs in our cheap clothing, but Shea conforms like a chameleon, and when I'm with her, she transforms me, too.

Someone even asks her who designed her dress, like we're attending some awards show. Shea replies that it was an up-and-coming designer named Hew Hew. French, she tells the woman. Talented and dreadfully overpriced, but worth every pressed penny. Then she winks at me. The woman believes Shea, just like I believe her. There is something about her that everyone trusts and falls in love with. It is her sincerity, her charm, and I suspect her special gift.

Looking around, I realize we're among the youngest partygoers here. Most people in our age group are broke from college loans, or probably still in college, doing keg stands to cheering crowds on a Friday night, not crashing luxurious wine dinners with billionaires. It's possible that Shea is still in college, I think, and realize that it's strange that it never occurred to me before. She's young enough, and I wonder if she's even old enough to drink.

She acts so young and naive in some ways, but so mature in others.

Now that she's opening up to me, the questions that matter in typical and normal relationships pour in. I was content to know little in the beginning, but now I'm frantic for more. Everything. I go to her and pull her away from her new acquaintances because I don't want to share. It's our first date, and I want Shea for myself.

She brings me a new rum and Coke, but this time it really has rum. I've spent this entire evening around people drinking, smelling it on their breath, and catching the scent of weed from dark corners of the party. So I finally do what I've been salivating to do all night—I stop thinking like I have wanted to do for so long, give in to the moment, and drink it because I want to stop being jealous and controlled, I want to have fun, too.

From the moment I finish the first drink and the liquor shoots through my bloodstream, everything unfolds quickly. I find myself caught up in the excitement of the party, and the exhilaration of being with Shea. We drink a lot. I'm loosening up like I always do: laughing, smiling, maybe even acting a little goofy. When I'm like this, I'm the life of the party. I even give Shea a run for her money.

We dance because she talks me into it. She's really soulful. Her hips sway and bump into mine, her moves silky and sexy. She grips my suspenders, somehow turning them into a tool of seduction. Every move she makes turns me on. We can't keep our hands off each other. With her next to me, she makes me look like a better dancer than I really am. I realize she just does that in general . . . makes me look like a better person. But I also feel like a better person. Somehow, a happier one.

The sunset fades, graduating into complete darkness, and the stars fight with the strung twinkle lights. The music stops and a man wearing a tuxedo walks on the stage, takes a microphone, and makes an announcement. "It's time to bless the wine!" Everyone cheers, including us because I think we're both drunk. It seems everyone is, and this is the highlight of the party. We go along with it.

A priest walks out, takes the microphone, bows his head, and says a prayer, while waving his hand over the top of a wide-open barrel of grapes. It must be fifteen feet wide, and it's set off to the side of the party. At the end of his prayer, the crowd shouts the word "amen" in unison. Shea and I shout the loudest. The announcer takes control again and asks for the women at the party to help crush the grapes. Shea is the first to slip off her silver sandals. I pick her up in my arms and lift her over the edge, wobbling as I place her inside the barrel.

The band begins playing a special song, something that everyone here seems to know and sings to, but I'm too busy staring at Shea. The twenty other women in the background are hazy, but together, in a dance of stomping, they crush the grapes beneath their bare feet. It's like I'm peeking through the lens of my camera and can only focus on her—singing, laughing, and turning the color of grape juice as it splatters on her, on me, and on everyone else. Shea's beautiful, and I want to reach out and take her again.

When the song is over, I do. I lift her out of the barrel and place her on the ground, then clasp her hand, pulling her inside with me through the large open barn doors that lead to the barrel caves beneath the chateau. Inside there are casks the size of trucks, and we slip behind them, against the far wall in the darkness where no one can see us.

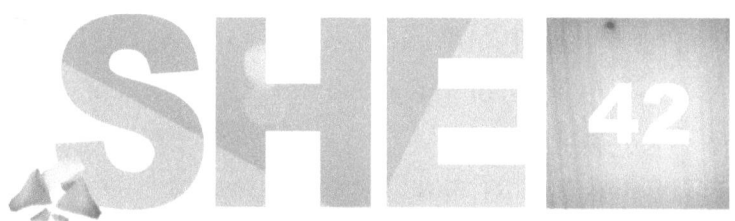

Hew presses me against the curve of a tall wine barrel and kisses me fiercely, and I welcome him. I want his arms tangled with mine, his warm breath rushing over my body, an intoxicating replay from this afternoon.

The alcohol has dulled my senses again and the truth is that I'm happy to release myself from always worrying if I'm doing the right thing, being the right person, making the right choices so that everyone around me is happy. I spent too long playing to the needs of others. All I need to do in this life is make myself happy in this moment.

"Come with me." This time I grasp his hand and race us back outside through the open barn doors into the party, weave around the dancers, the groups of people sipping wine, and finally away from the frenzy and into the dark quiet of the vineyards. Dirt presses between my toes as we run. By the time we stop, we can just hear a gentle buzz of music on the breeze. Dimmed yellow and white lights twinkle in the distance.

"Look at the roses at the end of each row of grapes.

Aren't they beautiful?" I drift to one, catching my breath before I lift a wide bloom and sniff.

"They are."

I glance over my shoulder to see Hew intently staring at me.

"I bet you know why they plant them this way, don't you?" Carefully I bend one stem, breaking it off the bush.

"I do."

"Tell me." I slink back to him, rolling the stem of the rose between my fingers.

"The winegrower uses the roses as an early warning sign to watch for mildew, since roses and grapevines react to diseases in the same way."

I stop and stand several feet away, soaking him in. Hew is handsome, sexy, sweet, smart, and charming, and I know I'm falling for him, too. There's no need to know his name; I know his soul, and it's beautiful. The rose drops from my fingers, and I reach for the tie holding my dress together. Taking my time, I unwrap Hew's masterpiece, never removing my gaze from his. Nor do his eyes waver from mine. That's how I know we want the same thing, to care for each other the same way.

With my body completely revealed, I let the tablecloth fall to the ground. In the breeze, it lands spread flat between us. We meet in the middle, only an inch apart.

"You're heaven to me." He brushes his palms down my bare arms.

Looking up into his glassy eyes, I see all of his concerns. He's always so understanding, so careful with me.

"Just stand still," I say, breathing the words against his chest. I unknot the bow tie, and then tug at his shirt, lifting it and sliding it from his slacks. One by one I release each of the buttons. Once his shirt is free, I spread it open and remove first one of his arms and then the other, before letting the fabric fall to the ground. But I leave the suspenders. I've been tugging and playing with them all night while dancing, and I'm not done with them yet. My hands slide over his defined pecs, and his chest hardens under my touch.

"You're driving me crazy." His lips brush my forehead.

Wrapping my wrists into his suspenders, I clench them with my fingers, binding him to me as I ease him to the ground. On our knees and face-to-face, unable to restrain myself any longer, I kiss him, needing to give myself to him completely again. I unbutton his pants, slide his suspenders over and off his strong shoulders, and free him and myself of every piece of fabric between us, until there is only air.

We're equal now, naked in the night. Hew takes the lead and I'm eager to let him. He reclines me to the ground, but takes his time. He reaches for the rose that I dropped nearby. With the flower he teases me, softly dragging the fragrant petals over my face, sliding it over my neck and circling my perky breasts. With each stroke, my body reacts, my back arching, stomach muscles tensing, skin shivering, and my hands clench the fabric beneath us. All of my senses amp up on overdrive. He moves farther south, gliding the petals over my hip bones and teasing the length of my legs in long, sensual strokes. At the end he switches to kisses, blowing and nipping while working his way back up my legs. Somehow he knows my most sensitive areas—ankles, the back of my knees, inside my thighs. My toes curl each time we connect.

Hew leaves no spot untouched or worshipped. And when he finally takes me, I willingly melt into him, merging together. Lust rushes through my body, and I allow the current to drive me over the edge of a waterfall.

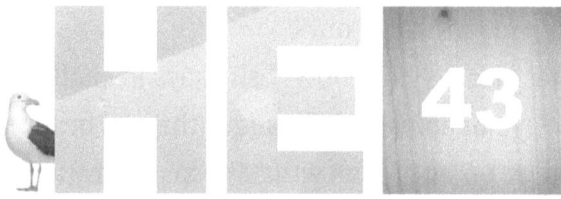

We lie in the vineyard, holding each other, drunk on each other. Shea's tucked into the curve of my shoulder. Nothing in my life has ever felt so right or so perfect. I kiss her head as she points to the twinkling stars. Just like the night we drove here, they and the full moon are shining down on her like they know what I know—she's special.

"What's that one?" she asks.

"What makes you think I know?"

"You seem to possess a vast knowledge of useless information."

"I'm not sure if that's a compliment or not."

She turns and gently bites my shoulder. "Tell me—tell me—tell me," she repeats in a monotone voice.

"Okay, well, that's Ursa Major. But I only know because along with all the other maps, I also had a map of the constellations."

"That one?" She points in a new direction.

"Lyria, Hercules, Corona Borealis, Virgo, Crater, Leo," I reel off as I trace my finger over different areas of the sky.

"Do you need me to go on?"

"What else do you know?" she says in challenge.

"The eye of an ostrich is bigger than its brain."

"Don't stop until I tell you." She kisses my arm.

"Astronauts can't cry in space."

She slides her wet lips over my shoulder and then dots my chest with kisses. Each unusual fact I share wins me more attention, but as she continues her quest, I start to mumble, losing my concentration.

"You're not done." She circles my abs with the tip of her tongue.

"Leonardo Da Vinci invented scissors . . . and it's impossible to lick your elbow."

This useless fact causes Shea to sit up and twist her arm in strange ways to force it toward her face. "You're right. I can't. You're so smart!"

"When a man anticipates sex, his hair grows." I continue with a smirk, hoping she will return to her previous agenda.

That bit of information has the desired effect and she lowers herself on top of me, pressing our naked bodies together. She runs her fingers through my hair, winding strands around her fingers. "It does look a little longer—and bigger," she concedes.

"Bigger?" I squeeze her. "And that's not the only thing." Then I attack her. She screams, giggles, and kicks but then gives in as I roll on top of her and pin her hands above her head, locking her hips down with my thighs. She's breathing heavy with laughter, and she's never looked as beautiful to me as she does tonight. I drag my palms down her arms, kissing her skin, and then we kiss again. With this introduction, I dive in, wanting to make her mine once more. This time is more playful, and I know we're making far too much of a ruckus, but it doesn't concern me. At least, not until I hear a noise that is not our own.

"Do you hear that?" I pull away from Shea and look for it.

"It's just a car." She slides her arms around my waist, her hands drifting to my ass.

A pair of headlights appears. They stop near us at the end of the vineyard.

"Oh no." Just as I say the words, a searchlight mounted on the side of the vehicle pops on and a beam of light cuts across the night. Dividing the dark, it scans the vineyard in our direction.

"We're busted!" I say. We jump up, simultaneously collecting our belongings.

"Run!" She laughs as she streaks across the field and I follow, my clothes balled under my arm. A spotlight swerves in our direction and catches us. The back of Shea's fleeing naked body is illuminated in the night. When our shadows cast long on the ground, she yelps and darts behind the shield of a row of grapevines, and I chase her. We race down the maze, making our way in the general direction of the party, and pass some departing partygoers along the way. They are too drunk to care that we're naked, and catcall as we streak past.

When the light first popped on, my heart stopped for a second time today. A run-in with the cops could totally screw me. But now that we're far away from the danger, where no car could easily chase us, I breathe a sigh of relief and return to this moment with Shea.

Shea makes it back to the car first, tagging the hood like we're running a race, returning to home base. She swivels just as I approach and I gather her in my arms. Even now, out of breath and scared out of my wits, heart hammering in my chest at the thought of being caught, I can't stop kissing her, wanting her, or needing her. If anything, I want her more. She gives in and we lean against the car.

"That was amazing. You're amazing." I breathe into her ear. Her mussed hair tickles my nose, but she pushes me away. At first I'm shocked, but then I see what she's up to. She fumbles for the car's door handle. Then she opens the door, grabs my arm, and tugs me inside, causing me to fall on top of her.

Even though the car is tiny, it allows for some interesting moves, and we finally finish what we started in the vineyard.

SHE 44

As I wake, I remember I'm in Hew's arms. I squeeze my eyes and peek with one to look through the dewy window of the passenger seat of the car. Outside it's dawn, and the birds in the trees around us chirp loudly. When I try to move, I'm stiff, and my mouth is dry. Hew stirs at my side, and I pull away from him to stretch out my arms and twist my back.

"God, I have such a headache." I rub my head.

"Ugh. Me, too." He moans.

"I think we drank too much." I chuckle, slowly remembering everything, as every detail rushes back. My head hurts until I get to the end of the night and remember the vineyard, and the car. I look down at my naked body, smile, and then take in Hew's lean, tanned muscles. I move in and give him a kiss. "Last night was amazing."

He looks down at me and grimaces.

"What's wrong?" He says nothing. "I look really bad, don't I?" I fuss with my hair and rub my face.

"No, it's not you." Hew rubs my arm. "You look beautiful. And yesterday was—wow."

We kiss again, but there's something wrong. I can sense it.

"You ready to blow this party?" Hew pushes back the seat, fishes for his slacks on the floor, and slides them back on. From his pocket he pulls out the car keys. He's being quiet, unlike his usual self, and I want to hope that this is just his cranky hangover personality. I mean, I get it. My head is killing me, too. I try not to dwell and wrangle the tablecloth, now covered with stains from the grapes and the grass, wrapping it around my body and tying it like a towel, just good enough to get back us to our room.

Hew starts the car and drives us back to Yountville, then parks at our B&B.

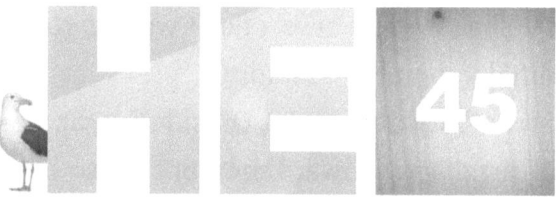

fucked up. I fucked everything up! Shea is sitting next to me in the car on our ride back to the B&B. She's humming and happy about last night, whereas I'm ready to drive myself into a concrete wall for being such a complete fuck-up by giving in and drinking.

My grip tightens on the steering wheel, turning my knuckles white. The voice that won't shut up is screaming at me, raging inside my body, whirling like waves in a storm, crashing and beating the sand over and over. I want to scream, punch, and kick myself the way Sollie Winters did. I deserve to be beaten like that every day, every hour, every minute and second until I'm nothing. It still may not be enough. Burning in hell wouldn't be enough.

Beth's youthful face flashes before my eyes. Her death was the wake-up call that forced me to want to make changes in my life. It dictated all the choices I made back then. I made a promise to her the night she died, the night I survived, and I just broke it for the sake of having fun.

Damn it!

I imagine slamming my head into the steering wheel and

I would if Shea weren't here. I don't want to ruin her moment with my complete stupidity.

We arrive back at the B&B. Outside the car, Shea grabs my hand, tugging me toward the front door.

"Why don't you go jump back in bed and I'll meet you there?" I try to keep my words level.

"You okay?"

"Yeah, just going to go grab a coffee at the shop we saw in town. You want something?"

"I only want you."

She lifts up on tiptoe and kisses me sweetly, and my heart breaks for letting her down as much as myself. If there were ever a new reason to finally break free of my addiction, it would be for her. What I did last night was a mistake.

"Hurry back." Her smile is lopsided and mischievous as she tugs the loose tablecloth tight around her chest.

"I will."

She strides away. When I hear the door close behind her, I make my way down the street and duck into the alley behind a retail shop. I finally allow myself to scream. The sound echoes off the buildings, shattering the early-morning peace. I kick the brick wall like I want to kick myself. I throw myself against the rough surface, trying to break bones, but I'm not that lucky. And then, like the grand finale for the fuck-up I am, my stomach turns with pain. The roil builds in my gut and explodes from my mouth, all over the concrete. Holding my knees, I hurl until there is nothing left inside. Finally empty, I fall against the wall and let the mortar bite at my skin as I slide to the ground and wail like a lost child.

I sit for an hour, wallowing in self-loathing. Depression, my old friend, creeps back, blackening my thoughts and killing my hopes. When people begin jogging and walking their dogs on the nearby street, I stand and steady myself. I need to get back to Shea. I know she'll keep me safe from myself.

Back at the B&B, she's sleeping. Thank God. I slip into the bathroom and clean up. My damaged knuckles, arms, and legs sting under the cold shower, but the water calms me, or maybe I'm just exhausted from only having three hours' sleep last night. I slide into bed next to the only positive person in my life and wrap my arms around her.

I feel like I've barely slept when I wake up sometime later, tangled in the bedsheets. Shea is already showered and dressed. She stands at the mirror in the room with dripping-wet hair and scissors in her hand. She pulls one strand straight and clips the length in one quick stroke. A long piece of hair flutters to the ground.

"What are you doing?" I shove a pillow out of the way for a better view.

"Cutting my hair. I've been wanting to for months."

"Why? Your hair is perfect." *And beautiful and I love the way it fans over your shoulders and down your back.*

"It feels good to have it short again, like it makes me stronger. I think I'll dye it, too. It used to be this really pretty ginger color and I loved it." She snips another strand.

"Red?" I sit up at this information. Watching her reflection in the mirror, I imagine her with slightly shorter red hair. I shake away the blurry image of another girl with red hair who appears in her place. She isn't my Shea. Thank God! But it seems a cruel joke of destiny that Shea would want to do this to herself now, after yesterday—last night! Even if she does it without knowing what it means to me or how it would haunt me.

She continues trimming. By the time she's done, the length is just at her shoulders. She's made it a little shorter in the back, and it does look great. Of course, she would look sexy in any haircut.

"What do you think?" She crunches her damp waves with her hands, looking confident and happy.

"I like it," I manage to say.

"Then why am I waiting for you to wink?" Shea settles herself in the bed next to me, her back pressed against the headboard. "You still have a headache?"

I wrap my arms around her waist and nestle my head into the pillow she pulls onto her lap.

"A little." It's not a lie, but I'm mostly still pissed at myself. That I gave in to the booze and not only took a drink, but then I took God knows how many more. Though parts are blurry, I remember most of the night. And after what

Shea and I shared, I can't believe that it's upstaged in my mind by my major fuck-up. Self-destructive emotions are bubbling to the surface again, and I force them down.

"You sure you're okay?" She strokes my hair.

"Never better." I take her hand and press a kiss into the palm. I'm trying not to let this change our mojo, but it's hard to hide the anger and disappointment when the don't-fuck-up voice is still yelling at me.

"There is actually something I wanted to talk to you about." This is as good a time as any. I swallow hard.

"Anything."

I clear my throat. "I got an e-mail from the company I interviewed with and they want a second interview. I'm one of three final candidates."

"That's great news!"

"It is, but I have to be back in San Fran on Monday, and at some point, I have to return home for my job."

There's a long moment of silence and she lifts her hands. Body language always says so much, especially with Shea. Just like I originally thought, all that we have teeters on the edge of that same knife. What she says now will decide if we tip over, slicing us apart, or if we will stay balanced for another day.

"You'll do great at your interview," she says and tentatively resettles her hand on my back.

Behind the words I distinguish sadness, and there is for me as well. I can't stand the thought of this ending so soon. Even now, after all we've shared, I don't know if she'll give up her game and finally tell me her real name when we have to part. Yes, I could tell her my name now, but that doesn't guarantee she will contact me. We can't go on like this forever, but I guess that was the whole point from the beginning. Her point.

"I know you don't want to plan anything, but I want to spend as much time with you as I can. I was thinking that we could drive back toward San Fran and maybe cruise some of the coast? I've heard it's really beautiful." I'm trying to turn this day around and make the most of our time.

"I've seen photos. It is," she adds in a steady but unenthusiastic voice, which makes me think I've lost her. Trying to show my sincerity, I sit up and grab her hands so she understands. "So, what do you think? It'll be fun."

She looks around the room, as if she's searching for the answer. When her gaze swings back to me, she finally nods with a smile.

"Great! I'll get ready and we can go."

I take my time getting ready, trying to joke and laugh with Shea, hoping our normal banter will reassure her, and that it will keep my anger leashed. To some degree it works, a little. I've pulled myself out of my own funk. Shea is more important than my stupid issues. I've started from day one before; I can do it again. I fight for the good thoughts that will move me in a positive direction. I can't let my problems ruin us, or the small amount of time we have left. But most importantly, I want her to stay put. Even now, she could take off running. I hide the car keys in the ice bucket when she's not looking, feeling more than a little paranoid, and I hope she doesn't know how to jump-start a car, but knowing her, she probably does.

When I step out of the bathroom after shaving and dressing, she's sitting on the bed watching me. With her hands shoved between her pressed knees, her little bags are packed and piled at her feet. I step closer and see that her eyes are red-rimmed and her face flushed, most likely from crying.

If she were a normal girl, or even my sister, I would ask her what's wrong without a thought. But this is Shea, so I must be careful about everything I say, especially if it may be of a sensitive nature.

I sit by her on the bed. "You in a rush to leave me or something?"

"No, just ready to go." Her answer is curt with no give.

Oh shit. I'm in trouble. I rush from this point on, packing and checking the room for anything we may have left. I grab the keys from the ice bucket when Shea walks out the door. I hope when we get into the car, things will be better.

When we step out into the hall, our crappy neighbor comes out at the same time. I'm surprised when it's the older couple and not the couple I thought.

Shea looks over at me. "Looks like you were wrong."

Her voice is level, bored even. This would have been the perfect opportunity for her to joke with me, tell me how much I suck. But instead, she darts down the stairs. Instead of having a moment of fun, somehow I've messed everything up just by being myself.

A few minutes later, I check us out and carry all our bags to the car. I make sure I'm driving. With the convertible top down and the sun shining on us, I settle in and drive south, the same way we came. Today the traffic is heavy on the 101, so we don't make it through the Golden Gate and down to coastal Route 1 until midafternoon.

We don't speak much. Honestly, I'm scared shitless about what I can even say. I try to joke in our normal ways, but nothing seems to stick. As the moments of silence pass, I tense with worry. My hands tightly grip the steering wheel, my arms locked and rigid. I stop at several outlooks, jumping out to shake myself out and take photos of the beaches, the rocky coast, the sea lions, and the zombie seagulls. Sometimes Shea joins me with her arms crossed, her new shorter hair blowing in the breeze, and sometimes she just stays in the car, listening to the radio.

When I get back in after stopping at Half Moon Bay, I decide to just get out all my worries. I'm working myself into a frenzy.

"Let's just talk about it." I turn to her after I shut the car door and settle the camera between us.

She's sitting in her seat with one knee bent while she

leans against the door. She's scratching her head, as if this is some kind of meditation to calm her. "Talk about what?" She doesn't look at me.

"Whatever it is you're upset about."

"I'm not upset."

"Then why aren't we talking and joking like normal?" She shrugs.

"Did I do something? Please tell me." I realize in saying this that I was a complete prick this morning and it was apparently contagious. I tried my best not to let it affect us. "I'm sorry for being a little off this morning. If I said anything bad, I'm really sorry."

"It's nothing, okay? Just drive."

Fine. I jab the key in the ignition and start the car. This day is turning into complete shit. She's not going to tell me until it just explodes everywhere, destroying this messed-up relationship that we've built. I can feel it and it makes me angry. We continue on our drive, but the farther we go, the less comfortable everything becomes. Every time I look over, she's winding her hair around her finger in a compulsive way, looking over her shoulder at the cars behind us, and checking her side mirror.

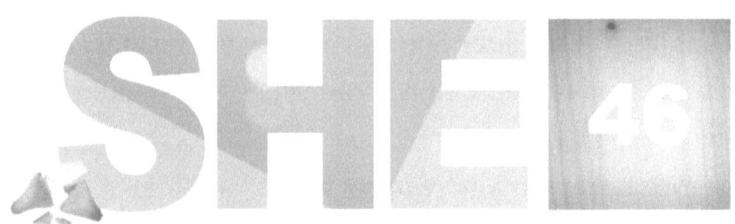

SHE 46

My head is clouded and I don't feel right. It may be because I've fallen for Hew and now that I've come down off my lust high, I realize that this will never work. I can't be in love or anywhere near love because I still have my Bren-and-Luke issue to work out. And now I've just made it all worse by adding poor, beautiful Hew to the mix. God, I don't even know his real name! He won't want me when he realizes the truth, even if that is all a little hazy right now. In fact, I sense that Hew's made up the whole second interview thing, just to get away from me. I don't even want to think about it, especially after I gave myself to him in the vineyards, our room, on the floor, and on the room's dresser.

My stomach turns over and cramps, and I grab my side as Hew flashes me a look. He's mad at me for not talking, for not laughing at all his jokes. Today, he's acting like Luke. Mean Luke. I wish he would just get it without me having to explain myself. Every day before now, he seemed to understand me. How could I have been so stupid to think that I could do this? That this ridiculous friendship, or whatever we have, could work?

I adjust in my seat, lean in, and look into the side mirror. The car behind us has been following us for miles, and I can't help thinking that it could be Luke. He found me in Napa, though I don't understand how. But then Hew had found me every time he wanted to. So how does that make sense?

Just as I try to control my breathing, to calm myself out of this frenzy growing out of control in my mind, the driver in the dark blue truck behind us flashes their high beams. What do they want us to do? Hew is driving well over the speed limit. I look back over my shoulder. When I do for a second time they bang on the horn, and I can't take it anymore.

"Pull over!" I point at the next park overlook. Hew does as I ask and as soon as he pulls into a space near the rocky cliff where tourists are gathered, taking photos and videos of the Pacific Ocean view, I jump out of the car.

Not surprisingly, the blue truck has followed us in. I don't have to see the driver to know who it is—the only person who is psychotic enough to act this way, to find out who I'm with and hunt him down, so he can hunt me down. God knows that Luke's government job gives him access to resources that would make regular stalkers giddy. Surveillance videos, e-mails, texts, bank statements—nothing is off-limits to him. Luke would only need to see Hew and me on a security tape to find him, and by extension, me.

Luke steps out of the driver's side of the truck and slams the door shut. He lifts his sunglasses on his head when he sees me, and crosses his bulging arms over his coral-colored shirt.

"I told you that you can't shake me, babe." He clenches his jaw. "I don't know why you can't get it through that thick-ass skull of yours." Luke steps forward with his long legs.

"Why the hell can't you just leave me alone?" I shout. "I don't want anything to do with you. It's over. It's been over for a year!"

Luke approaches like he always does—unconcerned with any of my feelings, and only worried about his needs. Selfish bastard.

I step back from him, ending up at the edge of the overlook, near the ragged rocks. Up here the wind whips around the ridge of the cliffs, blowing my hair in my face. I look down at the ocean raging below. The way it churns in angry crests, breaking against the cliff, is exactly how I feel about Luke.

I glance over to Hew, who is quickly shuffling out of his seat belt and jumping out of the car with a what-the-fuck-is-going-on look on his face.

Luke grabs me by the arm and clenches it tight enough to break it. He has before, along with other bones, so I have to be careful. He shoves me around like a rag doll.

Hew approaches us. He's asking questions, acting

strangely, but I just ignore him, trying to focus only on Luke. I need to deal with him before I deal with Hew, because everything seems to be combusting all at once and it's just too much for me to compute.

But Hew is demanding to be heard. I look to him.

"Hold on. Don't get so close to the edge, it's dangerous. What's going on?" he asks, waving his hands in front of him, beckoning us to come back. Isn't it obvious what's going on? Why is he asking such a ridiculous question?

Maybe he didn't realize that Luke is a real threat. I never explained the details to him, but he should get it now. As Luke moves us closer to the edge of the cliff, Hew reaches for my arm, trying to pull me back, but I twist away.

"Stay back! This is my fight!" I scream. "This is between Luke and me!"

"You're goddamn right it is," Luke says adamantly, and his confidence irks me.

But now, seeing Luke this way, compared to Hew, I know Hew is the only choice here. I've been an idiot all morning, thinking that I wouldn't be able to figure this mess out, but it's easy to see that Hew is the only one I want and need. With that certainty in my heart, I turn to Luke, ready to end everything once and for all, and in any way necessary. He's made me insane, messing with my mind and body for long enough.

I muster all my courage, setting my jaw, clenching my

fists, and readying my stance, calling forth all the feelings I've had this last week that make me stronger and more the person I was before Luke ever showed up. All the things Hew helped me remember. I'm a strong person, and I have the strength to get away from an abusive man.

"Luke, you need to back off," I demand.

"Over my dead body, bitch." He leans toward me, getting up in my face. Jaw set. Teeth gritted.

At that word, Hew rushes in again, but I extend my arm, holding up my palm to tell him to stay back. I need to do this myself.

"Hew is more of a man than you'll ever be," I tell Luke, gesturing to Hew.

Luke gives Hew the look of death. The realization settles in Luke's eyes—I've really and truly been with someone else. It's confirmed now. He probably never even considered that since he's so fucking full of himself. Immediately he steps toward Hew and I grab Luke's arm, swinging him back to me. I'm not done with him yet.

"Is this who you're cheating on me with? You always were a little whore."

I latch on to Luke's arm, unwilling for the two men to fight. "He treats me with respect and kindness, nothing you have ever shown without an agenda. So to answer your question, yes, he's the one. The only one! I'm done with you!"

With those words, I press both hands on his chest and

shove him with all the anger that's boiling over inside. He stumbles back, arms flailing at his sides to catch himself. On his face is a look of utter shock, because I've never stood up to him this way. Not with so much force. Not with physical force. I push him again before he's steadied his footing, but this time harder because I need to let him know that I'm serious. This time Luke isn't able to withstand me and gravity does the rest. He falls backward, sailing into the open air, right over the unprotected edge of the cliff.

The moment it happens, I can't believe what I've done. In shock, I step to the edge to see. My jaw drops and my hands clenching my screaming mouth as his screams fade into the thunder of crashing waves, several hundred feet below.

He's gone.

I killed him.

I just killed Luke.

With that understanding slapping me in the face, my temperature plummets and I feel nothing but icy coldness. My blood rushes to my feet, leaving me feeling sick and weak. Black spots race in from every corner of my vision, stealing my sight. My knees give in and I lose my balance, equilibrium tilts off, and the world folds over on its side. The last person I see before I black out completely is Hew.

hea jumps out of the car before I barely come to a complete stop.

"Why the hell can't you just leave me alone?" she yells. "I don't want anything to do with you anymore. It's over. It's been over for half a year!" She continues shouting as she circles the back of the Fiat.

I unlock my seat belt, open the door, and rush to step out, trying the figure out what the hell she's doing—who she's yelling at. She continues moving, now in front of the car, carrying on like a lunatic, waving her arms around and violently throwing herself from side to side, acting as though someone is attacking her.

But no one is there.

No one.

Only Shea.

My stomach turns into an acid pool, making me ill as I watch her act out.

Seagulls cackle, gliding on the ocean wind, like they are laughing at her—at me. Maybe they've been laughing at both of us all week. Tourists including families and re-tirees edge away from her. They point and watch as she has what I can only describe as a delusional panic attack.

I can't believe what I'm seeing. Can't believe that Shea is this broken, and I never even realized until now. Her strange behavior all this time slowly falls into place in my mind.

I move to her, trying to bring her back to reality. "Shea, what the hell is going on? Who the hell are you talking to?" I look around her, determined to see someone, hoping for anyone to appear near her that would explain her bizarre behavior. But there's no one.

She moves all the way to the edge of the overlook, near the cliff's edge, and with each second that passes, I'm even more worried that she's going to hurt herself. Unsure what to do, I try a gentler approach. I inch closer, knowing that one wrong move could set off her time bomb.

"Hold on. Don't get so close to the edge." I wave for her to return to me. "It's dangerous. What's going on?" My voice shakes with concern.

At the right moment, I rush in and grab her arm, but she fights me and twists away only to move closer to the edge. She's only a few steps away from certain death and my heart stops.

"Stay back! This is my fight!" she screams at me. "This is between Luke and me!" She then pauses, listening, as if she believes someone is responding to her. That they are arguing.

She shoots her gaze to "Luke" and then at me, giving

me a strange look—an adoring one, so far removed from the previous seconds that I think she's returned to reality, but the moment is short.

"Luke, you need to back off." She points a rigid finger at the air. Her face turns scarlet, her body tensing and her arms waving in angular movements.

I step toward her again but she holds out one hand, warning me away.

"Hew is more of a man than you'll ever be." She gestures to me and I step closer. I need to be in a position to tackle her at the right moment.

She scratches and clenches at the air. "He treats me with respect and kindness, nothing you have ever shown without an agenda. So to answer your question, yes, he's the one. The only one!" she yells, and with a loud grunt and with both arms extended in front of her, she pushes into the air over and over like some crazed mime, as if she's moving Luke away from her. When she has pushed as far as she can, tripping near the edge, she looks over the cliff and watches the water below. I think she believes she's just pushed "Luke" to his death.

My heart breaks into a million tiny pieces because I realize that all this time, Shea's world has been entirely make-believe. Everything I know about her has finally fallen into place. The fake names, the reluctance to share anything truthful about her life, the highs and lows, the multiple breakdowns, the well-used pill bottle, the grandiose stories followed by the winks—even us. Everything that has been a charming game of lies to me might be completely real to her.

She swivels toward me, her face contorted with horror, then it loses color, turning the palest translucent white. Her eyelids sink shut as her body plummets to the ground and I leap forward to try to catch her.

I try to open my eyes, but my world is blurry. At my small movement, someone squeezes my hand.

"Honey. You're all right. Open your eyes."

It's strange to hear this comforting voice now. I haven't heard it in a while.

"Mom?" The word breaks through my cracked lips.

Items around me come into view. A TV mounted across the room, sterile mint-colored walls, flowers and balloons, bland furniture, and a machine that I can't see, but it beeps nearby. My mom leans over and strokes my head with her palm.

"Mom?" I know she shouldn't be here. I'm not in Maryland; I'm in California with Hew.

"Hew!" I sit up, remembering his horrified face right before I passed out. I try to move, but I'm restrained by tubes attached in several places. I pull one out of my nose, rip another from the skin on the back of my hand, and throw the sheets off my body, determined to find him.

"No, honey, no. You have to stay in bed. You took a bad fall and had an episode." My mother holds me in place, trying to coax me the way she normally does. There's a sharp pain at my hairline. I reach for it, feeling a large bandage. I don't care; I try to get up again. My dad appears at my room door and runs to her aid, but I know I can fight both of them. I've done it before, and I can't give in when I have so much at stake.

"Hew!" I scream for him. I know he'll come. He's here; I know it.

"Honey, calm down," my dad says gently. "There's no Hew here."

"No!" I fight them. They're wrong! I swing my arms.

Nurses rush in to help restrain me, and now there are too many to win this fight, but I keep wrestling them for freedom. I need to find Hew. "Get off! Hew!" I smack and kick, becoming violent. Why are they doing to this me? I only want to see him. I scream and cry as the nurses quickly work together to bind my arms and ankles in restraints. I'm crying so much that soon I'm choking on my own snot.

Why won't Hew come?

A new nurse walks in and I know why she's here; I've played this game before. She stands at my bedside, prepping a syringe. Despite my pleas, she leans down and plunges the needle into the inside bend of my arm.

"You need to relax," she says in a soothing voice.

"I just need Hew."

I'm still battling, but I'm wearing down and soon

enough the drugs kick in, slurring my words. Before I sink under the veil, I see Mom and Dad across the room. Dad wraps his arms around her, rubbing her back because she's crying, too. And just for a moment, seeing those faces I love, like I have seen so many times before, I remember why I'm here and why they're doing this. I'm sick and in this fleeting moment of clarity, I wonder if Hew is just like Luke—a hallucination.

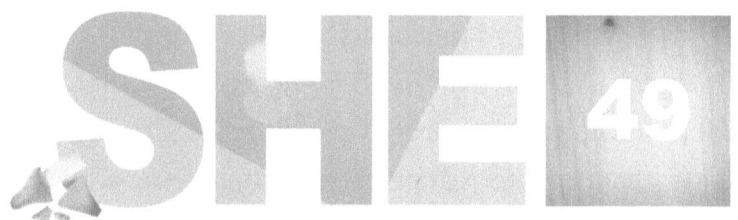

SHE 49

Five days later in Maryland

"So, it says here in my files that I should call you Shea now? Is that correct?" Dr. Leevy looks up at me over her wire-rimmed glasses. She smiles, and her dark cheeks bulge like apples. Even though I hate our sessions, there's something I like about her and her no-nonsense attitude. And though she's a hard-ass, I like her more than the others who tried to treat me before her. She's the only one who found a way through.

"Yes, it's a conscious name change, not a delusional one," I assure her.

"Okay, well, we'll talk about the name change tomorrow. For now, this is a quick interview for me to assess what's happened since we last saw each other"—she looks at her folder—"two weeks ago." She sets it back down and folds her hands on her desk. "Shea, I don't want to beat around the bush. You and I have a long history, and you know how I work. You're here for a ten-day observation period. According to the police report, some of the witnesses who saw your episode in California were under the impression that you were suicidal, and you wanted to jump from the cliff of the overlook."

"You know that's ridiculous." I roll my eyes.

For the first six months after the accident, I saw many doctors who were eager to pigeonhole me into any diagnosis that remotely applied—schizophrenia, paranoia, schizoaffective disorder, and atypical bipolar mood disorder. The truth is that I don't meet the basic checklist for any of those illnesses. Not even close.

When I met Dr. Leevy, she took a different approach. She was the first to take her time with me, to understand the complexity, the uniqueness of my condition, and explain that mental illness is not always black and white. My illness lingers in the shady gray areas that can't be completely explained by a textbook.

So, as of right now, she's given my illness no specific name. According to her, there are no cases that identically mirror mine—that she can find in research. The only thing we know for certain is that the hallucinations are a cycle. When I have an episode, my reality sometimes bends far from realism. Instead it's like a Salvador Dali painting of dripping clocks and eccentric landscapes of ever-changing objects that bend to my needs, acting upon my subconscious will, and torture or even save me when I'm not looking. But with all that said, I have never even come close to suicide.

"It does surprise me, yes," Dr. Leevy admits. "Even on your worst days, you never showed suicidal tendencies. But please, explain what you were doing."

I glance around the room, considering the right things to say. Being under medical attention and medicated regularly for several days now, I'm able to distinguish reality from fantasy—for the most part—though my brain is functioning in a familiar fog created by the pink pill.

"Well?" She leans back in her chair and crosses her arms.

"You know. The same as before." I shrug. When I think back on my episodes, I feel ashamed to talk about them. They have only ever been controlled my taking the pink pill regularly, something I was not doing in California, and only when *he* showed up.

"Luke?" she asks.

I nod, but don't make eye contact.

"Okay, so let's go over what we do know is true at this moment in time. Go ahead."

I sigh heavily and roll my eyes. If I had a pressed penny for every time that I've had to "bring myself to reality" in the last several months, as Dr. Leevy calls it, I could have hundreds of them, enough to fill a cigar box.

"Today, my name is Shea. By choice," I remind her. "And I'm here because roughly two years ago my fiancé, Bren, and I were on a date, walking around the Inner Harbor in Baltimore, when a woman driving a car swerved off Pratt Street and hit us." The bridge of my nose begins to burn, a cold burn, the way it always does when I get to this part of the story. "Bren." I tear up at the memories, my voice cracking as I fight to speak. "Bren and I were severely injured." My voice rises into a high-pitched tremor. I pause to compose myself, feeling every scar left on my body from that night throb with pain. "He died and I survived."

"Don't gloss over the details. This is important." She taps her finger on her wood desktop.

I sigh. I do it a lot during our meetings because everything we discuss, reliving all the pain over and over, chips off little bits of my soul. "I sustained severe head trauma, and afterward suffered from post traumatic stress syndrome, which in turn possibly triggered my hallucinations."

"Correct, and who is Luke?"

"Luke is a delusion. A coping mechanism, a paranoid invention." I use her words from earlier sessions and wipe my wet cheeks. "That I created because I couldn't believe that Bren would ever leave me—even by dying. In my mind, I created a fake brother to cheat with. That way I was the one leaving Bren on my own terms."

For the first year with Dr. Leevy, I didn't have the ability to distinguish fact from fiction. Luke was real and Bren was alive, and anytime someone suggested anything to the contrary, I became angry and violent, ready to defend my beliefs until I exhausted my body, my mind, my voice, and the people around me. It wasn't until several months ago that I started to have spots of clarity. In the breaks of light, Dr. Leevy presented me with piles of documented information, like death certificates and several meetings with Bren's family, for me to use to finally connect the pieces that had been warped or missing in my mind.

She believes I never had the proper closure for Bren's death, since I was in the hospital recovering my mind and body for over a year and a half. I didn't get to attend his funeral, and see for myself that he had really died. Even though I eventually accepted Bren's death, Luke had still been an annoying constant. A sucky souvenir from a bad trip. I even believed he gave me these scars; I still believe it sometimes.

Though the difference is that now I'm quicker to catch my blurred psychotic moments. An improvement that Dr. Leevy attributes to a new experimental medication I've been taking. Things were even going so well that I tried to break my relationship off with Luke and pull away from him in my hallucinations, but the paranoia of him became worse, like Luke was somehow fighting back, trying to cling to me. That is, until I pushed him over the cliff several days ago.

"Have you seen Luke since you returned?"

"No." I slouch in my chair.

Dr. Leevy leans forward and rummages through her files, then lifts a piece of paper that she scans. "What about this person you were screaming for in the hospital in California? Someone named Hew, it says here."

Even medicated, I still want to believe Hew is real. I allow everything we shared to play in my mind like a movie, from our unorthodox meeting, the no-name game, touring through San Francisco to his favorite places and then mine, our drive to Napa, the bike ride through the vineyards, kissing in the river, being dressed and worshiped by him the day and night we made love, at the party, in our room. And those were just events. What about the feelings and everything connected to them? The lust, the happiness, the comfort, the trust, and all the jokes and laughs we shared? *No. No!* I can't for one second believe I made all that up. My hands clench the handles of my chair as I fight my confusion.

Hew was complex and three-dimensional, while Luke was always so flat, just fragments of back story I contrived in my head to make everything fall into place and work the way I needed it to. I may have invented Luke to heal my mind after Bren's death, but Hew is the one who really saved me and healed my heart. He gave me the courage to fight off Luke and to finally free myself of him. I know Luke's gone now, and for good. The problem is that if I told all this to Dr. Leevy, I know she would tell me that Hew is another imaginary companion that I created to get rid of Luke, some kind of delusion of a boyfriend.

Every moment I spent with Hew felt so real. This information, though undeniable to me, could be dangerous to share because without any proof of his existence, who will believe me? This is how I felt with Luke in the beginning. The illness convinced me that my delusions were absolute truth. What if they are doing that again?

I try to make sense of the complexity in my sluggish mind, but I'm still confused because several unanswered questions remain. How did Hew always seem to find me in San Francisco, just like Luke always seemed to? And if he's real, then why did he leave me when I needed him most? Did I scare him? If I did, I understand, but where did he go? When I passed out after pushing Luke, I hit my head on a rock, slicing open my head. He wouldn't have just left me there to bleed to death. There is no record of him in the police report, or any man for that matter. I know, because I asked to read it. How could a person who stood by me for days while I cried my eyes out to him and told him nothing about myself, not even my real name, run away when I needed him most?

"I don't remember doing that. I don't even know anyone named Hew." I finally answer her question with a lie, playing it cool and staring right through her.

"I see." She punches the button on the end of her pen with her thumb exactly three times, every other time it's four—open, closed, open—like she always does before she jots her notes. I swear she has OCD.

"Other than the name change—"

"By choice," I interject.

"By choice." She shoots me her famous raised eyebrow. "Pending further evaluation, of course, I see no reason to hold you beyond the ten-day period."

I smile inside but I can't let her see, so I hold my face in an unreadable shield. Being free and at home will allow me to search for Hew and prove to myself that he's real, but most importantly, give me the chance to somehow apologize and win him back.

"Now, Shea. If this is approved, you will be released to your family, like you were before, and you will be expected to take your medication as prescribed and stay under the supervision of your parents. No more trips on your own. For now. Do you understand?"

I nod, and look down as I twist the hem of my hospital shirt.

"In the year and a half that I've worked with you, I don't, nor have I ever believed that you are a threat to yourself or others. In fact, your improvement, despite this little hiccup, has been a miracle. But for now, you must remain medicated. Say yes if you understand."

"Yes," I mumble.

"Good." She shuts the folder and rises from her seat in one fluid motion.

"And after you leave, I expect follow-up visits with you every week."

"Yes, ma'am."

She ushers me to the door. When she opens it, my male nurse, Ray, is waiting to take me back to my room.

"At our two o'clock session tomorrow, I want to dis-

cuss your trip to California in detail and your new name,"
Dr. Leevy reminds me, then shuts the door behind me.

Two months later, at home in Maryland

The floor of my bedroom in my parents' home is a mess. Scattered amongst the items are wedding binders with collages of my perfect wedding with Bren, unfinished party favors, bags of crafting materials from Michael's, sample invitations, and travel pamphlets for planning the perfect honeymoon that would tour us around the world. This is the second time I've looked at these items in two and a half months. But that last time was on the day Bren and I had planned to get married after graduation. I put on my wedding dress, like I was getting ready for that day, looked in the mirror, and proceeded to have the mother of all breakdowns.

I had only been home from the hospital for few months when it happened. Imagine my parents' shock when I ran out of the house in the wedding dress, crying, and hopped in a taxi that I had called, leaving them. Only to be notified a week later that I had been found on the cliffs of California, about to attempt suicide. That last part I still find ridiculous. If there's one person in the world who's thankful to be alive, it's me. Though I've had a tough time weeding through the garbage dump the ordeal has created in my mind, I'm slowly finding my way back.

Today, at Dr. Leevy's request, and for a lot of my own reasons, I'm packing these memories away. But I leave out the brochure on Paris. I want to go there someday. I owe it to Bren; I owe it to me.

I rise from the floor and drift to my window seat and sit, flipping through my brochure and looking at the glossy photos of the Eiffel Tower, the Seine River, quaint cafés, and museums. I set it aside for something real and glance to the window. Outside, the sun is shining but the leaves are falling off the trees.

I haven't seen Luke since California. Dr. Leevy believes that my "killing" him by pushing him over the cliff allowed my mind to free itself from the delusions. If it were that easy, why didn't she tell me to do that in the first place, I asked her. She said I needed to want him to leave, like asking a guest who's outstayed their welcome to go. Sometimes I think she makes everything up as she goes. It's easy to sound smart in hindsight.

To this day, I still haven't fessed up to her about Hew. As far as she knows, I traveled California by myself, which I feel like I may have done, too, because I've looked for him on the Internet, scouring everything I could think of to find the real Hew. But with no real information about him, not even his name, my searches have been useless.

Every day since I last saw him, I've even tried to conjure him with my mind through a delusion. He never materializes, not like Luke did. And because of that, there's been a huge void in my chest since I decided that he must be a hallucination, too. But if Hew was, then I decided I'd rather stay in that world with him forever. So over a week ago, unbeknownst to my parents and Dr. Leevy, I stopped taking my meds. There's a hard lump inside the window seat's cushion beneath me where I've been hiding my pills, until I can smuggle them to the bathroom to flush them.

I lean against the glass and huff my warm breath on the window. With my finger, I draw the outline of a heart, and then brush the moisture away. I close my eyes and attempt to conjure Hew once more. When I open them again and peer through the glass, a car pulls into the driveway. Whoever it is doesn't get out, they only honk the horn over and over. Then finally the driver leans forward and when I see his face, my heart absolutely stops.

Somehow I conjured him.

My palms are sweaty. They slip and slide over the leather of the steering wheel as I pull into the driveway. I haven't seen Shea since I ran away from her that last day in California. I had a reason, but even still, it wasn't fair to leave her like that. I've felt nothing but sick guilt since then.

These last two months, I moved out of my sister's basement and into a small studio in San Francisco for my new job. As I've been settling in, I've been trying to figure out if there's any possibility that Shea and I could truly be together. For me, I can't stop thinking there's a reason that everything happened the way it did, and in my mind, I'm constantly reliving every joke, every touch, every kiss, every caress, and every other second we spent together. But the question is: Will she forgive me when she understands how we're connected?

I turn off the ignition and decide to just blast the car's horn. If she's here, she'll see me. I lean in toward the windshield and look at the upstairs rooms. There, her beautiful face presses against the glass. She smiles and my heart melts with happiness, my eyes aching to look at her again. Several seconds later she pushes through the screen door, races across the porch, down the stairs, and runs barefoot across the browning grass. I jump out of the car and meet her in the middle of the front yard.

"Hew!" She screams so loudly that the birds in the trees take flight. As we're about to collide, she leaps into my embrace and locks her legs around my waist, anchoring herself to me. She doesn't waste time talking, she just kisses me and I comply, allowing her to mold our bodies together. Finally being with her again is like coming home.

"Shea!" her dad screams from the front porch. "What the hell are you doing? Don't you know who that is!"

Sollie Winters rushes down the steps, muscles tightening beneath his flannel shirt, ready to attack me the way he did several months ago when I came to meet Shea (who is not really named Shea) for the first time. Back then, I needed to apologize to her for ruining her life. Step nine of Alcoholics Anonymous—making amends. But the difference now is the last time I came I only wanted her forgiveness; this time I came to ask for her love.

Shea gives me one final squeeze before she slides down my body and I try to savor it, knowing that this may be our last. As I expected, she doesn't know who I am. She spent a year and a half after the accident in a hospital to heal her body and mind, and was most likely shielded from the outside world. She wouldn't know my real name, but she will in five seconds.

Sollie grabs Shea by the wrist, swinging her out of the way just before he cocks his arm and lands a punch square on my jaw. My head whips to the side and a spray of blood bursts from my mouth. Just like before, I don't fight back.

"Dad, no! Stop! What are you doing?" she cries out and pulls him by the shoulders, forcing him away.

I reach for my mouth to wipe the blood, but stand firm to meet his oncoming accusations.

"This guy was involved in your accident!" Sollie's arms swing at his sides, ready for another round.

Instinctively I cringe a little, but inside, I know I still deserve all his hatred.

"What? No, Daddy. This is Hew. We met in California. He's my friend."

"Tell her, you bastard!"

"Shea," I say softly, wanting to stall because I know how much this information will hurt her. How this could tear us apart forever. Now that I know who she really is, I know her back story and all the pain that I caused her, I know I ruined her goddamn life, killed her fiancé, and made her lose her mind. I know every single fucking detail. "This isn't easy for me to say."

Shea pushes away from her father, crying, "No, no, no." She covers her ears, swaying and turning back and forth, winding up like a spinning top at the thought of what I'm about to reveal. "No, it's not true. There was a woman driving that car. It can't be you!" She grinds her teeth and jabs an angry finger at me as her arms and body begin to shake.

"You're right," I tell her.

"See! Dad, you're wrong. You're wrong. Thank God!" She rushes to hug me, pressing her head on my chest, and my heart beats faster. I desperately want to return the embrace, but I know I don't deserve it. She still doesn't know everything.

This time I look over Shea's head to Sollie, whose jaw has dropped. He's stepped away from us in silence to stand with his wife, who has just appeared from the house. I think he finally sees right through me, through Shea. It's hard to deny when you see us together, even I can see it from within our bubble. We're in love with each other, but it's so fucking tragic, like a damn train wreck that you don't want to watch but can't pull your gaze from. We each fell in love with the person who ruined our lives—Shea through no fault of her own, and me for being in a stolen car for a joyride in a drugged-out drunk fest with my sister, Beth.

Shea and Bren were just standing in the wrong spot, having a romantic moment, kissing, and not paying attention to the car that lost control and swerved in their direction.

"God, I'm so happy to see you." Shea's hands are all over me, but she still hasn't lifted her head.

When I look over at Sollie, he simply gives me a nod, as if he knows that what I'm going to tell her will be enough to keep us apart forever. Shea is the only one who can make me stay away. Not him.

Sollie and his wife look at me with what appears to be pity on their faces, before turning around and going back inside. But they their maintain their watch over Shea from inside the house, their silhouettes framed within the front windows.

s he real? God, I hope so! I think the words over and over, rubbing my face against Hew's chest, trying to determine if he's really here.

He's going to tell me something bad; I know it. Something I may have fabricated for him to say in my fantasy world so I can push him away, and give myself reason to never see the hallucination of him again. I couldn't push him over the cliff like Luke; I love him too much. He would have to do something far, far worse to make me hate him.

Before I have time to organize my thoughts, Hew grasps my upper arms and sets me away. Frightened, I look up into his intense eyes.

"Shea." He swallows, and his Adam's apple bobs at my eye level. "What I have to tell you is difficult for me, but you need to know everything."

I shake my head; I don't want to know.

"Two years ago, I was a different person. A very lost person. I partied too much with my sister, I did drugs, became an alcoholic, and dropped out of college right before I graduated. I was a fucking mess."

Hew drops his hands and I step back. I can't believe

what he's telling me. He's too good a person for this. I know it. I've seen the proof of it in every second that we've spent together. He's lying.

"I had been two years sober when I met you, done a year in jail for stealing a car, got released on good behavior, and had a long bout of community service. I had even gone back and finished school while interning at a small company in Baltimore. Even though I moved in with family to make it work and save money, I'd gotten my life back, was moving everything in the right direction, and looking for a new job in San Francisco."

"Please, no," I whisper.

"Beth was my best friend and I was her younger brother." Hew's eyes begin to glisten. "Like so many nights, we'd gotten out of control. She and her boyfriend stole an expensive car from a ritzy hotel downtown. When they picked me up, Beth was driving, and she was smashed out of her brain. We went drag racing down Pratt Street. She ran a red light and swerved to miss a pedestrian. She ran off the road and . . ." His words drift off.

"No." I hit him in the chest. "No, I won't let you lie to me just so you can leave me. I can't let you leave. I love you!"

"I wish I were lying. I wish I could wink and make you believe that it may not be true. But I would never lie about this, you're too important to me. You're the only one who knows the complete truth."

I break down, simply fall to my knees and howl. I've been

through all kinds of pain, but not the kind where everything that's right and wrong with me collides into a horrendous mess.

He bends down. "That night, Shea, the car drove over the walkway, hit two people, and plunged into the freezing water of the harbor. When the car filled up, I quickly ran out of air, and I couldn't save Beth. I broke my way through the windshield and swam to the surface. Up top, Bren was barely holding your head above water and you were unconscious and badly injured. He asked me to save you, and I did. Even though I was fucked up, somehow I maneuvered your broken body to the ladder at a nearby floating dock, and lifted you out of the water. You had an open gash on your jawline, blood covering your face, soaked into your short red hair." He runs his finger over the old scars on my face and I jerk away. "But I knew I had just saved an angel from the pit of hell. It was the only thing that I had done right up until that point in my life. The only thing."

Every muscle in my body is rigid with anger. I step away, putting distance between us, but Hew continues to talk. It's like he won't shut up.

"That's why I left you in California. When you hit your head on the rock and the blood covered your face, I flashed back to that night. Maybe that and the combination of you cutting your hair shorter, like it was back then, and telling me you wanted to dye your hair red finally made me recognize you. My brain was so cloudy the night it happened from being so high and whacked out of my mind that I only remember all the blood and the hair. When I realized who you were, I was scared that you could never love the person who ruined your life, so I waited until I knew you were safe and then I left."

"Why didn't you save Bren? Why didn't you go back for Bren?" I charge at him to beat my tight fists into his chest and arms. He just stands there like an immovable wall, watching me, allowing me to hurt him, which makes me angrier.

"I did go back!" Hew says, finally defending himself. "I jumped back into the water but Bren was already gone. It was night and the water was too dark. I couldn't see anything. No one could find him. Not until the divers came."

"I hate you!" I lunge forward to attack him. "Leave!" I yell, shoving him again. "I hate you!" I scream so loudly that it feels as if my voice shreds my throat.

Hew walks backward, looking like a wounded animal, but he doesn't bother giving excuses or attempt to change my mind. He just slides into the driver's seat of his car and starts the engine, as if he has said everything he needed to say.

And he did. He said everything he needed to make me hate him and never want to see him again. Real or fantasy, I'm already trying to rip any part of him from my soul when his car backs out of our driveway and peels away.

swerve over the gravel and dirt road, speeding away from Shea's family farm. Screaming with anger, I bang the palms of my hands on the hard curve of the steering wheel until I can't take any more pain. When I'm a mile away, I slam my foot on the brake pedal, forcing the car to skid to a stop just off the street into a field of dying grass.

Did I expect her to take this information any other way? How could I possibly ask her to love me after I've ruined her? All of her scars are because of me. Me! And finally, after these two years I thought I was getting my life back and moving on? What a cruel joke. Now that I've met this stunning person, I'll have to lose her forever, just like I lost my sister. Shea was right on the first day that we met; destiny is a bitch and not only is this payback, it's torture.

I rub the heel of my palms into my eye sockets, then slide them up my forehead, trying anything that will re-lieve the extreme pressure building inside my skull. Any second now, I know I'll explode. So I do the only thing I can think to. With quick movements, I lean across the seat, pop open the glove box, and reach for what's inside. I hesitate, hand hovering for a moment over the silver flask given to me at a wedding years ago, before drinking was ever a problem.

Since that night at the party in California with Shea, I'm ashamed to say that I haven't exactly been on my best behavior. And every drink I've taken since then, I've hated myself a little more. My guilt about that horrible night in Baltimore has grown exponentially since falling in love with her. When I was in jail after the accident, my family told me what happened to the girl from that night. I felt remorse, yes, but now I bear a new level of pain. Before, my choice of coping was to try to repress everything that happened and control every aspect of my life, which was easy to do when you're in jail. But since I was released, it's been so hard to do, an exhausting battle that feels like it will never really end. From experience, I know that dulling my feelings is so much easier, and there's only one way I know how.

I snatch the flask with one hand and quickly open the driver's door. I jump out with it and take off running. In a full sprint, I rush across the field, dodging rocks and trees. I push my body to the brink as if this is some kind of torture session. I have a choice to make. I can be a better person, do the right thing, or easily slip back into the well-worn suit of the old me.

When I fondly remember how much easier and

carefree things were back then, the don't-fuck-up voice screams at me like a soul entrenched in the flames of hell, and says, "Remember where that got you the last time?"

With a quick decision, I slide to a stop, extend my arm behind me and whip it forward, throwing the flask into the air. It spins, arcing across the sky, and lands in a pond with a splash, disrupting the ducks floating nearby. Rippling rings expand from its impact point, growing until they reach the edge where I'm standing and violently shaking, trying to regain control over my body and mind. But the good news is that the voice has finally stopped yelling.

My shoulders slump. The tension releases and I drop to the ground, out of breath, out of energy, and finally ready to give in. This is it. I can't do this anymore. And though I've told myself this before, there is a new more prominent piece of this fucked-up puzzle, one more important than me—Shea. I owe her this, for everything I did to her, her fiancé, and their families. And for everything I did to mine.

My family.

I let those words settle on my tongue for a moment. They feel foreign. We haven't been anything that resembles a family since the accident. At least, not where I'm concerned. Out of fight, I fall to my side in the dirt, curl into a fetal position, and I cry for everything I've lost, including myself.

I want to be better.

I need to be better.

I will be better.

From here on out, I'll do everything in my power to be good enough for Shea. For me. For Beth. For my family or anyone else who decides to be in my life. I make the promise to myself.

The list of promises grows as I watch the sun set. When it dips behind the trees, closing the curtain on another day that I've ruined, or maybe managed to save, I pull myself together. I was supposed to be at my parents' home for Thanksgiving dinner over an hour ago. And though I'm sure they're not missing me, I decide that now, more than ever, is the perfect time to try to make amends.

As I stand outside my parents' home in Annapolis, I close my eyes and hear chairs screeching over wood floors, silverware clinking against Mom's holiday china, and the hum of pleasant conversation. Just as I step onto the stoop, everyone inside breaks out into laughter. Listening, I can make out the distinct sound of each family member's voice, and I ache inside. I lift a hand to my middle, feeling an actual physical pain at how much I miss all of them, for the loss of what we used to be, and for not really knowing what will happen when I walk inside.

I press my hand on the door and sigh. If I leave, a holiday can be happy for everyone else for once. They haven't seen me since I moved for my new job almost two months ago. My sister Ashley, who had been letting me stay with her before I moved, had extended the invitation for tonight. Even though she's the closest to me of all my family, she probably never expected me to actually show up. The truth is that I probably wouldn't have, if it weren't for making the trip to come clean with Shea.

Just as I turn to leave, the door creaks open. "Hi," a small voice says through the screen door.

I turn to see my sister Layne's daughter, my three-year-old niece, Beanie, her eyes wide and bright with happiness. She's too young to know to hate me like everyone else. She bases our friendship on the time we spend playing princesses.

On unsteady tiptoes, she reaches for the latch and the screen door pops open. Her little toes curl over the door's threshold. "Come play with me," she says with an adorable lisp. "I want to show you my new Barbie." Then she stretches out her tiny hand.

With her large doe eyes looking up expectantly, she might be the only person inside this house that I can't refuse. I reach out, and she wraps her small chubby fingers around one of mine.

Once inside the foyer, I see no one has noticed that I'm here. I pick up Beanie and settle her on my hip. It's a crappy move, I know. As if she's the armor that could save me from the ammunition bound to come my way when they see me.

I walk through the hall, stepping into the living area where I can clearly see the dining room. Across the open room, everyone in my family sits around the dinner table, carrying on and laughing the way families should.

Ashley sees me first. "You came!" She stands and pushes her chair back. As she moves to hug me, everyone in the room quiets. The awkward pressure that builds is so thick, it's hard to breathe. They know what my being here will mean—drama.

"I'm so glad you're here." Ashley hugs me and Beanie giggles.

"Who's here?" my dad says as he steps into the dining room from the adjoining kitchen, carrying a casserole dish. His head turns in my direction. When he sees me, his mouth immediately draws down at the corners and his jaw tightens. "What'd you come back for—your girl?" He slams the dish on the tabletop.

"Robert!" My mom stands and sends an admonishing look to my dad.

"Well, you know he didn't come back to see his family. Never puts his damn family first." He swings a pointed finger.

"You told them?" In horror I look down at Ashley, and she casts her gaze away. She never could keep a secret.

Damn it!

Ashley reaches for Beanie, picks her up and tucks her into her side, probably for the same reason I did earlier.

"I trusted you," I whisper with an edge of anger. I may have been drunk and lonely when I told her everything over the phone from California, but still.

"Sorry," she says and steps back. "They asked how you were and it just kinda slipped."

Ashley is the only person that I've confided in during the last two months. She knows about Shea, our time together in San Francisco, and who she is. The problem is that my parents and my oldest sister, Layne, blame me for Beth's death. None of my family, not even Ashley, believed that their sweet little Beth could be that bad of a person—to steal a car and kill someone under the influence.

Feeling guilty for everything, I had lied and told them I was the one who stole the car when I didn't, that I was the one who introduced Beth to drugs when it was really the other way around. That everything was my fault. After the accident, I didn't want the memory of Beth's short life to be marred by our bad decisions. Somehow it was easy for them to believe that I was the bad one, and that hurt me deeply. But being the one who survived, I could do what Beth couldn't. Take the punishment that I knew I deserved, go to jail, try to improve my life, and make amends for both of us. But I've never told them or anyone else the entire truth—only Shea knows the complete truth now, and she still hates me as much as they do.

Why did you save a stranger over your own sister? This was the one question they repeatedly asked me after the accident, and every time they've seen me since. I can't answer them. Being so messed up at the time, I don't know exactly why things played out the way they did, but I know I did all that I could under the circumstances. They make me question this. They hate me for this. And I hate myself for not doing more—for even being there.

The sad thing is that they even hate Shea for this.

If there were ever a future for Shea and me, it wouldn't include my family. They hate her because she lived and Beth didn't, even though Beth and I were to blame for the accident. They are the kind of people who can't see that Shea was innocent from the beginning. They are those asshole neighbors you hate because of their backward thinking, and no one will change their minds. They're unreasonable and selfish, and that's why they will never forgive me.

"I shouldn't have come." I let my gaze roam the room, jumping from one face to the next, searching for anyone who will protest and insist I stay, but there is no one here. Apparently not even Ashley. Even if she does want me here, she's too timid to speak up for me, and probably unwilling to tick off our dad.

I turn and walk back through the house to leave. Right as I grab for the front door handle, I stop. I need to say something and stop running from them. With determination, I stride back into the dining room with my fists balled at my sides.

"All of you suck!" I aggressively swing my arm over the group. "I've said that I'm sorry over and over again. I made a mistake. A huge fucking mistake! And I hate myself for it more than you do. None you have to live with this kind of guilt." I bang my chest with my fist. "But you certainly will never let me move on, will you? How is it right for you to steal my life away when I'm trying to get back on track and make amends? How are you helping me by hating me? You aren't! So now you have two children who are dead to you. But one is still gasping for air, struggling to survive and make things as right as he can. Yet you still sit there, watching me drown!"

It isn't much of a speech, but it's enough. Instead of letting them beat me down like Sollie Winters, like I always believed I deserved, or letting them pound the guilt into my skin like rusted nails, infecting my body and mind, I've finally said my piece and stood up for myself.

As I leave, racing out the front door, I hear Beanie crying. I feel horrible for scaring her, but I don't regret what I said.

A week after I see Hew, I come clean with Dr. Leevy. Since he appeared at my house, I haven't slept or eaten. My clothes are hanging off me, and dark circles line my eyes.

"I lied," I say to start out. "I did scream for someone named Hew when I was in the hospital in California." I chew the inside of my cheek, waiting for her reaction.

Dr. Leevy readjusts in her seat and leans into her desk, rolling her pen between two fingers. "Why did you lie?"

The tears fall before I can even attempt to control them. "Because I didn't know if he was real."

"Is he?"

"He is, but I wish he wasn't."

At her urging, I let the truth spill out, starting in San Francisco and ending with him telling me how he was responsible for my accident, Bren's death, and how he saved me from the water. It sounds ridiculous to my ears when I say it out loud. Though I admit that even still, I long for those easy moments in California when he was just some guy I didn't know, who I could have fun with and be myself with, free of any problems. And I know how messed up that sounds.

"Shea, are you absolutely certain that this Hew did not seek you out? Look for you for some reason?"

"He didn't."

"How can you be certain?"

"Because I was the one who talked to him first. He never approached me, not once."

She nods, taking notes. "So how do you feel about all that's happened?"

"How do I feel? How do I feel?" My words rise into a high-pitched shriek. I hate this question. Why must shrinks always ask it? I stand and pace the room, throwing my arms out in wild gestures. "How do you think I feel?" I turn to face her. The scene I make causes Ray, who acts like more of a bouncer than a nurse, to open the door and check on us, but Dr. Leevy waves him away.

"I feel like crap! I feel confused. More confused that I've ever been. I ask myself every second of the day why I'm being put through this torture. What kind of sick game of life would send Hew to ruin everything, let him save me, and then send him back for another round years later so that I would fall in love with him? How could this happen? It's impossible. I want him to be a hallucination."

Dr. Leevy rises from her desk and comes to my side, where I'm slumped over the back of a chair heaving ragged breaths as I sob. It's as though my heart had been ripped out, stomped on, put back in, and allowed to heal so that I could feel the blood of life pump through my veins once more before my heart is ripped out again and eaten.

She hands me a tissue. "Why don't you rest on the couch?" With gentle hands, she guides me until I lie down, settling on my side. She brings me a glass of water and sets it on the table in front of me, and then seats herself on the nearby chair.

"You've been holding back on me," she says but she doesn't seem angry. "And I can see that this is all confusing for you. There's no doubt that you've been dealt a very bad hand here."

She crosses her legs and continues. "I suppose I've experienced strange coincidences, myself. My husband and I met in another state, even though we were from the same town and lived a block apart. As young people, we had the same friends, probably even went to the same birthday parties as children, but never met. Not until we were twenty-five and fifteen hundred miles from home."

I look up at her. "Really?"

"Yes. In fact, it's one of our favorite stories to tell because it seems absolutely impossible, but it's true." With that glimmer in her eyes, it must be. "But with that said, I want to give you something to ponder." She becomes serious. "What's happened to you is awful. And I don't know if you believe in God, Buddha, Allah, the universe, life, or whatever, we haven't gotten to discuss that in our sessions. But I believe this—whoever you pray to, or whatever you believe in will provide you with what you need in this life to survive, to learn the lessons that need to be learned, and sometimes supply you with the tools to heal."

Slightly confused, I sit up. This bit of insight is unusual for our sessions. It's a personal thought, a friendly one, not a doctor-patient one. Something she rarely, if ever, shares.

"The world has moved in extraordinary ways to force you two together on so many occasions that I find it hard to believe it's random. There may be something in him that you need, and something in you that he needs. A yin and a yang. An ebb and flow. You see?"

I shake my head.

"Well, sometimes these things don't make sense until they do." She laughs at herself.

I fold my hands in my lap, trying to figure out if her words are plausible, if Hew was thrown into my world for a reason. "That doesn't sound very—" I pause, searching for the word, "scientific."

She harrumphs and steadies her cheek on her palm, staring at me with a smirk. "I suppose it doesn't, but not all answers can be found in science. Some things aren't tangible. Sometimes they're built on faith, and decided by your heart and soul."

know I'm dreaming, but it's the nightmare that I can never escape. It repeats, tormenting me. Everything is quick flashes, sharp angles, blasts of colors, and confusing memories.

Beth smiles. She's gripping the steering wheel of the stolen silver Porsche. She swears it belongs to a friend. I want to believe her, but I'm not sure. Her boyfriend, Mike, is in the backseat. They reek of weed; we probably all do. She's a mini version of me, grown up into a tomboy with her dark hair pulled back into a messy ponytail. She's my best friend.

I focus my attention back to the road and shriek, "Red light!"

Beth jerks the wheel. The car swerves, just missing people in the crosswalk. The front wheels jump the curb, and the car jolts violently. I bang my head and shoulders against the door and ceiling. We're on the harbor pathway when we ram a couple. Their impact on our windshield shatters it and makes us scream. Then we're gliding through the air and land on the surface of the harbor water, which is much harder than you'd think. I fly forward, smashing my head on the dashboard.

My next lucid thought is about how freezing cold the water is as it rushes around my chest. My muscles constrict, my breathing intensifies, and I scream but my voice goes nowhere. It's trapped with me in a sinking box. I'm disoriented and confused. Everything is blurry. I remember I'm with Beth. She's not moving. Mike's not moving. He's dead; I can just tell. His mouth gapes open, head tilted back, and there's a gash across his face. Blood's everywhere. Beth's head and body are slumped below the water.

I reach for her, and pull her head back. She's injured like Mike. I haven't put my seat belt on but she has. I fight to release the buckle, pulling at it with all my strength.

I need to save her.

I need to save her!

I'm losing the battle fast. I gulp my last breath of air. The water rushing in fills to the roof of the car. I'm going to die.

The doors won't open, and I don't know how to unlock them. I lean back and kick the windshield with my feet. It cracks further and finally releases. I don't want to leave Beth, but if I don't my lungs will explode.

I swim through the opening to the surface and pop above the water, violently gasping for air. Freezing sharp pains shoot through my lungs. Using my arms, I beat the water to keep myself from sinking.

"Help," a low voice says. I look around, thinking it's Beth, but it's not. It's a man holding a girl's head above water. "Help, please."

My head still muddled, I splash over to them.

"Save her, please."

I don't think; I just do. Despite my panic, I reach out to take the girl's limp body and drag her through the water. Eventually I knock up against the edge of a floating pier and somehow maneuver her and myself onto the decking. Out of breath. Freezing. I collapse. Is she alive? Am I alive? There's so much blood. On her. On me. Wet red hair fans over her destroyed face and broken body.

I roll back into the water, looking for the guy. He's not there. Sirens. People scream at me from a pier.

Then I remember—Beth is somewhere below, alone in this coldness. Guilt. Dread. Sadness. I wish I were with her. I give up, wanting to make the feeling a reality. I allow myself to sink into the murk. It's freezing. My muscles seize and when I finally gulp the water, sending rushing stabs of pain into my lungs, I allow myself to drown.

That's when I awake from my nightmare, gasping for air and lying tangled in sweat-covered sheets and pillows. I roll and sit up, lingering in a half dream state, reliving the rest of the night. I did give up in that water, inviting death like a long-lost friend. It greeted me with chilled open arms, pulling me with the slow current, flooding my lungs and sending me off into the quiet and painless blackness. If only the medics hadn't fished me out of the water and resuscitated me, I would be with Beth.

Looking back, I realize I was the one who gave Shea the scars that cover her body. The ones I hated that other man for when really, all my hate should have focused on myself. I was a coward the night I gave up in the water, and every night I've given in and drank. But I won't allow myself to be that coward anymore. Not ever again.

The clock flashes three a.m. I rub my face, stand, and walk across the small apartment. In a few steps, I flip on the desk lamp. Under the single beam sits a project I've been working on, a present for Shea, or maybe it's simply therapy for me. Either way, it's something to do to fill my time outside of work, a project that means something to me.

I seat myself on the stool and start where I left off last night after the last nightmare. Methodically, I glue pressed pennies into place on a piece of wood. Each of the hundreds I have pressed for this project have the second renewed life I long for. Many pieces are scattered around the desk and floor. They don't look like much now, but they will soon when they are glued together.

As I'm working, I remember it's Christmas Day, and

I'm thankful that I don't have to work today but sad that I'm alone. Ashley hasn't even called, but I don't blame her. I know she's controlled by our dad, like everyone else in the family. Though last week I found the perfect gift for Beanie, a princess tea set. I wrapped it up in Cinderella Christmas paper and mailed it. Who knows if Layne will actually give it to her, or tell her it's from me.

I wonder what Shea is doing. I wonder if she even gives me a thought anymore, if she'll ever forgive me, but I hope she will because everything about her is stuck in my head on permanent replay.

SHE

eeks later, I still don't speak about anything that's happened in the last few months, especially not during Christmas. It's swept under the rug like my illness, ignored as we carry on with holiday festivities, hosting family and friends at our farm. Everyone is happy to see me healthier, and though I'm pretending to be gracious and thrilled to see them, too, I'm still somehow hating but missing Hew at the same time.

For a little while, I think I've lost too much of my spirit in this fight—at least the little that I had stored up. But as the days go by and I see no hallucinations and feel stronger, I vow to move on and improve myself. Be a better person every day. I remember that I said that once to Hew and decide it's a respectable goal—a New Year's resolution. And though I feel ill at the thought of how Hew's life intertwines with mine, I liked who I was when we were together, even if I only want to remember it as a dream.

To pass the time, I take a cooking class and just try to live and be normal. Whatever normal is for someone like me. Like all things in time, I think I begin to heal.

Dr. Leevy says my unique case study could help others, that her colleagues are intrigued. She's even writing a paper about me for some medical journal, like I'm some messed-up guinea pig. I try not to think about it too much. I do have some confusion from time to time, but each day I do feel better.

More and more I fill my time with activities that interest me. They are the good minutes of my day. If I give myself one second of free time, I'm afraid I may slip back to that place where Luke may find me. For the first time since the accident, I think about my future. Once upon a time, when I was in college, I wanted to be an artist. But now I decide there is something to the idea of the wine and fortune cookie company, so I buy a book on starting a business, and spend all of winter and into early spring writing my business proposal, becoming consumed with the idea.

Dr. Leevy says she'll be my first customer. My dad says she'll have to fight him for the honor. I'm not sure which badass will win.

In March, I take the next step and begin to teach myself how to make chocolate-covered fortune cookies. If this business is going to succeed, I need to become an expert.

"Look what just came for you." Mom walks back from the front door with a large package.

"What's that?" I look up from mixing my fortune-cookie batter.

"FedEx just dropped it off. Has your name on it." She sets it on the kitchen table.

I wipe my hands on my apron and cross the room to investigate. There's no return address. Mom appears with scissors, which I remember were in fact invented by Da Vinci. I looked up the fact to see if it was true. With the blades open, I swipe at the seams of the box, slicing and releasing the tape. I set the scissors on the table and open the flaps. Inside, foam peanuts are packed to the brim.

"Who's it from?" Mom asks.

"Not sure. No note." I dig, sifting my fingers through the peanuts until I find something hard. I lift the heavy object from inside as Mom holds the bottom of the package down. When the peanuts fall away, I see what I've pulled out—a birdhouse. But this is not any birdhouse; this is *my* house. The one that Hew promised to build me.

"How beautiful!" Mom gushes, but she can't possibly understand the meaning or know how incredibly confusing this is to me.

I set the birdhouse on the table and drop into the seat next to it to stare at it, unable to take my eyes from it. As I examine it, I realize with sadness that every detail of the birdhouse represents something from the trip Hew and I took together.

This birdhouse is designed like my dream house. It's a San Francisco painted lady, a Victorian with gingerbread details, yellow with white trim. The door is purple with a hand-painted plaque on it with the words HE + SHE. Like, Hew + Shea, a strange coincidence, considering our fake names. The roofing is layered copper pressed pennies that give the appearance of shimmering fish scales.

I turn it. On one side of the house, a vintage-style billboard sign painted on the exterior wall reads, NAPA VALLEY WINE AND FORTUNE COOKIE COMPANY. Hew designed a logo for the company and it's perfect, exactly what I would choose.

My mom reads it out loud and turns to me, her eyes wide. "Isn't that what you want to call your new business?"

"Yeah." I gulp. "Do you see this, too? You're seeing this, right? It's not just me, is it?" My gaze rises to hers.

"Of course. Don't be silly," she says, and grabs my hand. I had to check, even though I was pretty sure. I've developed a paranoia about my everyday life being a hallucination. "I didn't know you told anyone about your idea yet," she goes on, saying what I want her to, but I remember that's how my delusions work. They make you believe with absolute certainty.

"Just you and one other person," I mumble.

"Then I guess we know who sent it." She pulls the box away and peeks inside.

"Yeah," I say softly, and spin the house to the back. On an open deck sits a mini bird Jacuzzi. Around the rim in tiny letters, it reads, FOR OUR FLAT ASSES. A burst of laughter escapes my lips and I cover my mouth, immediately angry with myself for letting it slip. I still want to hate him.

"Look, an envelope." Mom pulls it out, wipes off the peanuts clinging to it, and hands it to me.

I stare at it, unsure if I'm ready to deal with whatever it says. It's been five months since Hew came here to apologize.

The oven beeps, and Mom jumps up without a word to open the oven and check on dinner.

I decide that nothing can be worse than what I already know, what I've had to live with for months now. I turn the envelope over and slide my finger under the flap, then rip it open. Inside, there's a note that says, "For your zombie birds." There is also a plane ticket, some other smaller tickets, and an itinerary.

Mom turns back around and leans against the counter, watching me. When I look up at her in shock, she's already watching me with a smirk. I look closer at the envelope's contents.

"A plane ticket to Charles de Gaulle airport in Paris, a train ticket to the south of France, and an itinerary for a week of classes to learn about wine at a French winery." I look at her again and she looks away, as if she's trying to ignore me, which makes me highly suspicious. "What do you know about this?"

She shrugs. "I don't know what you're talking about."

She pivots to the sink and begins to fill it with hot water, then carefully squirts in a little dish detergent, as if washing dishes is the most important thing in the world right now.

I stand up and go to her. She can't lie without doing this weird thing with her facial muscles around her eyes. It's one of her tics. I know, because it's one of my tics, too. "Mom." I wave the ticket at her face. "What have you done?"

"All right!" She throws her sponge in the sink and splashes the water. "I told him I wouldn't be able to keep it from you forever. You know how awful I am with that."

"Keep what from me?"

"Shea." She still stumbles over the new name, just like Dad. She shakes her head and grabs my hand. "Sweetie, that boy has been trying to apologize to you well before you even met him. He had been here three times before you ever left for California."

"What?"

"Your dad ran him off every single time, angry at the sight of him, but thinking you were too fragile to speak with him."

"That doesn't change what happened. Hew was still involved."

"Yes, he made a mistake, a huge one. But at the same time, I've also never seen you as happy as you were the day he appeared here. You love him. He loves you."

"He stole my love from Bren!"

"Bren's gone. Hew is here."

My eyes burn and begin to blur at her words.

"Sorry," she says and rubs my arm, but doesn't take it back.

"Have you been talking to Hew?" My lips quaver.

She shrugs again. It's her go-to, her easy way out. "He made me promise not to tell you lots of things."

"Spill."

She sighs. "I met him in the hospital in California. I arrived at your room first. Thank God your dad was parking the rental car. He would have killed that boy if he saw him there."

"What was he doing when you found him?"

She tucks a strand of hair behind my ear. "Praying and crying. He was praying to God that you would forgive him. And crying that he was the one responsible for—" She turns away, uncomfortable just like she is every time she's forced to talk about my issues.

"And?"

"And when he saw me, he jumped up like I had caught him doing something wrong. I told him to leave before your dad showed up. I knew who he was from his attempted visits, and following some of his trial. You were in the hospital, and we cut you off from everything related to the accident then. There's no way you would have recognized him, unless you remembered anything about that night."

I shake my head. I did feel I recognized Hew in the beginning, which made me say hi to him in the first place, but I could never place him in my mind. Maybe I had somehow seen him the night he fished me out of the water. I can't know for sure; I was in and out of consciousness when it happened.

"Anyway, he left," she continues. "At the time, I didn't quite understand how you had finally met, but he contacted me a few months ago to check on you. He said that he had moved to San Francisco for a new job, and told me about your time in California and how he fell in love with you . . . and that he was still in love with you. He wanted to know if I thought you could ever forgive him."

I shake my head. "How can I?" Tears spill over my lashes and pour down my cheeks.

"I know, honey. Only you know what you can forgive and what you can't. In your heart, I know you're a forgiving soul. It's who you are. And even if you can't love him again, you can give him your forgiveness and let him know so he can at least move on with his life, even it you aren't in it." She rubs her thumb on my chin the way she did when I was little.

"I don't understand how you can even think I could consider this?" Somewhere deep in my heart, I hope she offers me the answer I need to get past this. Help me make sense of the confusion.

Mom's eyes fill up with tears. "I can't hate him completely when he kept my little girl alive. I owe him because if you would have died that night, your father and I would have died, too. You're our only baby." Her voice cracks, setting off a wave of tears. We both cry. She hugs me and speaks low in my ear. "Now you can live a beautiful life. It may not be exactly what you planned for, but it can still be something—something extraordinary. Bren would have wanted it that way. He was a good guy. He wanted you to live."

She does it. She says exactly what I need to hear her say. I could have died that night. But Bren reached out to Hew, and they both worked to save me. Together.

The first time I came to AA, I didn't even have the balls to say I was new and introduce myself. It was court mandated back then, and though I did want to be there, I was embarrassed for everything I had become. Two and a half years later and twenty-four weeks dry, I know the preamble and the twelve steps and twelve traditions book by heart, but I still, after all this time, have yet to share my story or my name with anyone. Even when I was sure the group wouldn't judge me, I haven't because maybe if I admitted everything that I had done, all the mistakes would make me feel more guilt.

But today, for the first time, I only feel like the truth could set me free.

The group sits in a circle. Most everyone holds a Styrofoam coffee cup. When the chairperson asks for volunteers to share their story, I stand up with confidence, give my name, and admit that I'm an alcoholic. Everyone collectively responds as they always do with "Hello!"

I have to give the CliffsNotes version of my story because my five minutes of sharing ends quickly. When I'm done everyone thanks me, and for the first time in years,

I'm relieved. After I sit, I reach to my side and grab my mom's hand. She tears ups, her smile reaching her eyes. She insisted on coming today, and I insisted on her being here for support.

"I'm so proud of you," she whispers and squeezes my clammy hand.

Mom appeared at my door on New Year's Eve with a suitcase. All she had to say was "I'm sorry" for me to fall into her arms. She said Christmas wasn't right without me there, and she would be here for me from now on.

This is her second visit since then. This time she spent the weekend trying to "fix" my apartment and make the five hundred square feet "livable." Now I have curtains, throw pillows, and towels. Okay, I needed the towels, but not the other stuff. I'll leave it out when Ashley comes next week, and maybe longer if it grows on me.

Layne and Dad are not as easily persuaded, but Mom promises that they'll come around eventually. I hope she's right.

SHE 58

It is April first—my birthday—a cruel joke of destiny for a girl who has a hard enough time deciding what's real and what's not. My mom is standing behind me with her hands covering my eyes. I'm waiting for a surprise, but I have no idea what they would be giving me that I have to see from the backyard.

"Can I open them yet?"

"Not yet," she says, but I hear the sound of Dad's truck. The roar of the engine is unmistakable as it drives past us, coming to a stop. The dogs bark, freaking out the way they always do when he returns home. I try to peek through Mom's fingers, but they're clamped tight.

The truck's door squeaks open and then slams shut.

"Go ahead and let her see," Dad yells from across the lawn.

They shout, "Surprise!" at the exact moment Mom lifts her hands, revealing my birthday gift.

"Oh my gosh!" I run to the little beat-up white camper hooked to the back of his truck. "It's exactly like the one I saw in the paper!" I open the door and a cloud of mold and dust hits my face and I cough.

"It looks like it because it is, sweet pea." Dad lifts his baseball hat from his head.

I turn and grab both my parents in a hug. "This is so awesome, the best gift ever!" I pepper them with kisses, and we all giggle with happiness.

I had clipped a photo of this exact camper out of the paper and pinned in on my new company's vision board, a bulletin board of inspirational quotes and photos to keep me focused on my new endeavor. I kept thinking back to the Feng Shui Taco truck in San Francisco, and how I could sell my fortune cookies the same way.

"I can see it already. I'll paint it a banana color, and put the logo on the side. Right here!" I stretch my arms, gesturing to the size and location.

"Well, that's a good color choice, since I already bought the paint." Dad pulls two buckets from the bed of his trunk, lifting the cans by their wire handles.

"You two are so sneaky! I love you!"

"We're just so happy to see you so passionate about this." Mom can hardly contain her smiles.

"And thank goodness the cookies are good, too," Dad says, then grimaces. "Except for those key-lime-pie-flavored ones."

Mom hushes him and smacks him on the arm.

"Thank you both, I love this!" I turn, taking in the whole thing.

We spend my birthday cleaning the camper from the

inside out. We open all the windows and doors, and turn on some music in the yard. Mom and I start inside, removing the cobwebs, spiders, and layers of dust. And Dad works on the outside, spraying it with a hose and scrubbing it with soapy water. Every so often he misses and sprays us through the windows, which makes my mom yelp and my dad laugh.

The interior is in decent shape, though I'll have to do a lot of modifying to make it work. It could take several months, but I'm happy to have something to look forward to—a project.

By the end of the week, the camper is cleaned up enough to paint the outside. We do it as a family. It's not only been good for me, but for all of us to connect again.

The next day comes too fast, the day that I'm supposed to paint the logo on the side of the camper, and I'm more than a little stressed. I sit on the wide steps of the back porch, looking out at the camper, holding up two computer printouts one at a time, squinting and trying to imagine each logo option on the side. One is a replica of Hew's logo, the one that he painted on the side of the zombie birdhouse. The other is the crappy logo that I designed, a wine bottle and pixilated fortune cookie that I found online, montaged together with some text in a paint program on mom's old computer.

Staring at the two on paper, I can't help feeling that I'm not just making some kind of choice between the two logos. I obviously know which one is better and it isn't mine, but I wonder if I'll be able to live with the choice the rest of my life, always looking at *his* logo, remembering who it represents. What it represents.

I've been thinking a lot about what Dr. Leevy, Mom, and I discussed over the past few months—obsessing over it, really. And I think I want to forgive Hew. I feel that if I don't, I'll never be able to clear the slate in my own heart and move on. We don't need to be together, but I need closure. He wants closure. I don't want him to live with the pain that I've been fighting in my heart and mind. I can't do that to someone else, even if they took away the most important person in my life. I'm just not built that way.

With the help of a projector shining Hew's logo on the side of the camper, Mom helps me outline the design in pencil and then we paint the outline in black, let it dry, and then fill the shapes in with color. And when it's done, I know I've made the right choice. My soul feels free.

It's sunny but chilly today. From the backyard shed, I grab my new lemon-yellow beach cruiser bicycle—I needed something to match the camper—and drop a backpack and a bunch of flowers in the front basket. I pedal from our home down a dirt path, leading south, bumping over the rocks and potholes while listening to the breeze rush through the green spring leaves.

I'm still undecided if I'll use Hew's gift, a trip to France, but I have to decide by this weekend. My dad says that Hew's trying to buy my forgiveness. I don't argue because I know the truth in my heart: he didn't intend it that way. Despite what he's done, he cares about my dreams and me, and I think, like my mom, that he wants to see me live, even if that means he's not part of my life.

A few moments later, I turn my handlebars down a new road and ride for several miles through the countryside until I reach All Hallows Parish. I circle the historic brick church and stop next to the back steps, where I leave my bike.

I'm here for a lunch date. I gather my items and cross the cemetery until I reach the headstone next to a small dogwood tree that marks Bren's grave. I remove the dying flowers from the vase at his grave and replace them with a bunch of wild black-eyed Susans.

Then I unpack my bag, lay out a quilt, and sit down with my lunch. The only problem with this lunch date is that he doesn't talk back. This would make Dr. Leevy happy, but not me. If Bren could answer, I would ask him what I should do about Hew. Bren would know; he was always my sounding board, my cheerleader, the person I dreamed with, and my best friend.

I'm long past crying at these meetings. It's been two and a half years now, and though I desperately miss him, his passing doesn't consume my life like it did when I finally understood he was gone. He's fading from my mind, but not from my heart. There will always be a part of him in me.

I tell him about my week. "I've officially mastered fortune-cookie making. I've even developed a few different flavors of cookies and icing. Mom's favorite so far is a red velvet cookie dipped in a cream cheese shell, but Dad still likes the maple dipped, sprinkled with bacon chips. I guess that's more manly than red velvet." I ramble on, knowing that he's listening.

"But that's just filler information. You know why I'm here. I need to learn the other part of my business—the wine part. It just doesn't seem right to take this gift from Hew without you on board with the idea." There is silence, of course. "This is the part in the movie where you give me a sign—a rain cloud opening up and pouring on me, or even the cliché lightning strike—but not too close. I'm tired of being in the hospital."

But still there is nothing. And I take the silence as a no. "It's okay, I get it. I'm not sure if I'm ready to let go yet either. I mean, I feel like I'm leaning that way, and I know you'd be okay with it, want me to move on and all that, but it's not easy."

I don't talk anymore. I just finish my sandwich, then lie down next to him in the sunshine, partly covered by the shade of the tree. Above me, birds hop from one branch to the next, building a nest. I lace my fingers behind my head and stretch my legs while enjoying the warmth on my face.

Relaxed, I close my eyes and fall asleep, only to wake up sometime later to a loud bang. I shoot straight up and look around. The gardener's here now; a ride-on lawn-mower rumbles beneath him. Cut grass and dust shoots from the side of the machine into the air. I think it must have backfired and woken me. I feel groggy but need to get back home.

Reluctantly I collect my things, shove them into my backpack, and shrug the straps over my shoulders. I kiss my fingertips, then reach down and rub the smooth top of Bren's headstone.

"I had fun today. I'll see you next week." Since Bren didn't give me a sign, I've decided not to go to France. If he's not ready, then I'm not ready.

I walk to my bike, passing a group of gardeners, and say, "Hi." I nod to them, but they're snickering, and I have no idea why. I ignore them, find my bike, and head back home. When I pull up to the house, Dad and Mom are in the front yard planting flowers. I stop near them, set my bike on its side, and kneel down to help them.

"How was your visit?" Mom asks without looking at me as she presses dirt down around the base of a pansy. I lean in to help.

"Bren talked my ear off."

They each give me a sideways glance.

"Just kidding. I swear." I hold up my palms. That's when they both sit up and stare at me, then begin laughing hysterically. My dad laughs so hard that his face turns bright red and tears rolls down his cheeks.

"I knew I was funny," I say slowly, looking from one to the other in confusion, "but I didn't know I was that good."

Dad places a hand on my shoulder. "Trust me, honey, you're not that good."

"Then why are you laughing?" I look between them.

"Do yourself a favor and go inside and look in the mirror."

I raise my eyebrow at this, but jump up and run up the stairs. Just inside the front door, a mirror hangs on the wall. When I see my reflection, I scream and then burst out laughing, too. My hair and dress are covered in bird crap.

I laugh . . . I laugh so hard it hurts. It feels good. Bren sent zombie birds after me while I was sleeping; I know it. This is his sign.

I'm sitting on a bench in Paris, looking across the Seine River. Tourists shuffle across Rue Lagrange, making their way toward Notre Dame Cathedral. I've been roaming the streets admiring the details of the architecture all morning.

If Shea decided to come to France, I have no way of knowing. We didn't have the same flights, and I haven't talked to her mom since before I sent the birdhouse. For all I know Shea could have thrown the thing out. But if she did come, I couldn't stand the thought of her being here without me, even if we never see each other.

I'm still hung up on her smile, our time together, and the way we are when we're together. For some reason, being in the same city, looking at the same Eiffel Tower, the same Arc de Triomphe, and the same stars at night gives me comfort. I tell myself it's not stalking if I don't seek her out, but I toss a pressed penny into every fountain I see, asking destiny to send her my way one more time if it's meant to be. And I apologize for calling her a bitch.

After a while, I stand up and dip my head into the loop

of my camera strap, then settle it on my chest. I stroll the path along the Seine, snapping shots of the architecture, the river, the bridges, and the people sunning along the banks or painting at easels. Paris is alive and beautiful. It's Shea's kind of day.

I wander to the Louvre, which is even busier. I mill around the plaza, looking for the best shot of the glass pyramid, designed by one of my favorite architects, I. M. Pei. At the perfect spot I crouch and lift the camera to my face. Through the viewfinder, I find perfection but it's not in the architecture—it's a woman standing in the water in the middle of a large fountain that wraps around the glass triangle. She dances with slow, graceful movements, beckoning the crowd gathered around her to cheer at her show. A security guard yells in her direction but she ignores him. I walk to the fountain to get a closer view. She spins, arms spread wide, disturbing the still water, but stops when she sees me. She raises and lowers her arms like wings of a bird as she glides toward me until we're face-to-face.

"Hi," she says. I didn't realize when I wished for Shea by throwing pressed pennies in every fountain that I would actually find her in one. Destiny works in mysterious ways.

"Hi." I grin and watch her struggle to step out of the fountain. I reach out my hand, helping her to the ground where she's dripping wet, wearing a tank top and days-of-the-week underpants. She drops a pink backpack on the ledge.

"Every time I see you, you're wearing something unexpected," I say, remembering the conversation when we first met.

"How many times have you seen me?" Shea wrings out her shirt and pulls it over her head. Wearing only her bra and panties, she's completely comfortable with her near nudity, and she has every reason to be. Every milky curve of her body is still utter perfection.

"Too many times to count," I offer from our original script.

"Really?" She leans away from me to dig into her backpack, and I see her panties have MERCREDI embroidered on the ass. Wednesday in French. This girl still makes me smile, which is what I've missed most about our time together. She turns and shrugs into a gingham sundress that makes her look fresh and radiant.

"I think destiny keeps pushing us together," I tell her.

"Maybe," she says with a shrug.

"I have a confession to make."

She shoots me a sideways glance. "I guess it's good that we get these little confessions out of the way. Maybe that's what we do on this trip. We only tell the truth."

"I came to Paris hoping that we might meet."

"Shocking. That's not much of a confession." She wraps her hair into a bun. "But just remember, we're just hanging out and having fun, no attachments, no e-mails or texts after whatever this is is over." She jabs a pointed finger in my direction.

"Your statement implies that we've started a 'whatever this is.'" I raise an eyebrow.

"We have. We're friends. That's all." She slices the air with her hand. "I just want you to know that I forgive you, that I want to know the real you, and then we can see where this goes." She shrugs as if what she just said didn't just change the trajectory of my life for the better.

I'm beaming inside, but trying to play it cool, I say, "I accept your rules." I can't believe she's standing in front of me, talking to me. "So if we're friends now, don't you think we should introduce ourselves?"

"You first." She juts her head in my direction.

"I'll do you one even better. I'll tell you my name and one truth about myself."

She agrees to this with an unsure nod.

I reach out my hand. "Hi, my name is Hew and I have a drinking problem, but I'm doing all I can to fight it."

Her eyes widen. She, of course, knows my truth already, but I'm unsure if she has researched my real name. "Your name is really Hew? You didn't lie?"

"Who in the world would purposely choose to be named after a computer?"

"True." She laughs. "It's a very uncool name."

Everything I told her from the beginning was the truth

because all I've ever wanted was to know her, have her know me, and fall forever into her radiant little world. It's all I wanted since we met. She is my addiction now.

"I warned you when I bought the lottery ticket that I wasn't good with the dreaming stuff."

"You still have it?"

I slap my back pocket. "It still goes unchecked, and I still continue to dream about what you and I could do with that money."

"Well, it's nice to meet you, Hew. Mr. Possible-million-aire." She bites her lip and finally lifts her hand, fitting it perfectly within my grasp. The energy we once shared is still there, surging from me and into her. I'm reminded of how we were, and the possibility of what we could be again.

"So now it's your turn." I look at her.

"Okay. My truth first." She rolls her eyes. "In San Francisco, when I was supposed to drive to either the fortune cookie factory or the Palace of Fine Arts, I drove to both places. I wanted to spend more time with you."

"You didn't leave it to destiny?" I'm giddy inside, knowing that she made the conscious choice to be with me. My heart swells.

"Of course not. She's a bitch."

We laugh.

"And your name?" I press her, wanting to hear her say it. Of course I know it already, but if she tells me this time, I know she's truly forgiven me, giving me a chance to make things as right as I can between us.

I focus on her lips, waiting for what feels like eternity. Her mouth forms the shape of a circle, releasing the sounds, and as she does, everything around me slows. When her real name finally rolls over her tongue, I see our past, I see our future, and the all-consuming love I feel for her.

But most importantly, I see *Hope*.

THE END ♥

HE+SHE

NAPA
VALLEY
Wine &
Fortune
Cookie Co.

Choose Happy

MICHELLE WARREN

REVIEWS

If you enjoyed Hew and Shea's story, please take a moment to write a spoiler-free review on the site where you purchased the book. By sharing your feelings in a review, on your blog, on social media, or with a friend about the book, you support this independent author.

Please join Michelle Warren's mailing list to learn about future novels and sales. Use the your QR code scanner to open the form and join, or use this link: HTTP://TINYURL.COM/PKQHSPL

AUTHOR'S NOTE

To my knowledge, the mental illness Shea suffers from and is treated for in this story is fictitious. Real-life research and case studies were an inspiration, but I bent and shaped the information for the needs of this novel. If you would like to read in depth about similar topics, refer to the extensive textbook, *Delusional Disorder: Paranoia and Related Illnesses* by Alistair Munro.

Unfortunately, I can't say the same for alcoholism. It is a real disease that affects many families. If you know someone who suffers from substance abuse and you need assistance, please contact *www.aa.org,* or find a treatment center here:

www.findtreatment.samhsa.gov

ACKNOWLEDGMENTS

A big thank-you goes out to my beautiful beta readers. They are my super troopers, suffering through incomplete, error-ridden drafts that bear no resemblance to the final product. Thank you for telling me when I suck because you only make me better. I love you! Tabitha Preast, Jenn Sterling, Michelle Mankin, Amy Bettwy, Nikki Shaw, Melissa Brown, Melissa Perea, and Deena Baily Graves.

Pam Berehulke from Bulletproof Editing is my extraordinarily kind, patient, and talented editor I want to tell every author about, but also hide her away because I want to keep her all to myself. I'm greedy that way. Thank you, Pam, for your awesomeness!

And to my husband, Warren (the namesake of my pen name), who always gets the short end of the stick: I owe you for all the evenings you sucked it up with takeout (though you know any food is better than mine), and the nights you gave up and went to bed without me while I tapped away on your laptop. You handed over our precious time so I could pursue my passion. And most importantly, you gifted me the five-year anniversary trip to San Fran that inspired this book about the city we love. When we saw the naked bikers, visited the Palace of Fine Arts, bought dirty fortune cookies, drank wine in Napa, and cruised the California coast, you and our love inspired me.

A spontaneous, offbeat **romance**

FIND MORE INFO ONLINE AT:
MICHELLE-WARREN.COM

FACEBOOK:
www.facebook.com/MichelleWarrenAuthor

TWITTER:
www.twitter.com/@MMichelleWarren

INSTAGRAM:
www.instagram.com/MMichelleWarren

PINTEREST:
www.pinterest.com/michellewarren

GOODREADS:
https://www.goodreads.com/author/show/4097828.Michelle_Warren

JOIN MY MAILING LIST:

HTTP://TINYURL.COM/PKQHSPL

ABOUT THE AUTHOR

Michelle Warren didn't travel the road to writer immediately, first she spent over a decade as a professional illustrator and designer. Her artistic creativity combined with her love of science fiction, paranormal, and fantasy led her to write her first YA fantasy novel, *Wander Dust*. Michelle loves reading and traveling to places that inspire her to create. She resides in downtown Chicago.

Other books by Michelle Warren include:

THE SERAPHINA PARRISH TRILOGY:
Wander Dust
Protecting Truth
Seeing Light

COMING FALL 2014:
Miami Hush Club

www.ingramcontent.com/pod-product-compliance
Lightning Source LLC
Chambersburg PA
CBHW020229180626
46810CB00006B/2094